I0695117

Merry Christmas
AND A HAPPY NEW YEAR

KISS HER ONCE FOR ME!

ELIZABETH
My brother was getting married.
At Christmas no less.
The holiday I hated the most.
Let me list all the reasons why this will be the worst season yet:
One would be my luggage not arriving.
Two would be being told I had to find somewhere else to sleep since my room was occupied by family members.
Oh, and now I am forced to stay with my brother's best friend.
The man who broke my heart seven years ago.

NATE
My best friend was getting married.
I was happy for him.
Until I had to offer his sister my spare bedroom.
It'd be fine, two weeks and she'd be out of my hair.
But the thing with Elizabeth was that she pushed every single button I have.
She gets under my skin in the best ways.
All we have to do is survive the wedding and the holiday.
Then she'll be gone yet again.
Unless maybe, just maybe, my wish of having her comes true.

BOOKS BY NATASHA MADISON

Only For Series
Only For Tonight
Only for Love
Only for Her
Only for Him

Dream Series
Shattered Dreams
Forbidden Dreams
Buried Dreams
Stolen Dreams
Forgotten Dreams

Meant For Series
Meant For Stone
Meant For Her
Meant For Love
Meant For Gabriel

Made For Series
Made For Me
Made For You
Made For Us
Made for Romeo

Southern Wedding Series
Mine To Kiss
Mine To Have
Mine To Hold
Mine To Cherish
Mine To Love
Mine To Take
Mine To Promise
Mine to Honor
Mine to Keep

The Only One Series
Only One Kiss
Only One Chance
Only One Night
Only One Touch
Only One Regret
Only One Mistake
Only One Love
Only One Forever

This Is
This Is Crazy
This Is Wild
This Is Love
This Is Forever

Southern Series
Southern Chance
Southern Comfort
Southern Storm
Southern Sunrise
Southern Heart
Southern Heat
Southern Secrets
Southern Sunshine

Hollywood Royalty
Hollywood Playboy
Hollywood Princess
Hollywood Prince

Something Series
Something So Right
Something So Perfect
Something So Irresistible
Something So Unscripted
Something So BOX SET

Tempt Series
Tempt The Boss
Tempt The Playboy
Tempt The Hookup
Tempt The Ex

Heaven & Hell Series
Hell and Back
Pieces of Heaven
Heaven & Hell Box Set

Love Series
Perfect Love Story
Unexpected Love Story
Broken Love Story
Mixed Up Love
Faux Pas

Cover Design: Jay Aheer
Model Photo: Wander Aguiar
Cover Illustrations by K.B. Barrett Designs
Editing done by Karen Hrdicka Barren Acres Editing
Editing done by Emma Gilmore
Proofing by Ashley Carey
Proofing by Judy's Proofreading
Formatting by Christina Parker Smith

HOLIDAY Unscripted

NATASHA MADISON

One

So This Is Christmas

Elizabeth

November 2nd

"SO THIS IS *Christmas.*" I roll my eyes when I walk into the doctor's lounge and hear the soft sound of the music coming out of the radio.

"Ugh," I grunt, looking over at Ty, my coworker who's sitting at the table, scrolling on his phone while he eats his breakfast bowl. "Isn't it a bit early for this?" I point to where the music is coming from, just in case he didn't know what I was talking about.

"It's perfectly okay for Christmas music to be playing at the beginning of November," he says, his Australian accent annunciating "ah" instead of "er." "It's kind of a global rule."

"Who said this?" I ask, taking off my white doctor coat and opening my locker. "I want to know their actual names and not something you just made up."

"Society," he informs me and I roll my eyes as I hang up the jacket before grabbing my big tote bag. "I'm pretty sure society as a whole."

I put the bag over my shoulder. "We should have a rule made where there should be no Christmas music playing in the common areas until the first of December. Or if we even want to tempt fate, dare I say, two weeks before Christmas. Just enough time for us to not be sick of it."

"As soon as Halloween is done, it's fair game." He grabs a forkful of eggs, shoveling them in his mouth.

"How can you even think Christmas when it's hot outside? When you think of Christmas, you think snow and cold." After living in Australia for the past seven years, I'm still not used to it being summer during Christmas celebrations.

"That's just in movies." He winks at me, and if we didn't work together, I might maybe, just maybe, think of hooking up with him. But I've seen it time and time again, nurses and doctors getting involved with each other and the breakup is felt through the whole department. It's just too small a circle. So, I've made it a strict rule that I will never get involved with someone I work with. Not a nurse, not a doctor, not anyone who I will be seeing more than once in my workspace.

"Are you the kind of person who puts their tree up the second week of December and then takes it down the day after Christmas?"

"Pfft." I fold my arms over my chest, shaking my head.

"As if I put up a tree!" I shake my head. "I'm the type of person who likes to enjoy life and I value my time, so I do not even try to attempt to put up a tree," I tell him. "Besides, for the last five years I've done nothing but work the whole two weeks around Christmas and then I take a glorious month off." I exhale. "You should try it."

"I love Christmas," he says. "I can't ever imagine not being able to have Christmas dinner with my family."

"I'm feeling nauseous," I tell him, making fun of him and putting my hand to my stomach. "I'm tired, so I'm going to head out, and you can enjoy your breakfast"—I point to the bowl—"and all things Christmas." I hold up my hand to the sound of the music playing. "I think my ears are going to start bleeding soon." I stick my hands over my ears, making him chuckle, as I walk out of the doctors' lounge and notice the nurses changing shifts.

The whiteboard that hangs right in front of the nurses' station is being tended to by Gayle, the head nurse in charge during the 8:00 p.m.-to-8:00 a.m. shift. She's making sure she writes all the notes for the day nurse who is coming in to relieve her. "I'm off," I tell Gayle, and she looks over her shoulder at me. Her black scrubs have prints of colorful Band-Aids all over them.

"See you tonight," she replies and I nod my head.

"Just so you can be ready and prepared"—she moves the paper in her hand toward me—"my Christmas scrubs are coming out."

I groan. "I might have to take this up with HR," I stop and tell her and she just smirks at me. "I don't know if I can work in these conditions."

"I'm just giving you the heads-up so you can properly prepare yourself."

"I'm going home right now and getting scrubs that are the color of the Grinch."

She tosses her head back and a bark of laughter comes out of her, making her light-blonde bob move just a touch. "That will look like snot," she states. "Highly do not recommend." She smiles. "But I don't know what the cool kids are wearing these days. You do you."

"Great," I mumble as I walk out of the swinging doors of the emergency room and head for the front of the hospital. The hustle and bustle of morning has people arriving as I head out after my twelve-hour shift. Nothing like walking out into the bright hot sun after spending the night going crazy in the darkness that is the emergency room night shift. I squint just a bit as I head over to the side of the parking lot where the staff parks.

I rummage through my big purse, tossing things aside and grabbing my keys and unlocking the door to get in. I start the car and roll down the windows as I pull out of the parking spot. Stopping at the closed barrier to scan my parking pass, I wait for it to open up so I can drive through.

I pull out of the parking lot, turning on the radio and listening to the non-Christmas songs as I make my way home. After a long night shift, I'm ready to be in my apartment. I drive up to my apartment complex, park in my assigned spot, and wait for the window to roll up. I grab my bag and head toward the stairs that lead up to my door. The stairs open to both sides, each floor has two apartments on it, four floors per unit. I walk up the two flights of stairs, finally making it home. The rug at the door is a gift from my brother Jack and his wife, Evie, when they came to stay with me for a week on their way to New Zealand. Jack and Evie met when they were both in the hospital at the same time for cancer treatments. They became the best of friends; they even had nicknames, Jack was called Jumping Jack and Evie was called Easy Evie, because she was so easy to make happy. Jack was lucky that our father could afford the treatment. Evie's family were not as lucky, but my father made it possible that she got treatment also. They only found out when they both turned sixteen that our dad made it so Evie could afford the care. From then on they were even more attached at the hip. Then it quickly went past the best friends stage and they finally caved to their feelings. She and Jack finally got married six years ago and are looking at adopting their first child.

Welcome-ish, depends on who you are and how long you plan to stay.

I press my code into the door pad and wait for the lock to unlatch before turning the handle and stepping in. The shades are still drawn from when I left thirteen hours ago. I dump my bag off at the door and kick off my sneakers.

I make my way over to the living room, opening up the blinds before walking into the kitchen and doing the same thing to the window by the table. I walk into the back of the apartment, where my room is, heading straight for the shower. Opening the glass door, I turn on the water before undressing out of my scrubs.

I let the warm water wash over me as I put my head back and water runs down the nape of my neck. I close my eyes and exhaustion washes over me. Getting out I grab a towel, wrapping my hair up in it before grabbing my white robe.

I walk over to the chest of drawers and take out a pair of boxer shorts and a tank top before returning to the kitchen and opening the fridge. I move things out of the way, trying to decide what to eat for dinner. It's breakfast for certain people, dinner for me. The last snack of a protein bar, between patients at 4:00 a.m., wore off about thirty minutes ago. I'm starving and exhausted, so whatever is going to be the fastest to heat up is what I'm going with.

I take out one of the prepared meals I usually order when I'm working for the week and turn toward the oven, starting it. As soon as I place it in the oven and start to make my way back to the bathroom to comb out my hair, the phone rings from beside the door.

I walk over, grabbing my bag and closing my eyes for a moment, hoping it's not the hospital calling me in for an emergency. Turning it over in my hand, I see it's my mother FaceTiming me.

Smiling, I slide the green button to the side and wait until her face fills the screen. "She's alive!" she shouts over her shoulder, and I roll my eyes at her.

"Where has she been for the last week, Elizabeth?" I hear my father, Zack, shouting from somewhere in the house.

"Your father wants to know," she starts, as if I just didn't hear him shouting from the other side of the room. I see her sitting down in the kitchen, all the lights on in the room.

"Yeah." I laugh. "I heard him. I was working. Plus, with the time difference, I would pick up the phone to call you and it would be in the middle of the night over there."

"You know that wouldn't happen if you lived closer to us." My mother smiles at me. "We could even work side by side."

I inhale deeply, my mother is the head of the oncology department for the children's hospital in New York City. It's where she met my dad many, many moons ago, when he came in with my big brother Jack who was fighting cancer. She got him on an experimental drug; my father would have done anything to save him. We are thankful every single fucking day that it worked and he went into remission.

In the end, she fell in love with my dad at the same time. He was also playing hockey with my uncle Max at the time. Now that they are both retired, he heads up the Horton Foundation, which helps a few children's hospitals across the states, and my father runs the arena that has been in my aunt Allison's family for generations. It's where most of my cousins who play for the NHL go in the summer to get fit. Or if they are rehabbing an injury, they go to him to get back into shape. "Mom, we have this conversation monthly." I put the phone down on the counter in the bathroom and pull the towel off my long, light-brown hair that has streaks of blonde woven into it. Picking up the leave-in conditioner, I start spraying. "I love living in Australia."

"But we would love you living here," she pushes and I laugh.

"Noted," I tell her. "Is that what I owe the pleasure of this phone call?" I put the conditioner back down and start to brush out my hair. "Usually this is a Sunday phone call. After you have the family dinner, you call and let me know I'm missed and it isn't the same without me."

"It's almost Sunday," she replies and I snort.

"It's literally Tuesday over here, so it's Monday where you are since you know I'm in the future." I look at her. "I will say nothing bad happens, so you are still all safe."

"Very funny," she retorts sarcastically. "Anyway, I was calling you to remind you…" I stop moving as I listen to her, knowing she is probably going to tell me something she reminded me about at least five times, but the minute she said it, I most likely forgot about it. "…that you need to buy your plane ticket."

I slap my forehead with the palm of my hand. "Shit," I swear, "I had it written down on a Post-it at work, and I think I threw it out."

"Your brother is getting married," she huffs, "and you forgot!" The last part is shrieked out.

"I mean, it's not like I won't be at the wedding." I try to calm her down. "Or that there are no planes to America."

"Elizabeth Parker Morrow." She uses my full name,

letting me know she is either deeply upset with me, or she's about to lose her mind. Actually, when she's about to lose her mind, she says my name with clenched teeth, so I think I'm fine…ish.

"Here we go," I groan. "Mom," I say softly, "I will get online right now." I grab my hair in my hand and twist it up before clipping it to the back of my head. "And I'll get my ticket."

"Don't bother," she grumps, "I already bought your ticket." I smile at her. "Don't you dare smirk at me, young lady."

"I'm smiling because I'm happy that in less than six weeks I'm going to be seeing you," I tell her. "I'm so excited I get to spend Christmas with you." I hold up my hands and jump up and down. "Yay, Christmas."

"Zack," my mother shouts for my father, "come and speak to your daughter."

"Mom," I say her name, "you're the best." I lean on my elbows in the middle of the small island and wait for my father to come to the phone.

"Here." She thrusts the phone at him. "She's exactly like you."

He chuckles and I see him sit down on the couch next to my mother and lean over to wrap an arm around her shoulders. "Hey, if it isn't my favorite daughter."

"Um, I'm your only daughter," I remind. "Unless someone comes to the door and, ding-dong, you have a long-lost daughter you didn't know about. How awkward would that conversation be?" He gasps. "Don't even try it, you were a very good-looking man back in the day, and you played professional sports. God knows where you put that thing." I suddenly fake gag.

"Why am I even talking to her?" My father looks over at my mother, who is now biting her lip. "I told you just buy her the ticket and send her an email, but no, you wanted to call her and then she's all like this."

I laugh. "I love you too, Dad," I tell him and he side-eyes me. "But yes, send me the details. I am going to put in for time off. Fingers crossed I can get it."

"Your brother is getting married!" my mother shouts. "My son is getting married. I'm already a mess that I'm losing him, and you aren't helping."

"Okay, let's relax and not talk like he's going off to war. He's getting married and they bought a house one street over. I think you'll be fine."

"That's right. The only one breaking my heart is you."

"Smooth," I say when the oven beeps. "I will get the time off. I will be on the plane and his wedding is going to go off without a hitch." I smile into the phone. "Now, I have to let you go so I can eat and get my ass to bed. I love you. It's always nice seeing you." I blow a kiss and then hang up the phone, and the text comes in right away.

Mom: *Text the hospital now for time off.*

I roll my eyes but I pull up the rotation for the holidays. I pull my name off and block three weeks off for the insane amount of wedding activities the soon-to-be newlyweds have planned and leave a note that my brother will be getting married. I walk over to the fridge and grab the bottle of wine out and pour myself a glass. "It's going to be fine," I tell myself before I take a gulp of it. "So this is Christmas."

Merry Christmas

AND A HAPPY NEW YEAR

Two

It's Beginning to Look a Lot Like Christmas

Elizabeth

"HOW WE DOING?" I ask Gayle as I make my way around the nurses' station, going to the computer and pulling up the patient's name I just treated in one of the exam rooms.

"We have three more," she reports and I look up at the clock to see it's almost eight, and I'm going to be late leaving again today. Nothing new when it comes to the holidays. The number of people who end up in the emergency room during this time is called the "holiday surge."

"What are we looking at?" I ask her as I fill in the notes for the patient I just saw and had to stitch up because he decided it would be a good idea to cut down his own Christmas tree with a fucking saw that slipped.

"Two of them have broken bones," she states. "Last one, two sisters were sort of arguing and one punched the other one in the face when she took the last cookie." My head whips around seeing Gayle, who is smirking, as she holds a paper in her hand and she works on the whiteboard. Her scrubs today have a slew of Santas all over them. Bright and cheerful, unlike mine that are all black. I actually tried wearing the snot-green ones, but they were so bright I just couldn't take myself seriously.

"Who says holiday cheer is dead?" I snicker as I complete my notes and then get up to walk into another exam room.

The phone buzzes in my back pocket and I ignore it as I greet the patient. "Hi." I smile at the man lying on the hospital bed. "I'm Dr. Morrow."

An hour later I'm pushing open the on-call room and moving my neck side to side to get the kinks out of it. It looks like Christmas threw up in here. There is a Christmas tree in the corner of the room that looks like it's seen better days, and right across from it is a menorah with blue-and-yellow Happy Hanukkah letters right above it.

"Hey," Ty says, shrugging on his white coat before reaching into his locker and grabbing his stethoscope to put around his neck. "There she is"—he smirks at me—"the Grinch of the emergency room."

I hold up my hand to flip him the bird. "I've been working twelve-to-fourteen-hour shifts straight for the past fourteen days," I explain to him, "to make up for the three weeks I'm taking off for my brother's wedding."

He reaches into his locker and pulls out a small box. "I made you these." He hands me the red box with HO

HO HO written across it.

"What is it?" I ask him, pulling the top off and seeing Christmas cookies in there. "Are these homemade?" I pick up one and bite into it.

"Yeah." He smirks. "I like baking, it relaxes me."

"These are really good," I compliment, putting down one and then picking up one that looks like a chocolate cookie with white dusting on it. "I'm impressed."

"It's a family recipe," he says. "When do you leave?"

"Two days," I tell him, putting the rest of the cookie back in the box to enjoy when I sit on the couch in a bit.

"You excited?" he asks me and I shake my head.

"I love my family, I do," I say and he chuckles, "but they can be a bit overwhelming, and then add in my mother is becoming a momzilla and going nuts. My brother is trying to make sure everyone is happy. His future bride is constantly posting videos of updates no one is really asking about. I've silenced the bridesmaid chat because I just need to know when to show up."

"A wedding on Christmas Eve, no less," he teases me as I open my locker and toss the box of cookies in my bag, "you must be dying."

"The only thing I know about the wedding," I inform him, "is the color of my dress. Which is a bright red and not green—thank God for that—and that it's open bar." He laughs at me. "And that I'm going to be seeing all my family. So liking two out of three isn't bad."

"I'm afraid to ask which one it is you don't like." He shuts his locker and nods at me. "I can't wait to see pictures."

"I'll be sure to post them on social media right away," I joke with him.

"The last thing you posted on social media was two years ago and it was you at the beach with some of your cousins."

"I've been busy." I take off my stethoscope from around my neck and put it in my jacket pocket before shrugging it off, as he opens the door and leaves me alone. The Christmas music plays softly from the little speaker in the corner and I have to wonder if it's on loop somewhere just to drive me crazy. Once my shift is over, I'm out the door. Some like to sit and relax, some even shower here, but I'm always ready to be home as soon as possible.

Gayle is walking out at the same time. Her lunch box is in one hand and her purse is in the other as we walk out of the emergency room and into the sun. "It's going to be a hot one," she observes. "See you tonight."

"Two more days with me, Gayle," I tell her, "and then what will you do without me?"

"Enjoy singing Christmas songs without being told to shut up." She side-eyes me and I laugh as I walk to my car. The phone rings as soon as I get behind the wheel.

"Good morning, Mother," I greet as the phone connects to the Bluetooth. "Shouldn't you be in bed or, I don't know, winding down."

"There is so much to do for the wedding still." She ignores my sarcasm. "Anyway, are you packed?"

"Mom, I leave in two days," I tell her, "that's a tomorrow problem, or an if-I-can-push-it-to-the-day-I-leave problem."

"Why are you waiting until the last minute?"

"Mom." I scan my pass and wait for the barrio to open. "I'm coming home, if I forget anything, I'm sure I can get it there."

"Ugh," she huffs, "whatever. I'll call you tomorrow night to check in."

"Or how about I just see you in three days?"

"Whatever," she repeats and hangs up the phone on me.

I pull up my brother Joshua's number and he answers after one ring. "What are you doing to our mother?" I ask him and he laughs.

"She's acting like I'm the first of her kids to get married. Jack got married and she was fine."

"No, she wasn't," I snap out. "She cried for about a month straight. She had to keep putting ice cubes on her bottom eyelids and we made fun of her for it, don't you remember? She said if you made fun of her one more time, she would kick you where the sun doesn't shine and you'd need your own ice cubes."

"Oh yeah." His deep laugh fills the phone. "I told her whatever is going to happen will happen."

"That's the worst thing to tell our mother," I bite at him. "It's like you don't even know her."

"I just don't want her to stress. Instead of her not stressing, she's big-time stressing and that is stressing me out. It's stressing Macy out"—he mentions his fiancée's name—"and Mom's calling Jack and now he's coming to me and I'm going to Dad. It's a vicious cycle."

"And people want to know why I live on the other side of the world."

"Tomorrow we are going to have brunch with her and tell her to lay off a bit." I snort, laughing when he says this.

"Can you please videotape it? I've never actually seen steam come out of Mom's ears in real time. I've heard about it like a myth, but I've never seen it live."

"You really think she's going to freak out?"

"You really think she's *not* going to freak out?" I laugh. "That's an amateur move. Her baby is getting married."

"One, I'm not even the baby of the family; you are. Two, I'm not dying," he clarifies. "Anyway, I have to go and calm Macy down because she has been nursing a bottle of wine all night long."

"Maybe she's having second thoughts," I joke with him and he growls at me. "See you soon," I say and hang up the phone as I make my way home.

Two days fly by and I'm waking up at 4:00 a.m. to pack my suitcases right before I have to leave to get to the airport. I park in the long-term parking lot. Grabbing my checked bag and then putting my carry-on on top of it, I slowly make my way into the airport.

I don't know why I'm expecting the airport at 6:00 a.m. the week before Christmas to be chill, but that's on me. As soon as I step foot inside, I know I was dead wrong, and the chaos of the holiday crowd hits me. People wearing Christmas hats and sweaters while I'm wearing yoga pants and a T-shirt. I make my way over to the counter, seeing the line looks wrapped around another line.

The sound of children crying and the song "It's Beginning to Look a Lot Like Christmas" being blasted out of the speakers add to the already noisy scene as people try to make their way to security. I get to the counter and check in my bag. "You might be cutting it close," the girl states, wearing Christmas tree earrings dangling and a Santa hat.

I smile at her as I watch my bag with the priority sticker get jammed up on the conveyer belt. "I somehow thought I would be avoiding the rush of the holiday travelers."

She smiles at me, and it's a smile I sometimes give to patients when I want to tell them they shouldn't listen to Google when it comes to treating their ailments.

She types away at her computer. "Your flight is taking off from gate sixty." She types more. "The lounge is available, but I'm not sure how much time you are going to have."

"That's okay," I say nervously, looking around now and seeing the line to security getting longer and longer.

"You are all set." She finally hands me my paper boarding pass, even though I have it on my phone. "Your luggage tag is on the back." I nod at her. "Have a great travel day and happy holidays."

"Thank you. Happy holidays," I mumble to her as I grab my carry-on bag and hike it over my shoulder and walk toward the gate. I take a picture of the chaos that is the airport and send it to my mother.

Me: The eagle is in the airport.

I send it and she immediately sends me a picture of her with a smile.

Mom: My daughter is coming home. I'm going to have all my kids together for Christmas. My heart is full.

Me: Knock it off.

Mom: Okay, fine, but I make no promises there won't be tears.

Me: Don't make me accidentally miss my connecting flight and stay in LA with Ariella.

Mom: Joke's on you, she's going to be here for the wedding.

I put my phone away and head toward security, which takes me over an hour, and I have to run to catch my plane. I'm one of the very last people to get on the plane and the girl who was at the counter when I was checking in is somehow now here to basically gloat at me. "This is why we ask that you get here three hours before the flight." She holds out her hand for the boarding pass and then turns it upside down as it pings to let me walk on to the plane. "Have a safe flight."

"Thanks." I grab the paper and head down the ramp toward the plane, thankful my mother booked me a pod instead of teaching me a lesson and having me sit in the back of the plane. I store my bag by my seat as I get settled in. By the time I'm taking off, I'm ready to relax. The thirteen-hour flight flies by since I sleep the majority of the time, only waking to eat. When we land in LA, there is no gate agent waiting for us. We arrived at 6:00

a.m., and by the time they get someone there, we are waiting for over forty-five minutes. Something about the latch or whatever. I have to run again to catch the connecting flight. Customs, luckily for me since I have global entry, is a breeze, but I don't even have a chance to text my mother when I finally sit down, again one of the last people on the plane.

After traveling for the past fifteen hours, I'm starting to feel gross. The airplane air getting to me. The last six-hour flight is the longest part of it all. I keep looking at the plane on the screen and each time it feels like we're stuck there. Every minute feels like an hour, and I'm anxious to finally get home and recover from the travel. We touch down in New York and when I look out I see the snow and close my eyes. I look down at the sweater I'm wearing, hoping my mother has brought a jacket for me.

I'm one of the first people off the plane, and I smile when I walk toward the exit and baggage claim. Stepping onto the escalator that takes me down, I am bouncing on my feet, suddenly excited to finally see my mother. Waiting for the escalator to descend feels like eighty-four years passing, and finally, I can see people waiting for their family members. I look left and right, searching for her.

I finally step off the escalator and walk over to the baggage carousel, waiting for my bags. I look around as my phone switches from airplane mode to get service. I wait until I see a couple of bars for signal before dialing my mother and putting the phone to my ear. I look around for her to see if maybe I can spot her in the crowd when she answers after two rings. "Seriously," I goad when I hear she's not in the car, nor the same noise I'm hearing around the airport, "you can book my ticket, but then you forget to come and pick me up?"

"Oh my goodness, have you landed already?" I hear her rushing on her end and then I hear voices over an intercom.

"Yes, I'm here and you're not. Tell me I'm the middle child without telling me I'm the middle child."

"One, you aren't the middle child."

"I've been awake for eighty-four years, Mom. I'm delirious. This feels like a middle child thing." I correct myself, "It's actually even worse, I'm the baby of the family and you forgot me."

She cries out, "There was a pipe that busted at the hotel, and your brother slipped. They think his foot might be broken." Her voice goes higher and higher.

"Oh damn, that's going to suck in pictures if he's going to have to get a boot," I mention as a buzzer rings and the belt starts to move. "I guess I'll get a cab there," I tell her. "Don't come down for me. I'll be fine."

Of course you will," my mother confirms. "I never have to worry about you."

"You literally tell me the opposite every single chance you get." I shake my head. "I'm waiting for my luggage. I'll see you soon."

"Okay," she replies, disconnecting her phone, and I look down to see a picture of the five of us taken two years ago on my screen saver.

"I guess it *is* beginning to look a lot like Christmas."

I chuckle and shake my head.

Three

ALL I WANT FOR CHRISTMAS

ELIZABETH

December 14th
First day of hell

I LOOK AROUND as more and more people start to come and wait by the belt, and people from my flight start to arrive at the carousel as they wait for their luggage too.

The first couple of bags come out and I'm ready to jump at any moment, especially since I have a priority sticker on mine. Five suitcases come out and then it stops for a good fifteen minutes. The same bags going around and around again. Everyone is looking around and the frustration level rises, along with the fact it looks like another flight has just landed and their bags are also coming to this carousel.

I pull out my phone and text my brother Jack.

Me: Mom forgot me at the airport.

Jack: Boo hoo, you're old enough to know how to

get home.

Me: Wow, someone is salty today.

Jack: While you've been relaxing in business class and your own pod, I've been trying to deal with all the relatives who have descended on us and now have to be housed in different places.

Me: Well, you sound like you need some Christmas cheer.

Jack: Fuck off.

Me: Now this is what I'm talking about. Merry fucking Christmas.

Jack: I'll see you soon.

I decide to text my father next.

Me: When are you coming home? We miss you so much. Home feels so empty without you here. Does that sound familiar? Because that's what you guys tell me at least twice a week. Now that I'm here, you guys forget to pick me up at the airport. Nice. Good parenting. Father of the Year award goes to… NOT YOU.

Daddio: Will you ever forgive me for not picking up my adult child, who lives across the ocean and is her own person? Her words not mine.

Me: Well, now I know what I'm going to be discussing at my next therapy session.

Daddio: You go to therapy?

Me: You pay for it.

Daddio: Wait, is that the charge of one hundred and eighty-five dollars every month?

Me: That is correct. It's because of you I'm in there in the first place, you should be paying for it.

Daddio: Maybe you're in therapy because you miss us and want to move back home.

Me: Definitely not. Especially not now that you FORGOT your daughter at the airport!

Daddio: I didn't forget you anywhere. Your mother once forgot you at school, now that is forgetting you. But you getting on a plane and landing isn't us forgetting you.

Me: Wow, this is why my therapist says you gaslight me.

Daddio: WHAT!

I laugh and I'm about to answer him when my brother texts me.

Jack: What did you just tell Dad?

Me: I have no idea what you're talking about.

Jack: He just asked me if he gaslights me.

Me: You're welcome.

I stop talking to him when the carrousel makes a buzzing noise and then it starts to move again. The first couple bags start coming out and then forty minutes later new faces fill the carousel, and a couple of people from my flight are still lingering. I look around and see the counter for the airline, pick up my carry-on, and put it over my shoulder before going over to stand in line.

Fifteen people are in front of me, another man comes over to help, and I literally feel like I'm going to fall on my feet. I'm so tired. I blink as my eyes start to get dryer. I put my bag down and kick it forward when the person in front of me walks ahead. It's almost an hour later by the time I make my way to the counter.

"Hello," the woman greets me. The happiness and cheer she probably started her day with is now gone, and who can blame her. How much does the job suck when you get yelled at hourly?

"Hi." I smile at her. "My bag didn't arrive," I tell her and she looks at me with a blank expression on her face.

"Where did you originate from?" she asks me and holds out her hand to me, expecting something.

"Do I have to pay for this?" I ask her getting my wallet, and she snorts.

"Girl, I wish," she replies, shaking her head and laughing. "No, I need your baggage ticket."

"Oh." I laugh at her. "Got it." I grab my big tote bag to fish for the paper ticket I stuck in there. "I've been up for twenty-four hours now," I ramble as I rummage through and find it at the bottom, "not that anyone seems to care."

I hand her the ticket, and she turns it over. She clicks on her computer. "Hmm," she says and then I hear her nails on the keyboard doing it again. "Are you sure this is the right ticket?"

I stare at her. "That is what she gave me," I tell her. "She said this is for your bag."

"There is nothing in my system," she reports and now my mouth hangs open.

"Excuse me?" I blink five times, not sure I actually heard what she is saying.

"There is nothing in my system," she repeats the words slowly.

"Yeah, I heard you the first time. What I mean is what?" I ask confused. "You see, I got to the airport.

Gave my bag." I start to motion with my hands. "She put a luggage tag through the top of my luggage and she put an orange tag that said priority on it, and then away it went."

"Yeah"—she nods—"but there is nothing in my system to say it even scanned in."

"What does that mean? So you don't know where my luggage is?"

"Technically"—she looks at the screen—"no." She then looks at me. "Usually when it goes in, it's scanned and whatnot, but it doesn't even show that it made it on your plane in"—she looks back down—"Australia."

"I don't know what the screen is telling you, but what I'm telling you is I checked in my bag, and now I have no bag. You can see from the sticker she gave me that I checked a bag, I didn't make it up."

"We can fill out a lost bag report," she offers. "They usually turn up…" I let out a sigh. "…in a couple of days."

"A couple of days," I say, flabbergasted.

"With the holidays"—she starts to type, ignoring looking at me—"it could be longer."

"Great. How does this happen?"

"Could be a whole slew of things. One could be that your tag literally just ripped off." She shrugs one shoulder. "Another could be that it got onto the wrong belt."

"And my bag could be sitting anywhere right now?"

"That would be correct." She smiles. "Okay, so I'll ask you a couple of questions."

"Great."

"Was there anything on the bag besides the tag?"

"Yes," I reply. "There was the luggage tag on there. It's from Coach and it's blue with sparkles. It has my name and address on it. I think even my phone number."

I put my elbow on the counter and form a fist, leaning my forehead on it.

She types away on her keyboard. "Okay, what size and shape is it?

"It's black and it's a suitcase."

"Black." Her face makes a grimace. "For the future, never go with black."

"Noted."

"What is inside of it? A list of things in case"—she looks at me and is almost afraid to say the words—"the bag opened somewhere and things are out."

I put my hands on my cheeks, sort of like Kevin McAlister did in *Home Alone*, right before he yelled at the top of his lungs. "Things are out?"

"Sometimes zippers break and by accident there are items that come out. Of course, not at the fault of anyone. These things just happen."

I look up at the ceiling and try to calm myself down. "Well, there were clothes, a pair of high-heel shoes, Louboutins, size seven." She tilts her head to the side. "I'm here for my brother's wedding."

"Yikes," she squeaks. "Anything else?"

"I don't know, really. I know I brought a couple of pairs of jeans. A couple shirts," I tell her and she nods at me.

"Okay," she says, "I'm going to need a contact number."

"Great," I reply and give her my phone number.

"Here is your ticket number." She hands me the white ticket. "Also, this is a little something to tide you over." She hands me a little bag. "It has some toiletries in there."

"Thank you," I say, shaking my head, "but I won't be needing that. My parents have things at their house."

"Well then, you have a great day." She smiles. "Happy holidays."

I pick up my bag and head toward the exit, my phone in my hand as I brace for the cold. The wind whips my hair to the side as I walk toward the taxi line. I'm waiting in line, going from one foot to the other as I wait for my turn. I'm literally shivering when the SUV stops at the curb and I get into the back seat.

"No luggage?" he asks me as I rub my hands together.

"Santa Claus won't make me happy with a toy on Christmas Day" blares out of the radio.

"No, they lost my luggage."

He hisses, "That's not good."

"Yeah, you're telling me," I grouse and give him the address to my parents' house.

An hour and forty-five minutes later, he's pulling into the end of the driveway since it's packed with cars. All the lights in the house are on. He stops the vehicle, and I take my credit card out and pay the fee before grabbing my bag and rushing to the front door.

I turn and push open the door but the door is locked. "You've got to be fucking kidding me," I grumble and then ring the fucking doorbell.

"I've got it," I hear my father yelling and then he comes to the door and swings it open. "Oh my gosh, Elizabeth." He reaches for me and pulls me to him. "You're here." He hugs me and the warmth of the house hits me. "We've been calling and calling you and it's going straight to voicemail."

"That would happen," I snap and put my hands on my hips, "when you've been flying for twenty-four hours and your phone dies."

"Why didn't you charge it on the plane?" He shuts the door behind me.

"Yeah, why didn't I do that?" I throw up my hands. "I should have done that," I say sarcastically, kicking off my sneakers. "I don't know why it didn't dawn on me to do this before."

"I'm sensing sarcasm," he replies, smiling at me. Even though he retired from hockey a long time ago, he's stayed fit.

"You would be sensing right," I retort and then I hear my mother shrieking when she runs into the room.

"My baby," she wails, running to me. "My baby is home."

"Oh, now she cares." I roll my eyes as she hugs me and swings me from side to side.

"It's been two and a half hours since I landed, and instead of you guys tearing up the country looking for me, you're all here. I could have been kidnapped and taken to some cellar somewhere."

"Okay, let's simmer down." My brother Jack comes

into the room, a huge smile on his face. He looks exactly like my dad. "I think you're giving yourself a lot of credit."

He takes me in his arms and gives me the biggest bear hug ever. "I'm prime picking." I look over at my father, who rolls his eyes, and then at my mother, who smiles through her tears.

"All my kids together."

"What took you so long?" Jack asks when he lets me go.

"They lost my luggage," I reply and my mother gasps. "I know, so much for packing early."

"You must be starving. Let's get you something to eat," my mother says, grabbing my hands and pulling me into the kitchen where I'm greeted with about forty family members. It takes me forever to make it through to everyone and then stop beside Joshua, who has his foot up on the table with a bag of ice draped over it. "Oh, here we go." I roll my eyes. "What's wrong with you?"

"It's badly sprained," he states as I bend to hug him and then ruffle his hair. He tries to get away from me, but given the fact he has one foot, it's easy for me to fuck with him.

"You better go rub some dirt on that and get your ass up. Lots to do." I clap my hand sitting next to him. "Chop-chop, groomzilla."

He laughs at me and I can feel eyes on me. My head turns to the side and there he is. My brother's best friend. My brother's very hot best friend. The same best friend who shared one night with me right before I decided to go away on my semester abroad. The same guy who I had a crush on my whole teenage era. "Nate." I nod my head at him, the same guy who ghosted me when I left. "Surprised to see you here."

"I don't know why." He smirks at me, and his chestnut-brown hair is brushed to the side from his fingers, those green eyes of his shine bright. I could never forget those eyes. They change from green to gray to yellow depending on the moment. "I'm usually always here." He is not lying. He and Joshua are almost joined at the hip. My whole childhood has stories with him in it. When someone was teasing me in ninth grade, it was Joshua and Nate who made sure the guy stopped. When I got drunk at a party and needed a ride home, I would call him before I would call Joshua. He's also the only man I think I've ever sort of loved...until he fucking ghosted me and now shall remain public enemy number one.

"Yeah," I respond, and then my mother calls my name.

"Elizabeth." She comes to me, with a plate in her hand. "Here, eat something."

"Mom," I say, looking at the plate of pasta, "I would love to, but I'm exhausted. I've been up for twenty-eight hours. I just want a shower and a bed." I get up. "So if you'll excuse me, I'm going to head to my room."

"Um…" She hesitates, looking at me with wide eyes as she looks over to my father. "About that." I tilt my head to the side.

"About that what?" I ask, not sure I want to know, but somehow thinking I'm going to be sleeping on the couch tonight.

"You see there was a water pipe valve that exploded at the hotel," my mother starts.

"Okay," I say, not sure why this has to be part of the story.

"And, well, the guests have to be—"

I hold up my hand. "Are you saying you gave away my bedroom?" I point to myself. "Like my bedroom with my stuff in it?"

I can hear Nate snickering from beside Joshua. "Snap," he says under his breath.

"It's okay. I think you can, maybe, stay with one of your uncles, but with the hotel being shut down, everyone is trying to get situated and accounted for."

"Did you not think that I needed to be accounted for?" I ask her but she doesn't say anything, just wrings her hands nervously. "So I have nowhere to stay?" I look at her, then at my father. My mother's mouth hangs open as she tries to find the words and she looks at my father, who looks at her, both of them with eyes that look like they are about to explode from their heads.

"I mean," Nate now starts, "if you want, you could stay with me." My eyes look over at him. "I have a spare bedroom, and it's not claimed, so it's all yours."

Four

IT'S THE MOST WONDERFUL TIME OF THE YEAR

NATE

"SO I HAVE nowhere to stay?" My eyes train on Elizabeth, who stands there looking like her head is about to explode. You know, like in the cartoons when the character's eyes widen and then they start glancing side to side, only for their eyes to pop out of their sockets and then steam comes out of their ears. I have to roll my lips together to stop from bursting out laughing as she looks at her mother, who has her mouth hanging open. Her mom looks over at Zack, who I think looks like he's about to have a stroke.

"Oh my God," she shrieks and throws her hands up in the air and then back down again.

"I mean," I speak up before her voice rises louder and all of Macy's family looks over here and the person who actually took her room starts to feel uncomfortable, "if you want, you could stay with me." Her head turns toward me so slowly, it's as if she's the evil doll from a scary movie. They look all innocent and beautiful, then they feast their eyes on you and, boom, you're dead. "I have a spare bedroom and it's not claimed, so it's all yours." I want to tell myself to shut the fuck up, but my head and my mouth seem to be off course with each other.

I look over at Denise and Zack, who both take a sigh of relief. "Oh my goodness," Denise says coming over to me, her hands extending as she points at me. "Nate," she says with glee, "Nate has a room for you."

"No." She immediately shakes her head, and I raise my eyebrows and smile at her, waiting to see if she is going to tell them why she refuses to stay with me. Has the day finally come when she acknowledges that we had one night together? Who knows? She sure as fuck forgot about it the day after when I came over to see her and she pretended I didn't exist.

"What?" Zack asks. "Why not?"

"Yes, Elizabeth"—I tilt my head to the side and watch her—"why not?"

"Well…" She folds her arms under her chest. "For one, he's the best man."

"That makes no sense," Joshua scoffs, "it's perfect." He looks at both of us. "I am surprised we didn't think of it earlier. But we were going crazy to figure out where to put Macy's family."

"Nice to know I came as an afterthought." Elizabeth looks at her parents. "It's Jack." She puts her hand higher than her head. "Then Joshua." She moves her hand down a little. "And then Elizabeth." She bends her knees to put her hand near the floor.

"Can we be more dramatic?" Joshua snorts at her.

"We can, actually," she gladly admits. "We so can. I've been up for the last two days it feels like. I've had to run for every plane I was on. My luggage and all my clothes are, I don't even know where right now. Could be in Australia or could be in Bali, what is for sure is that it's not here."

"Did you fill out a form?" Zack asks her like she's not having a meltdown right in front of him.

"No, Dad, I just left the airport, and I'm expecting the airport fairies to find it and bring it to me—"

"It's Christmas," I cut into the conversation. She again turns to look at me. Actually, *look* is too nice of a word; she turns to glare at me, her gray eyes fixated on me in a way that screams *shut the fuck up*. "You should have used Santa to deliver it on Christmas Day."

"Nate," she says my name and smiles at me. I've seen this smile a lot over the years, usually right before she tells me to go fuck myself. "Why are you here?"

"I'm the best man." I slap Joshua's shoulder, and he holds up his fist to me. "I'm everywhere."

"Can you not be?" Her teeth clench as she says it.

"Is that any way to talk to the man who is rescuing you from sleeping on the street?" Denise says. "You need to be nice to him."

She shakes her head. "I'm going to call the hotel."

"Um," Joshua starts.

"Shut up," she snaps at him and takes her phone out of her bag and shakes it in her hand. "I need a phone.

Someone get me a phone."

"The two hotels in town are all booked up," I speak up and she, of course, ignores me. "It's the busiest time of the year, plus with the wedding… They have been booked up for months."

"Then I'll go and stay in New York City," she stubbornly retorts, ignoring me completely.

"It's Christmas, you think you'll find a room in the city?" I can't help myself from egging her on and I can see her jaw tighten, but she avoids even looking at me.

"If I stab him, I'll probably go to jail," she announces to the room and not to anyone in particular, "but then I'll have someplace to stay." She looks at me and all I can do is smile at her, which makes her even angrier. "I hate fucking Christmas." She looks up at the ceiling.

"Sweetheart." Zack goes up to her, his voice is soft as he takes her arms in both of his hands. "It's going to be okay. You are tired and probably starving. They don't feed you much on the airplane."

"She flew business class," Joshua interjects. I look down at my lap, not sure I can stop myself from bursting out laughing, which would probably anger her even more and make her a bit more stubborn than she normally is. "She had cutlery and real plates."

"Joshua," Denise says, her voice warning him to stop talking.

"I'm just saying, Mom." He holds up his hand. "Listen, you think we wanted to rehome two hundred guests?" he asks her. "We literally have people staying everywhere."

"Whose fault is that?" She turns her wrath on Joshua. "Who gets married at Christmas?"

"Lots of people," I chime in.

"Again, Nate, you would be wrong, since December is the least popular month to get married."

"Who told you that?" Joshua asks her.

"Google," she hisses at him. "Why can't you be normal and get married in the fucking summer like everyone else?"

"We wanted to be different," Joshua replies, looking over at Macy, who is socializing with her family and has no idea this showdown is taking place. "Macy loves winter."

"What's going on over here?" Jack comes closer to us and falls onto the couch next to Joshua. "It looks serious."

"Mom and Dad are throwing me to the wolves," Elizabeth exaggerates.

"Wow." I look at Joshua, who laughs. "Suddenly I'm a wolf."

"We are not throwing you to the wolves," Denise clarifies. "She's going to be staying with Nate." She points to me.

"I never agreed to that." She shakes her head. "I can stay with Jack."

"I have two bedrooms and both are taken by Macy's aunts."

"Great, so you don't care about your little sister"— she lays it on thick—"who spent the whole day flying."

"In business class," Jack and Joshua say at the same

time and then share a high five.

"I hate them." She looks at her father.

"Okay," I start, getting up and looking at her, "let's all calm down."

"I'm cool," Joshua says, "as a cucumber."

"No one asked you," she hisses at him. "I should kick your foot and see how calm as a cucumber you are." Her eyes dart to him and then his foot, and he sits up ready to defend himself.

"Why don't you go and get something to eat?" I look at her, ready to face her wrath. "Then we can go, I'm sure you're tired."

"Yes," Zack agrees, "let's go and get you something to eat. You sound hangry." He laughs at his own joke. "And then Nate"—he points at me—"will take you to his house and tomorrow maybe we'll have news about the hotel and, hopefully, everyone can go to their original assigned places."

She looks down and then looks back up again. "I'm going to find another place to stay."

"Why are you being so pigheaded?" Joshua asks. "Just stay at Nate's house."

"Yeah." I sit back down next to Joshua and extend my arm across the back of the couch. "Just stay with me."

We have a face-off in the middle of living room, with all eyes on us. "This is so much fun," Jack goads, "the two of you." We both look at him. "You guys always were like water and oil."

"More like fire and ice," Joshua corrects.

"You two," Denise grits through clenched teeth,

pointing at Jack and Joshua, "enough poking the bear." She then points at Elizabeth.

"So now she's a bear," Jack teases, getting up and putting his arm around her. "Come on, sister," he urges, "let's get some food in you." He slowly walks away with her.

The minute she's in the kitchen and Macy's parents go up to her, she smiles at them and I hear Zack and Denise let out a huge sigh. "Thank you so much, Nate," Denise says. "We owe you big-time."

"Don't mention it." I look at them and smile. "Glad I can do something to help."

"You saved us." Zack nods at me.

"For now," Joshua adds, and Zack shakes his head, then turns to walk into the kitchen to see how Elizabeth is doing.

"Whatever you need"—I look at Joshua—"just let me know."

I get up and make my way to the kitchen, when the front door opens followed by a loud commotion. "Well, well, well." Their uncle Max comes into the kitchen, followed by his best friend and brother-in-law, Matthew. From the stories everyone tells, the two of them started out as enemies. Then Max dated Matthew's sister in secret, which made them even more enemies, until push came to shove and now they are inseparable. "We have arrived."

"Max," Denise calls, going to her brother and they share a hug. "Where is Allison?"

"She's going to come down tomorrow with everyone

else," he explains. "We came so we can help out with carpooling to make sure everyone is taken care of."

"Isn't that special," Elizabeth deadpans as Max walks to her and hugs her, kissing her on the top of her head. "They forgot about me, didn't even pick me up at the airport." He gasps. "I was going to have to sleep on the street," she tells him, "in the freezing cold."

"Never," he declares to her, "I would never let that happen."

"At least one person loves me." She wraps her arms around his waist.

"I'm ready to go when you are," I say quickly. I don't know why I say it, but I do.

"Fine," she huffs. "Denise." She looks over to her mother, who gives her a look. "Would it be possible for me to borrow a pair of pj's until I can get myself to the store tomorrow?"

"Yikes," Max notes, "she used your first name."

"That is never a good thing," Matthew adds going over to Jack and slapping him in the stomach. "How's my man doing?"

"Sweetie," Denise says to Elizabeth, "do you want to go and choose something?"

"No." She shakes her head. "The last time I opened a drawer in your room, I had blood leaking out of my eyeballs for a month."

"I told you it was a neck massager," Denise defends. "Do you think I would leave my toys out in the open?"

"And now my ears are bleeding," Jack grumbles. "She said toys. Like plural." He fake vomits. "I'm never even going in their bedroom anymore."

"Get your head out of the gutter," Denise scolds. "I just heard they were called that. Uncle Matthew threw out Aunt Karrie's toy chest."

"Oh my God"—Elizabeth puts her hands to her mouth—"what is happening right now?"

"Bet you want me to take you away now, don't you?" I ask her and she glares at me, which makes me laugh. I wink at her, which makes her glare at me even more.

"You do know that she is secretly planning to kill you in your sleep," Zack leans in to whisper in my ear, "and she's been watching those murder documentaries with her mother since she was like ten, so she can get away with it."

I laugh as Denise comes back down with a bag. "Here you go, sweetie." She hands her the bag. "There were a couple of things that you left here the last time you came to visit."

"Well, now that I'm thrown out of the house"—she grabs the bag from her—"I don't know when I'll be back."

I walk back to Joshua. "You call me if you need anything." I hold out my hand for him to shake and he slaps it and then we fist-bump. "I'll see you tomorrow."

"Will do," I affirm and then walk toward the kitchen and give Elizabeth a chin up before holding out my hand to her.

She looks at me and then my hand. "You think I'm going to hold your hand?"

"Do you want me to carry your bag?" I ask her, and

she ignores me and turns to walk toward the front door.

"Have fun." Jack slaps me on the shoulder. I follow Elizabeth out, my eyes going to her ass and then flying right back up before someone catches me looking at her like that.

I reach for her big carry-on bag while she slips her shoes back on and I look at her. "Don't argue with me," I warn her. "You've had a long day."

"Whatever," she mumbles and opens the door to walk out of the house. "Which one is yours?" she asks of all the vehicles parked.

"The black truck." I point to the pickup at the curb. "Right over there."

"Figures," she mutters as she walks toward it, "big truck." She looks over at me, eyes landing on my crotch with a smirk, as she opens the passenger door. "Must be making up for something."

"We both know I have nothing to make up for." It's been over seven years, and this right here is the first time I've ever spoken about that fateful night.

"We'll agree to disagree," she mumbles but avoids looking at me as she gets in and slams the door shut.

I open the back door, tossing her bag onto the seat before getting into the truck and starting it. She looks out the window the whole time, neither of us saying anything to each other as I pull up to my house.

"Welcome to my home," I tell her, and she reaches for the door handle and steps out. I grab her bag and head to the house with her following me. "I take it you aren't up for a tour."

"You would be correct on that," she mumbles. "I need a shower and a bed. So if you can point me to that direction."

I unlock the front door and push it in, excited paws running towards us echo in the entryway.

"Hey, boy." I put Elizabeth's bag down and he immediately goes to sniffs it before coming to me and I rub his neck. "This is Whiskey," I tell her, and she smiles and looks down at my golden retriever dog, who now wags his tail even more when she bends to pet him. "Let me just let him out and then I'll take you to the room." She nods at me as I kick off my shoes and head past the staircase toward the back door, opening it and he runs out. I turn around and see her still waiting for me at the front door. Her shoes are now off with mine, her bag's in her hand waiting for me. "This way," I say, walking up the steps to the bedrooms.

As soon as we make it to the top of the steps, I look back at her. "This is your bedroom." I open the door to the right which leads to a room with a queen-size bed that is never used. "Shower is right there." I point to the door beside her bedroom.

She walks past me and sits on the bed and collapse on it, outstretching her arms to the side. Bean, my cat, jumps onto the bed and just looks at her. "That's Bean," I say of the golden cat I rescued not too long ago. "She has trust issues," I mention when she jumps down off the bed and scurries to her hiding spot. "Do you need anything?"

She gets up on her elbows and looks at me. "No," she replies, "I'm going to take a shower and then go to bed."

I nod at her, my heart suddenly hammering in my chest. "I'll get out of your way, then," I say and turn back to walk down the stairs to retrieve Whiskey, telling myself this is going to be okay. It's the happiest season of all, isn't it?

Merry Christmas
AND A HAPPY NEW YEAR

Five

A Wonderful Christmas Time

Elizabeth

I WATCH NATE walk away from me and make his way down the steps. Turning back to look at the bedroom, I take in the queen-size bed sitting in the middle of the room framed by a gray headboard with brown undertones, coupled with matching nightstands. A lamp sits on one of them and the other is bare. The shades are halfway drawn. I use my foot to kick the carry-on into the corner of the room. Looking through the bag that my mother packed, I snatch out a pair of pj's before dragging my ass to the bathroom.

"Did you have a party while I was out?" I hear Nate speaking and then I hear the dog bark back at him, as if he's answering his question.

I step into the bathroom and turn on the light. I yell when I see something gray runs right past me over the tops of my feet. "You okay up there?" I look out of the bathroom and down the steps to see Nate, holding on to the wall with one hand and the banister with the other.

"There was something in here." I turn around in a circle, searching for where it went. The door is open to another bedroom right before the bathroom. "It was gray. I think it might have been a rat. Could be a raccoon."

He laughs and my body shivers at his rumble. "That's Baby Cat," he informs me. "His name is Ghost but he's the baby of the cats, so I just call him Baby Cat."

"How many animals do you have?" I ask him.

"Two cats and the dog. I would have more but—"

"Spoken like a true vet," I tease him as I turn back to the bathroom and shut the door. I open the glass shower door before starting the water. My hand is out to test to make sure it's the right temperature and I'm about to undress when I remember my toiletry bag. "Fuck," I swear, walking back into the bedroom and to my carry-on. The small white toiletry bag with little blue flowers all over it sits near the top. Thank God I packed it in my carry-on since it's filled with the essentials, as well as my toothbrush and my toothpaste.

When I go back into the bathroom, the gray cat is sitting on top of my pj's on the counter. "Hi, Baby Cat," I say closing the door and then undressing. "You can sit on those, but when I get out, I'm going to need you to find someplace else to sleep."

The shower feels like heaven. I hold my head back and let the warm water run over my face. A tired itchiness fills my eyes, and my eyelids are getting heavier and heavier, making them hard to keep open. I walk out of the shower and find the cat is now sitting on the clothes I just took off. I dry myself off just enough to slip on the black boxer shorts and yellow tank top. I turn on the water at the sink before putting toothpaste on my toothbrush and then putting it in my mouth, moaning when I taste the mint on my tongue. I have just enough energy to comb through my hair and grab my clothes, finally ready to walk out of the bathroom and climb into bed. The lights are still on downstairs and I just walk into the room and toss my clothes on top of my bag. Walking over to the bed, I see Baby Cat there now. "Okay, so I'm going to bed," I tell the cat, "and you can stay or you can go." The cat just looks at me as I move the covers and get under them. "Good night," I tell the cat, who's stretched out on his side and not even bothering with me.

My body relaxes into the bed. I think it takes me less than ten seconds to fall asleep. I don't even know how long I've been asleep, when my eyes flutter open. I feel heat enveloping the top of my head. When I look up, I see that Baby Cat is sleeping on my pillow, literally around my head. "Um, we are going to have to talk about invading one another's space," I inform the cat, who opens his eyes and then closes them back down as he sinks deeper into the pillow.

I look toward the bedroom door, finding it's closed almost all the way but with just enough space for the cat to come and go. I lift my arm up to check my watch and the black screen greets me. "Great, I don't even know what time it is." I look over toward the shades to see the light coming in from around the curtains. My bladder now makes it known that it needs to be emptied. I toss the covers off me, get out of bed, and tiptoe to the door to see Nate's bedroom door open but the room still dark. I move as quietly as I can to the bathroom, not turning on the light until I quietly shut the door behind me. I go to the bathroom, washing my hands and my face before brushing my teeth.

When I turn off the light and open the bathroom door, I hear noises coming from downstairs. I awkwardly make my way down to the kitchen. I walk down the steps and down the long hallway, noticing there is not one picture hanging on the walls. I wonder why that is, then I remind myself I shouldn't care about anything involving Nate. The hallway opens to the kitchen and dining room area on one side and the family room on the other.

Two big floor-to-ceiling windows are on either side of the fireplace that has a television mounted above it, facing the light gray couch with a circle ottoman in the middle on a light gray plush rug. "Good morning," I mumble when I turn and see Nate behind the island starting the coffee. He is wearing shorts and a T-shirt. His hair sticking up from sleep. "Did I wake you?" I ask him and then the sound of scratching makes me look past the dining room table that is right in front of the kitchen, toward the back door where Whiskey is waiting to come in.

I walk to the door and open, the cold air sweeping in as soon as I open it and he comes in. "It's freaking cold out there." I shiver, as Whiskey steps inside. He excitedly goes around my legs in a circle and then between them, his tail slapping me at the same time. "Good morning," I greet him, leaning down and rubbing his soft neck. "I guess it isn't too cold for you out there," I mention when I touch the cool air clinging to his fur. "What time is it?" I look up to see Nate leaning against the back counter, one hand outstretched beside him while the other hand holds a cup of coffee in his hand.

"Almost nine."

"Shit." I get up. "I slept for twelve hours."

"Just about," he says as I walk toward the dark-gray, almost black, island with the double sinks in the middle of it. "I take it the bed was comfortable."

I nod at him. "I woke up with Baby Cat on my head," I tell him and he smirks.

"He feels comfortable with you," he replies to me. "He has never gone in that room before."

"Good to know," I mumble. "I thought I was sleeping on his bed at one point."

"Would you like coffee?" he asks me.

I pull out one of the light-gray fabric stools and slide on it. "I would love coffee," I answer him as he walks over to the side counter right next to the fridge, where the coffee machine is. Opening the cabinet right on top, he grabs a mug before filling it. "Milk?" he asks me, and I nod my head as he walks to his white fridge with brass handles, pulling it open. The fridge and stove are the same color, matching the top cabinets, but the bottom cabinets are a soft walnut color. The black counters and the backsplash make the colors brighter. Whiskey walks into the kitchen, following Nate around before lying at his feet.

He hands me the coffee and I reach out for it. "Do you want a robe?" he asks me, and my eyebrows pinch together.

"A robe?" I ask him confused as he looks around me but not at me.

"You're naked," he explains and I snort.

"I don't know how long it's been since you've seen a naked woman"—I take a sip of the hot coffee and sigh—"but this is actually not naked."

"I can see right through your tank top." He looks to the side.

"Oh please." I look down and see that maybe you can see through it. "They are just nipples." He looks up at the ceiling. "Everyone has them. If you don't like them, don't look at them."

"It's kind of hard when they are right in my face."

"They aren't in your face," I refute and his eyes bore into mine. "If you don't like them, close your eyes." I poke him even more. "Every single person has nipples, including you."

"Yes, but I'm not flaunting my nipples."

"If it makes you feel better." I put the cup down on the counter. "I'd be okay if you came down with your nipples completely out." His eyes come to mine and I can't help but smirk at him. "You can take off you shirt now if it would make you feel more comfortable."

"I'm good," he grits between clenched teeth.

"Suit yourself." I pick up the cup and take another sip. "But if you like, you are more than welcome to whip them out any time you feel the need to." I try not to laugh at his scowl.

"What time do you start work?" I ask him.

"I took the next two weeks off," he tells me. "The pros of owning your own vet clinic." I nod. "Are you hungry?"

"I am, but I don't want to put you out."

"Then go and cover up," he tells me and I smile big.

"Are my nipples insulting you that much?" I ask him and look to see a sweater he tossed on the back of the couch. I push away from the counter, and the minute I do, Whiskey is on his feet looking around to see what I'm doing.

I grab the sweater and pick it up, smelling it to see if it's clean at least before putting it on. It falls past my thighs. "Is this better?" I hold out my hands to the side. "All nipples are put away and not visible."

"Now it looks like you are wearing nothing but the sweater."

"Oh my God." I throw my hands up and Whiskey walks over to me and sits beside me. "You'll survive."

"Will I?" he jokes with me, and I have to remember I don't like him and wipe away the smile that was starting to form.

"Do you want me to make breakfast?" I ask him. His phone rings from upstairs and our heads both look over at the hallway. He walks past me and jogs up the steps, and I hear his voice. "Does he make you cover your nipples?" I ask Whiskey, who now lays his chin on his paws and closes his eyes.

"Yeah, she just got up," he says coming down the steps. "She's fine. Why would you think she isn't fine?" He puts the phone on speaker and Joshua's voice fills the kitchen.

He laughs. "I wasn't worried about her. I was more worried that she killed you in your sleep." I shake my head and walk over to the counter, grabbing my coffee cup. "We're going to head out to my parents' to have breakfast," he shares.

"Am I invited to that," I snap out, "or did you guys forget I'm even here?"

"That's why I'm calling. Mom and Dad have been beside themselves with guilt since you left."

"Good," I retort. "I didn't sleep all night." I look up at Nate, who rolls his eyes.

"I heard you snoring from my bedroom," he states and the glare is on in full force. "We'll get dressed and be right over," Nate relays and disconnects the phone and tosses it on the counter.

"I don't snore," I hiss at him. "Now, I'm going to get dressed," I inform him. "Don't worry, I'll make sure to cover my nipples." I turn to walk out of the room. "Wouldn't want to offend you."

"Don't cover them on account of me," he replies before I walk out of the kitchen, "but it is cold outside. Not sure if nipples can survive."

"I hate you." That's the only comeback that comes to my mind.

"Good to know. I shall keep that in mind." His face fills with a grin.

I take a deep inhale and walk away from him, mumbling, "I need to find another place to sleep." I look back over to the hallway. "We're definitely not having a wonderful Christmas time."

Six

Jingle Bell Rock

Nate

December 15th

I WATCH AS Elizabeth walks out of the kitchen, then hear the muffled sound of her moving through the second level as I look over to Whiskey, who is watching her walk away. "If you go with her, you're a traitor." I point at him as he sniffs the air, then looks back to me. "Yeah, you picked right," I say, walking to his food bowl that I keep under the sink. I fill it with kibble before putting it on the floor and giving myself a minute to get my body under control.

My cock's at half-mast from her sitting there in her see-through top. I grab my cup of coffee, bringing it to my lips. "Jesus." I shake my head. "I'm going to need you to get a hold of yourself." I look down at my cock, but Whiskey looks over at me like I'm talking to him.

"You too, buddy." I motion with my chin. He ignores what I'm saying as he puts his snout back into the bowl and finishing all his food. I grab his bowl, rinse it off with water in the sink, and then put it in the dishwasher, before turning and making my way to my bedroom.

The spare bedroom door is open, but I hear Elizabeth moving in the bathroom. I walk into my bedroom, heading straight for my en-suite bathroom. Brushing my teeth, I then grab a pair of jeans and a T-shirt before slipping a sweater off the hanger and putting it on.

When I walk out of my closet, Whiskey is in the middle of my bed, stretched out on top of the dark blue down feather duvet that feels like you are lying on a cloud. "Let's go." I motion with my head toward the door. "I'm going to put you out before we leave."

He follows me out of my bedroom, stopping to sniff under the now closed spare bedroom. The soft scent of Elizabeth's perfume lingers in the hallway as I walk down the steps and make my way to the back door. I get it half open before Whiskey is running out into the yard.

I make my way over to the side door where the laundry room is and get the cat food ready. Filling the bowls and walking out, I hear her come down the stairs. I peek my head around the corner and see her dropping her bag by the door. "Are you escaping?" I ask her, motioning to her bag.

"Yes." She turns and walks back to me, holding my sweater in her hand. She's wearing a pair of jeans and a thick sweater now, thank God. "I'm taking it with me, in case I get my bedroom back, I won't have to come back here."

"You haven't lived at home in at least seven years," I point out to her as she puts my sweater back to where she got it from before.

"The first six months didn't count. I didn't know I wasn't coming back, so it's six and a half years," she corrects me, "but it's still my bedroom."

"I'm pretty sure once you move out of your parents' home, the bedroom you had is no longer yours."

"My stuff is in there." She's never going to let you get the last word. Never. Never did. Never will.

"What stuff?" I ask her as I walk to the back door when I hear Whiskey scratching on the glass door.

"It's none of your business what stuff." She folds her arms over her chest. "It's private."

I chuckle sliding the door open and watch Whiskey step one paw in and then another one before going straight for her. His tail wags back and forth, as she bends and rubs his neck. "We should get going," I tell her, and she gets back up and then walks in front of me.

"How did you have a change of clothes?" I ask her as I take her ass in and then my eyes quickly fly up to her head.

"I left these here the last time," she explains, grabbing her sneakers and putting them on. "Present me is very pleased about past me's decisions."

I shake my head, not even sure how to handle that comment as I move to my boots and slide them on before grabbing my jacket and shrugging it on. "Are you going to be okay with just a sweater?" I ask her, about to hand her a spare jacket.

She shrugs. "I have a jacket at home, unless they decided to lend it to the person who is staying in my bedroom."

I snort as I turn to look at Whiskey, who is sitting there in the hallway. "I'm leaving, buddy. I'll be back soon."

"That's so sad." She looks at me. "He's going to be all alone."

"He's got the cats," I joke. "Plus he's in a warm two-bedroom home with two big beds and endless spots for him to lie down, without having to worry about paying the mortgage. I think he'll be okay." I open the door, and she looks at me and then back at Whiskey.

"Bye, Whiskey." She waves her hand at him. "Chew on all his things," she whispers to him, but it's loud enough for me to hear.

She's about to bend to grab her bag when I beat her to it. "Get in the truck," I hiss at her and then look at Whiskey. "Don't you dare chew anything." He tilts his head to the side as if he's going to think about it.

We walk out and she rushes to the truck, opening the door and getting in. "It's freezing."

She rubs her hands together, while I start the truck and put her bag in the back before making our way over to her house.

When we pull up, there are even more cars in the driveway than last night, if that is even possible. "Is the wedding today?" she mumbles as she looks at all the cars. "Like, are we late?"

I can't help but laugh at her. "Maybe it's a big family breakfast," I tell her. Her family has come to have these big family dinners on Sunday where they basically invite just about anyone over. When summer months come around and most of the family comes to town to train or just relax, the dinners are even bigger.

She gets out of the truck. "Don't forget my bag," she reminds me.

"How about this," I start, walking to meet her in front of my truck, "if by chance the hotel got the pipe fixed and then all the carpets are now dry and there is no damage…" Her eyes get smaller and smaller as I talk, the glare more vicious. "…making it so you get your room back, I will gladly come back out and get it for you."

"Have I mentioned that you're the worst?" She tilts her head to the side, not waiting for me to answer her before she walks up her driveway and to her front door.

"More times than I care to remember," I mumble, following her up to the front door where she pushes it open. The sound of people talking echoes all through the house. Kids are running up the stairs that lead to the basement and then toward the kitchen. A couple run past us and quickly say hi.

As we get closer to the kitchen, the sound of plates clinking together becomes louder. "Oh, she's here." I stop behind Elizabeth as Denise comes toward her. "We were worried about you. We kept trying to call you and it went straight to voicemail. You didn't charge your phone."

"I forgot," she admits, "and you obviously weren't

that worried about me, you didn't even blow up his phone." She points over her shoulder at me.

"I tried to take good care of her, Denise," I say, walking past her. "Don't ask me how I did it, it was hard." I kiss her cheek. "Smells good."

"The caterers just got here," she states, and I look at the massive island they have in their kitchen that is now filled with serving plates.

"Just got here?" Elizabeth questions. "People are eating."

"Well, they were hungry." She throws up her hands. "Anyway, the older generation is in that room." She points over her shoulder to the formal living room they only use on holidays, such as Christmas or birthdays. "The wedding party"—she smiles at us–"is through there. Grab a plate and get on in there."

"Mom," Elizabeth says, "how's the hotel doing?"

"Oh, good news," she starts, "they were able to have a whole floor dried out overnight, so it can have some guests check in."

"So, I can have my room back?" Her voice is hopeful, but the look on Denise's face shows she is, in fact, not getting her room back.

"This is incredible," she mumbles as she walks away from her.

"She'll be okay," I assure Denise. "Just don't expect her to come back and visit for a few years. Closer to five, but not more than ten."

"Great," she says as she looks at Elizabeth, who is now scowling at her father who has taken her in his arms.

Her arms are to the side like they are limp. "Just great."

I shake my head and start toward the food, grabbing a plate and filling it with scrambled eggs, bacon, and sausage. Leaving room for pancakes on the side, I walk into the room where the bridal party is assembling and see Joshua sitting at the head of the table with Macy beside him. Two chairs are empty on his right side, so I walk up and pull out the chair. "Hey."

"The best man has arrived," he announces, slapping my shoulder and then squeezing it. "He lives." I look over at him and he smirks.

"With the way Elizabeth was, it was a toss-up if she was going to slaughter you in your sleep or not."

I chuckle at him. "I did sleep with one eye open, just in case. But she made me bring her bag on the off chance her room was free." I grab the fork and cut the pancake.

"Incoming," he warns, looking up and I feel the chair beside me being pulled out. "Hey," he says to her, "you look nice."

"I know," she answers, making me burst out laughing. "You don't, you look like shit."

"He was up all night, icing his foot," Macy defends from beside him and puts her arm around his shoulders, then uses her other hand to hold his cheek. "You look handsome." She smiles at him.

"I'm about to throw up and I haven't eaten anything," Elizabeth deadpans, "he didn't even offer to feed me." She points to me and I gasp.

"I made you coffee and then he called to invite us over here," I defend myself and she just shrugs.

"Let's just say he's not the friendliest host." She side-eyes me and it's my turn to glare at her. "He even made me wear a robe."

"Bastard," Joshua says. "Be better," he scolds and then we eat in silence.

"Okay," Macy says, clicking her fork on her cup, "if we can have everyone at the table's attention." I sit back in my chair and look up at her. "Before we start, we just want to thank everyone for being part of our special day." She looks at each of us and smiles. "I am so lucky that in nine days, I'll be marrying the love of my life." She bends to kiss Joshua, who just beams up at her. "We know some of you have come from far and wide to be here with us." She looks at Elizabeth. "And even though things are not going like they should be…" Her voice trails off and I see her bottom lip quiver. Joshua gets to his feet and then winces when he remembers about his foot. He whispers something in her ear, and she smiles at him. "With that said"—she turns and reaches into her bag beside her and takes out a manila folder—"we have the final itinerary." She jumps up and down with giddiness.

"Itinerary?" I hear Elizabeth from beside me. "I thought we just had to, like, show up and look pretty." She looks at me. "Well, not you obviously. We don't have time to do anything with that." She uses her hand to do a circle at my face, making Joshua snort out laughing. Macy walks around the table handing out white papers to everyone and stopping behind Elizabeth, handing her the paper. I hold out my hand for my own and look down and scan it quickly. "Um," Elizabeth says, looking to Joshua, who avoids looking back at her.

"We are in for a treat," she chatters, "there are so many fun activities from snowman building to a gingerbread house competition to ice hockey fun and so much more." She puts her hand on Joshua's shoulder. "Starting tonight at our first event at the karaoke bar." It's like she took happy pills this morning. "It's a little meet and greet to get to know everyone." She looks around the table. "It's going to be so much fun."

"I pretty much know everyone," Elizabeth retorts. "I mean, I have jet lag, you know flying across the world and all. Time change."

"You'll be fine," I assure her, looking down at the paper.

"Don't you have something else to do, like I don't know, stop talking?" she asks me.

"Didn't you work the night shift?" I look at her and her head turns around. "From what your father told me, you slept the same hours they slept."

"Don't believe everything he says," she snaps between clenched teeth. "He also said I would always have a place here and he was wrong."

"Okay, well," Joshua says, breaking up our little fight, "you can spend the day resting so you will be in tip-top shape for tonight."

"I don't have anything to wear." She shrugs. "My bag got lost." She looks around the table and people avoid looking at her.

"Give it up," I lean in and mumble in her ear.

"You give it up," she hisses at me. "I have to find

someone who can take me shopping," she says smiling. "See everyone tonight." She looks at me and grits her teeth at me. "Even you."

I look down and hide my chuckle for fear she will stab me with a fork "by accident."

"This looks like fun." I look at Joshua, who shrugs and I know he isn't the one who set this up. He is doing whatever Macy wants to keep her happy. "I'm looking forward to the tree farm."

"I heard you can cut your own tree down," Macy chirps, "and there are little trees for the people who are staying in the hotel that they can take back to the hotel and decorate in the lobby."

"Fun," I reply, looking back at Elizabeth. "You can help me decorate mine," I tell her, smiling even bigger when I see her get even more annoyed. "You're welcome."

Merry Christmas
AND A HAPPY NEW YEAR

Seven

Baby, It's Cold Outside

Elizabeth

I LOOK IN the mirror at myself, fluffing my hair on one side as I spray it with hairspray. "This is as good as it's going to get." I look over at Baby Cat, who jumped off the counter when I sprayed my hair the first time. I look at my hair that is blonder than before thanks to the hair appointment my mother made for me right before she took me shopping and insisted she pay for all my stuff. The least she could do after everything that's happened since I got back.

She ended up dropping me off at Nate's place and I walked in with four big bags of clothes. I dumped them all in the spare room, where the bag I forced him to bring with us this morning is now waiting for me. Needless to say, there was no room for me at my house.

Now I am putting the final touches on my makeup and turning to see how my hair looks from the back. I also get on my tippy-toes to see how my ass looks in these jeans. I bought them today just for tonight and they fit me like a glove on my hips and ass and then go straight down, stopping at my ankles where I am wearing little black booties with a small heel. It started to snow a bit when I was out, and the last thing I want to do is slip in heels and end up breaking something, so I went with comfort instead of sexy. The black bodysuit is tight and is off the shoulders. "What do you think, Baby Cat?" I turn back around. "Good enough, right?" The cat just looks at me and then gets up to go to the bathroom door where he scratches it with one paw, then looks at me to let him out.

I open the door, and he scrambles out towards the stairs. I look over at Nate's room and notice the door is open and the lights are on. The need to move over to his room and stick my head in is strong. I can smell a hint of his cologne in the air, so I know he's already downstairs. I follow Baby Cat down the stairs and hear the back door open, then shut. Strutting down the hallway, I stop when I see Nate look up at me while he rubs Whiskey's head. He's wearing a pair of dark blue jeans that hang annoyingly perfectly on his hips. A dark-blue knitted sweater is pushed up at the sleeves to his mid-forearm, the crewneck of his white T-shirt peeking out also. "Ready?" I ask him and he nods, giving me his grin.

"I charged your phone," he says, getting up and walking over to it. "You left it on the counter when you walked in, and I figured you might want it charged." He looks at it and then looks at me. "I think your boyfriend is trying to get a hold of you." He hands me the phone and I look down to see Ty has texted me, his text on the top of the text messages.

Ty: Are you alive????

"He's not my boyfriend," I mumble to him opening my text app, "we work together. Not that I owe you an explanation."

"If you say so," he replies and my head whips up.

"What does that mean?" I ask him and he avoids answering me.

"We should go before we're late." That's all he says, turning on the light over the stove before walking to the wall and shutting off the bright light that was on before. He walks past me to the front door with Whiskey following him. "Be good." He rubs his neck. "And stop trying to get into the cat's room," he scolds as I reach for my black jacket that I hung up when I got here.

Nate opens the front door and waits for me to step out before turning and slamming the door behind him. He presses something on the keypad before we walk to the truck together, neither of us saying anything. "Can I have the code for the door?" I ask him. "You know, just in the event I want to Irish goodbye."

"No," he states. "You want to Irish goodbye, let me know and I'll leave with you."

"What if you are having the best night of your life?" I say exaggerating a bit. "Then I'm going to put a damper on it."

"I'll survive," he deadpans, starting the truck and backing out of his garage.

"Suit yourself," I huff out and then look outside. "It's

probably one-two-three-four."

"Yes, how did you know?" My head whips around to look at him and I see he's smirking.

I roll my eyes and look out the window as the snow falls softly, hitting the street and then melting. After a silent ride to the bar, he pulls into the parking lot and there is a big sign in the front that says: Closed for a Private Party.

Once he turns the truck off, I get out and my phone buzzes in my hand, I see Ty has texted me again.

Ty: We're taking bets on how happy you are to be home.

I snort and take a picture of myself with my thumb down and send it to him.

Me: Who has horrible as the winner?

"Texting your boyfriend?" Nate asks from beside me.

"No, he's now my husband. We got married while I was in the truck with you." I pull open the door. "At this rate, I might be pregnant by the end of the night." I hold up both hands and cross my fingers. "I think it's happening right now." He looks right at me. "I would look away if I were you."

"Hey, you two." I look over to see my brother Jack walking to us, wearing his jeans and an untucked white button-down with a bottle of beer in his hand. "Was wondering when you would show up."

"She took forever to get ready." Nate shocks the fuck out of me. "I was waiting for an hour."

"Um, excuse me, I didn't know we had a set time to leave." I shake my head.

"I don't know about you," Nate says, grabbing a bottle of beer from the side of the bar that is there for us to take, "but when it says seven thirty, it means you have to be there at seven thirty, not leave the house at eight."

"You could have left me at your house," I remind him.

"If you want to be home alone in my house," he replies, bringing the beer to his mouth, "all you had to do was ask."

"I don't even know what is going on right now"—Jack looks at us—"but I don't want any part of it." He looks at Nate. "You're like a brother to me and she's my sister."

"Eww," I say, grabbing my own bottle of beer and bringing it to my lips as he walks away.

"You didn't exactly say eww that night," he mumbles and my head whips over to look at him, shocked he's bringing it up again after all these years. All. These. Years. Later. After everything that went down. The nerve of him.

"You said nothing the next day," I throw in his face and shock fills his features, "or the day after that or the day after that." I take five pulls of the beer and put it on the bar top, grabbing a shot from a waiter who is going around with them. I take the shot and cough as soon as I swallow it, looking around for a bottle of water and not seeing any.

"You better not throw up in my truck." He sits on a stool, bringing his beer to his lips. His legs are open and perfect for me to step in between them. I look away as soon as the thought pops up in my head, blaming the alcohol.

Turning back to him, so as not to let him have the last word, I snap, "You better not bring anyone home so I have to hear you doing the nasty, which will in fact make me throw up." I pick my beer back up trying to change the taste in my mouth from the vile tequila I just drank.

He doesn't have a chance to say anything to me since Joshua and Macy come up to us. Joshua is wearing the "I'm the Groom" shirt while Macy wears "I'm the Bride."

"It's a good thing you have those shirts." I motion to Joshua with a chin up. "I'd be confused on who is who."

"Yeah," Nate interjects, "she gets confused often." He motions towards me with his head. "Your sister got married on her way here."

I roll my eyes. "Wait, you're dating someone?" Joshua doesn't get the sarcasm. "Why didn't you bring him to meet the family?"

"I'm not dating anyone," I deny. "Nate is just being pissy because he can't bring anyone home tonight since I'm staying with him. Where are all our cousins?" I ask looking around.

"They get here in two days," he informs us. "The hockey season only ends the twenty-third, so a couple of the wives are coming down and then everyone else is coming when the games are over, since the last games are played on the twenty-second."

"What song do you want to sing with me?" Evie asks me when she comes up to my side. "It's between 'Girls Just Want to Have Fun' and 'Dancing Queen.'"

"Oh, I would love 'Dancing Queen,'" Macy says to us.

"I guess that's our answer." I look at Evie, who nods at me.

"What are you two going to sing for us?" Joshua looks at Jack and Nate.

"Yeah," I push, "what are you two going to sing for them?"

"Um," Jack starts mumbling.

"I think you guys should sing 'Shallow.'" I point my bottle of beer at them.

"I think they should do 'All The Single Ladies.'" Evie gets in with me.

"I think you need to stop talking," Jack tells her as we hear someone tapping the microphone.

"Okay, everyone," one of the waitresses starts, "we are ready to kick off karaoke night with soon-to-be Mr. and Mrs. Morrow." She points at them and Joshua raises his hands in the air. "Let's kick it off with them singing 'You're the One that I Want.'"

We cheer for them as they walk over to the stage. Joshua is limping as he follows her up on the stairs. I can't help but burst out laughing at them as they get up there and try to do their John Travolta and Olivia Newton-John impressions. Most of the time, Joshua is falling to the side since he can't put too much weight on his foot.

Everyone cheers them on as they finish with him grabbing her around the waist and dipping her for a kiss at the end. "Try to top that." I push Nate's shoulder. "I think you need to just grab Jack and lay one on him."

"As hot as I think you are," Jack says to Nate, "you're like a little brother to me, so that would be eeew."

All of us burst out laughing as the girl now calls Evie and me to the stage. "Here we go," I say, grabbing a shot on the way to the stage. "This is going to be fun."

"You should introduce yourself," Macy yells from her table and I look over at Evie.

"My name is Elizabeth," I start, "not Lizzy. Don't call me Lizzy, I will throat punch you." I point to everyone, and they laugh. "I'm the groom's favorite sister. I'm also his only sister, so there's that." I point to Joshua. "And this is my favorite sister-in-law"—I point to Evie—"for now." I wink at Macy, who holds up her hand and points to her finger. "She's also my favorite because she didn't force me to do karaoke when she was getting married."

The two of us start to sing and go off-key as soon as the chorus starts, making me laugh so hard I'm crying by the end of the song. Evie holds up her hand for me to give her a high five. I look back over to where we left Jack and Nate and see Jack on his feet standing and clapping, while Nate is leaning on the top of the bar, talking to the maid of honor. Saying something that makes her laugh, she puts her hand on top of his arm, which I know is fake because he's not funny at all.

I shake my head and try not to let seeing him with her bother me. It's been almost seven years since we had one night together. I walk down the steps and look around. "I'm going to the bathroom," I tell Evie, and she nods at me as I walk to the back of the bar.

I push open the door and walk to the sink to rinse my hands, looking down at the water and I'm taken back to that one night, the one night that will forever be one of the best and one of the worst nights of my life. More so the best than the worst, even though we haven't been the same since.

Nate and Joshua had just gotten home for winter break after beating the number one team to move up in the standings. Nate wasn't even supposed to be at the bar that night. He had plans to go with Joshua and Jack to join our cousins at the hockey rink that night for a pick-up game. But now here he was with a couple of his friends from high school just sitting on a barstool laughing. It was the first time I'd seen him since he was back.

"Hey." I walked up to him and smiled big. My heart hammering in my chest as I walked into the middle of his legs and leaned in to kiss his cheek. It was something that I don't think I've ever done before. I mean when he'd come into the house and seen me after a couple of days, he would always give me a side hug or sometimes hold up his hand so I could give him a high five. This was very different and for the life of me I don't know why I did it. I just did.

"Hey," he said smiling at me, "this is a surprise." He hadn't seen me since he headed back to school at the beginning of August.

"You can say that." I looked at the guys next to them remembering them from coming to my house a couple of times, but whose names I was blanking on. It could be

that it was because I was still in the middle of Nate's legs and my hand was on his thigh. It was an intimate gesture that I'd never done before.

"Hey." I held up one of my hands to the guys who are around us. They replied back with a chin lift instead of any verbal words. I was about to move away from Nate and head back to my friends when a guy who was walking past us was pushed into us and Nate wrapped his arm that was holding the beer around my waist and pulled me to him while he extended his other hand to protect me from anyone else that was going to bump into me.

"Watch it," one of Nate's friends told the guy and all I could do was look up at Nate.

"You okay?" he asked me and all the words that I learned my whole life were just stuck and jumbled in my head. The only thing that I could do was nod my head.

He smirked at me and the hold around my waist relaxed a bit but it didn't let me go. "You want something to drink?"

"Sure," I said and then someone called my name from across the bar, and when I looked up, it was one of the girls that I came with. "I should"—I pointed to the girl, my mouth dry—"get back to my friends."

He looked straight into my eyes and butterflies took flight in my stomach. "Yeah, you should," he said, bringing the beer to his lips and then his tongue came out to lick the drop of beer that was on his bottom lip. My hand itched to come up and hold his face and kiss him, but I knew that I needed to get away from him before I did something that I would forever be embarrassed about.

"I'll see you around." As soon as the words came out of my mouth, I groaned inwardly at them and he chuckled.

"Yeah," is all he said as I slowly disengaged myself from him. I walked back to my friends and the whole time I felt like his eyes were on me. One look over my shoulder when I got to my friend proved to me that I was right.

I spent the night chatting with my friends, in between looking over to where he was, and it's as if he knew when I was looking at him because his eyes would come to mine and we would share a look. A couple of times it was reversed, and I could feel him staring at me.

I saw him put the beer down on the bar and he got up, shaking his friends' hands before I saw him walking over to me. My heartbeat hammered so hard, it's a wonder that it didn't come out of my chest. His eyes stared into mine as he made his way to me. *"Do you want a lift home?"* he asked when he was leaving, and I nodded my head, even though I was not ready to go. I said goodbye to the girls who all looked at me as if they knew something was up, but also knew that Nate was like a brother to me.

I smiled up at him. *"Lead the way,"* I said and he slid his hand into mine and pulled me with him as I followed him out.

I thought once we were outside he would let my hand go, but he didn't; he kept it in his until we got to his truck and he unlocked the doors. *"Get in, Elizabeth."* His voice was tight.

I got in and watched him walk around the front of the truck before opening his own door and getting in. He *started the truck and then looked over at me. "You look really good tonight." His voice was husky. "Actually, you look good all the time."*

"You're one to talk." I tried to flirt back but my flirting game was at a solid two. He reached for me at the same time I reached for him, and in the middle of the parking lot, we shared our first kiss. His tongue slid into my mouth as his hand went to the lever under his seat to push it all the way back as he pulled me into his lap. Our mouths never letting the other go as the kiss was everything that I've ever thought it would be and more. I shivered on top of him, and it had nothing to do with the fact that it was freezing cold outside and all I had on was a tank top and an oversized zip-up sweater. It had to do with the fact that his hands were now moving from my hips to my ass.

"Fuck," he hissed out as my eyes slowly peeled open, "Elizabeth."

"Nate." I put my hands on his chest, as I felt his heart hammering as much as mine was.

"You want to come home with me?" The question was one that I thought I would never hear. It was also one that I knew the answer to without even having to think about it.

"Yes." I said the words out loud and then I kissed him again. This time it was me who kissed him first, but it was definitely him that ended the kiss, only to put my ass back in my seat and drive us to his house.

The bathroom door is pushed opened, ripping me from the past, and Macy comes in with another one of her bridesmaids and I just smile at them. "Your performance was so good," Macy compliments me. "Thank you for doing it for me."

"Of course," I reply and then shake the water off my hands, before grabbing a couple of paper towels to dry them off. I pull open the door and step back into the bar. My eyes roam over everyone, but I know I'm looking for him, even if I want to tell myself I'm not.

He and the maid of honor are exactly where they were before, this time the two of them have their heads closer to each other, and I don't even know why but my stomach sinks. "Hey," Jack says, walking out of the bathroom, "you okay?"

I swallow down the lump. "Yeah, just jet-lagged," I tell him and put on a fake smile, trying not to look over at the bar.

Eight

NATE

"YOU COULD MAYBE tell a couple of stories of when you were both growing up," Belinda leans into me to say because the music is so loud. One of the ushers is with his wife, screaming into the microphone. The two of them are dressed in matching outfits so we know they're together. "And if you have any pictures, we could maybe throw them together to do a slide show while we tell the stories."

"That sounds like a great idea," I tell Belinda, the maid of honor, who asked me if I wanted to make a speech with her at the wedding. We've been putting it together a bit while we've been together the last couple of weeks.

The sound of applause now fills the room, and I look over, clapping my hands with everyone else. My head starts to throb. "The next ones up are," the emcee says, sticking her hand in the bowl and pulling out the paper,

"Belinda and Jenny."

"It's your turn to shine," I say. Jenny rushes over to come and grab Belinda.

"They will be singing"—the emcee smiles at the crowd—"'Run the World (Girls).'"

She looks over her shoulder at me. "I'll see you tomorrow at the bowling thing," she says. "We can work on it more then."

"Sounds good." I lean into the bar and then look around for Elizabeth, who is now sitting at a table with Jack and Evie as they laugh at something. I grab my beer and head over to their table, pulling out the chair next to her. She looks up at me. "I was wondering where you were."

"What?" she questions, her eyebrows pinching together. "Where did you think I would be?"

"I don't know," I tell her, "one minute you were on the stage, the next—poof like a puff of smoke—you have disappeared."

"I'm sure you were really watching," she goads, "at the same time you were trying to pick up the maid of honor." She points to the bar. "I didn't think you wanted me as a wingman."

"What the heck are you talking about?" I ask her, seeing Jack and Evie exchange looks, their eyes wide at our exchange. Their heads bobbing back and forth like they are watching a tennis match. If I think about it, we have never ever not bantered back and forth. Well, except for that one night we spent together. Her mouth was too busy doing other things to sass me. A vision of her ripping off her shirt once we got into my apartment now fills my head. The smirk she gave me before sliding down to her knees is etched in my memory, as if it was yesterday and not seven years ago.

"Are you okay?" Jack asks me. "Your face went like really red there for a minute." He puts his hand on my shoulder. "Do you need water?"

"I'm fine." I turn back to look at Elizabeth and her bare shoulders and I have this sudden need to bite her. "I have no idea what the hell you are talking about."

"Well, you were flirting with her." She leans back in her chair, tapping her finger on the table in front of her. "Or at least you were trying to. The reason I know this is she laughed at your joke." She tilts her head to the side. "And, well, between me and you; you aren't funny at all."

"For your information," I snap at her, "we were collaborating."

"About how you wanted to get her in your bed?" She snorts. "I know, I saw."

"For a speech," I hiss at her. "For the maid of honor and best man speech." She nods her head at me like sure. "Do you think I would try to pick up the maid of honor?"

"Yes," she snorts out, then she whips her head to Evie and Jack, slapping her hand on the table. The smile is gone from her face and in its place is a look of seriousness. "Wait, is she staying with you guys?" she asks Evie and Jack. "Because if she is, maybe we could do a swap or an exchange, one girl for the other."

"She is not staying with us," Jack answers, trying to

hide his smirk.

"Fuck," she swears, and I just shake my head.

"Sucks for you." I point at her. "You're stuck with me."

"It does suck that your pickup game is lame." She laughs. "See what I did there? I rhymed."

"You are the only one laughing at your joke," I inform her.

"Evie"—Jack turns to proposition his wife—"would you like to come to the bathroom to make out with me?" He gets up and she smiles up at him.

"That's disgusting," Elizabeth says. "Go make out in the corner like normal people." She points to the corner. "Or you can wait until you get home."

"Yeah, but then I have to sit here awkwardly with the two of you as you trade insults with each other."

"Um, that's insulting," Elizabeth informs him. "I'm the only one trading anything at this point; he can't even do that right." She folds her arms over her chest, and I have the sudden need to kiss the shit out of her if only to make her shut the fuck up.

"Okay, everyone." The emcee comes back to the mic. "It's time for some holiday sing-along."

"No, absolutely fucking not." Elizabeth shakes her head. "I'm leaving. I'd rather sit outside on your front steps than stay here to sing 'Winter Wonderland.'" She gets up. "This is my Irish goodbye," she states and she literally looks around once, not saying anything to anyone before she just heads for the fucking door.

I look over at Joshua and motion to the door, and his

eyes catch the back of his sister's head. He gives me a chin up and then I turn and rush out of the bar, seeing her walking to the truck. "You were so sure I was going to follow you out here?" I say, unlocking the door.

"No"—she looks over her shoulder—"I was going to actually wait in the truck until you were ready." She pulls open the door. "Which it looks like you are ready now." She gets in. "Unless you want to try to stay and see if Mindy is going to come home with you tonight."

"First off," I start, opening my own truck door, "her name is Belinda." I really fucking hope it's Belinda since I called her that five times.

"Is it?" She tilts her head to the side. "Are you sure about that?" She puts so much doubt in me that I pull out my phone and search up her name in the wedding emails we've been getting weekly.

"Aha," I say, turning it to face her, "says right there Belinda, maid of honor."

"Made you look." She claps her hands and laughs. Her phone rings from her back pocket and she pulls it out.

"Is that your boyfriend?" I ask her, gripping my phone tighter.

"It is," she confirms and then answers it, "Hey, sugarplum."

"Hey yourself," I hear a female voice. "Ty said you are having the best time you've ever had in your life," the woman says and Elizabeth bursts out loud laughing.

"Is that what he bet?" she asks the phone.

"I'm having the worst time," she tells the woman. "I

was kicked out of my house and left to fend for myself. And to top it all off, I have to stay with my brother's best friend, who I don't really like."

The woman laughs. "I just read that romance book."

"Did it involve murder?" She looks over at me.

"Let me see what he looks like," she urges and I shake my head, but she turns the phone on me and I see the woman wearing a robe and glasses staring at me. "Hello," she says, putting her face even more into the screen, "aren't you a tall glass of water?"

"Hi." I hold up my hand and smirk at her. "It's nice to meet you."

"Honey"—she winks at me—"the pleasure is all mine." Elizabeth turns the phone to look at her. "So you are having a good time."

"What part of anything I just said makes you think I'm having a good time?" she inquires, and the woman laughs.

"I'll just pay Ty his twenty dollars and say he was right," she announces, "and you have all the fun tonight. You've earned it."

"Goodbye." Elizabeth hangs up on her. "That was Gayle." She looks over at me. "She's my triage nurse who runs the board and me, and basically everything else." Her voice trails off and she yawns as she looks out the window. I acknowledge her statement with a hum and we settle into silence for the rest of the drive.

We pull into the driveway, and she gets out and walks around the truck. "This was super fun," she deadpans. "Loved the way you got up on stage and belted out your heart."

"I was going to, but you didn't give me a chance to do anything because you were all 'peace out, bitches.'"

"Okay, for one, I would never say that." She snorts as I walk to the door and then cover the keypad with my hand as I put the code in, making her push me to the side. "That's not fair."

"If you have the code," I tell her as the sound of the lock starts working, "then what would you need me for?"

I turn the knob and then look at her. "Nate." She puts her hand on my chest, and I can feel the heat from her hand come through my sweater and my T-shirt. "I still wouldn't need you, regardless of if I had the code or not."

"So you'd freeze outside?" I ask her and she chuckles.

"I bet you one hundred dollars"—she folds her arms over her chest—"one of your garage doors is unlocked." I glare at her. "And I know this because you and Joshua always left it open for the other person."

"You don't know me," I scoff at her as she turns and stomps down the stairs and heads to the garage. "The dog," I yell out when I look over and see Whiskey stick his head out of the door and sniff the air, "he's going to run away."

"Yeah, right," she says, turning and coming back, "you owe me a hundred bucks." She taps my cheek with her hand. "I take cash." She smirks. "Hello, Whiskey." She squats to rub his neck. "Did you have fun tonight?" She gets up and walks into the house. "Did you chew any of his things?"

I walk in after her and shrug off my jacket as she

walks to the back and opens the door for him. "Do you have to go to the bathroom?" she asks him and he just sits by her feet. "Did you pee in his bed?" she whispers to him. "It's okay if you did."

"Are you done with that?" I ask, pulling the sweater over my head and tossing it on the sofa, leaving me in my white T-shirt. Her eyes roam from my head to my shirt and then back up again. I can see the fire in them, and she catches me watching her with a smirk on my face. "You hungry?" I ask her instead of saying, "Do you see something that you want?"

"No, not really." She breathes out a big sigh as she walks to the front door, taking off her boots. I walk back over to the staircase and the two of us walk up the steps together, almost in unison. Our arms rub against each other's, and my heart starts to go nuts in my chest. Not a word is spoken, only the sound of our breathing can be heard. We get to the top of the steps.

"Do you need anything?" I turn to ask her, wanting to drag her to my room and ask her why our night meant nothing to her.

"I think I'm good." She nods. "Night," she says and turns to the spare bedroom, closing the door behind her.

I stand here watching the light come on under the door and then turn to look down at Whiskey, who is waiting on the top two steps to see if I'm going back downstairs or to my bedroom. "Let's go, boy." I motion with my head. "Time for some shut-eye."

I listen to her moving around in the bedroom as I head to my own. I leave the door open, and notice her walk out of the bedroom and then head to the bathroom. "Should I go in there?" I ask Whiskey, who jumps on the bed. "Yeah, that's what I think too. Not the best idea."

Nine

Elizabeth

December 17th

THE PURRING IN my ear gets louder and louder as I slowly open my eyes. Gray fur fills my eyes as Baby Cat tickles my nose. I move my head away from him and mumble, "Good morning to you." His head is lying on his paws as he purrs, not even bothering to open his eyes. I close my eyes and then turn on the side to see if I can fall back asleep. I give up after a couple of minutes and then stretch my arms over my head once I'm on my back. Baby Cat finally pops his head up but only to side-eye me for waking him. He then turns to his side and stretches out on the top of my pillow. "Dude, I'm sharing this pillow with you and not the other way around." I arch my back, stretching again and the soreness now makes me wince.

My calves ache, my arms feel tight, and my head is slightly throbbing. My eyes also feel like they're filled with sand, burning from either exhaustion or the fact it's been two nights in a row that I've gone out and had alcohol. I toss the covers off me and slide one leg off the bed and then the other. I sit up and then look back over at Baby Cat. "Am I the only one getting up today?" I ask him as I stand up and it fully hits me that I feel like someone ran over my body.

I walk out of the bedroom and stop when I see Nate casually walking out of his. The shorts he's wearing are hanging on his hips. His chest is perfectly sculpted and on display, with Whiskey gingerly walking by his side. "Oh no." I hold up my hand, blocking my eyes but still catching one more peek of his abs that are on point, and I have to wonder how many times a week he works out. "My eyes." I turn my head to the side. "I'm seeing nipples."

I hear the rumble of his laugh, and I turn to look back at him as Whiskey comes over to me, his tail wagging in excitement. "Seriously, put them away." I point with one finger to his chest while the other hand pets Whiskey. "Or is this one of your sexist ideas where I'm not allowed to show my nipples because I'm a girl, but you can because you're a guy."

"Someone wise once said they're just nipples." He shakes his head as he walks over to the stairs.

"I don't know who told you that," I say to his bare back, my eyes lingering on his ass, "but that person sounds really smart."

"She's okay," he tosses over his shoulder. "A shit bowler, but you can't win them all."

I gasp, "I will have you know that I'm a fantastic bowler."

"Maybe down under…" His voice trails as he gets to the bottom of the stairs and turns to walk down the hallway, as I walk over to the railing and look down at him.

"I'm jet-lagged," I defend myself. He looks up at me, his eyes twinkling and the sleep now gone from his eyes.

"If you say so."

"I am," I tell him, "and that is all that matters." I don't wait for him to answer me before turning and storming into the bathroom. "Jerk." I head to the bathroom, washing my hands and face right after before walking out and seeing Baby Cat stroll out of my bedroom.

"Good morning, Your Highness," I greet, picking him up in my arms and he immediately twists in my arms to jump out. "Yeah, I'm kind of not liking you either these past couple of days." He runs into Nate's bedroom and I'm almost tempted to follow him in there, but then I smell coffee.

I think about going to put on a sweater to cover my nipples, but then I turn and walk down the steps. "If he can be bare chested, I can be wearing a tank top." I look down at my light-yellow tank top with little light-blue flowers. The matching shorts aren't tight but instead are loose and float around my legs. The cold air hits me right as I turn the corner and start to walk into the kitchen. Nate's standing at the back door, closing it now that

Whiskey has come back in.

"It's cold out there," I say and he looks back at me.

"Yeah." He smirks and his eyes trail over my face to my now pebbled nipples.

"Look at your own nipples," I tell him as I walk into the kitchen and head over to the cupboard that the mugs are in. "Did you make your coffee yet?" I ask him and he just shakes his head.

"I was too busy tending to the animals," he replies as Whiskey goes over to his bowl filling the room with the sound of him crunching on his breakfast.

I pull down two mugs and groan. "My whole body is sore," I mumble as I pick up the pot of coffee and pour one for him and then one for me. "It feels like I just did a huge workout."

"Um." He leans a hip against the counter next to me. "Did you forget what you were doing?"

"What are you talking about?" I ask him as he pushes off the counter and heads to the fridge to grab the milk.

"You spent the beginning of the night bowling like a normal person." I watch him. "Then the rest of the night you were trying to get your ball to spin."

I open my mouth. "Um, Nate, I was there, and it did spin."

Last night's event was bowling with the bridal party, and I would say I'm an okay bowler, but I'm highly competitive. Like, I'm not losing; I don't care who you are, even if you're a kid. If we're playing a game, I'm aiming to win. You can cry in your Wheaties if you have to. "It did not spin." He shakes his head as he adds milk to his coffee and then looks over at mine and waits for me to give him the go-ahead.

Being the stubborn person I am, I grab the milk from him and wince. The throbbing from my wrist now comes through. "Oh, it spun," I affirm, so sure of myself, but there were bottomless margaritas, so anything could be possible. I have vague memories, snippets, more or less. "I think someone has a video."

"Yeah, they do." He nods, grabbing the milk from me to pour it in my coffee as I argue with him. "I do. I also have one of you running in the other lane trying to blow on the ball to get it to spin."

"You know what? Your nipples are distracting me." I hold up my hand. "You should put them away."

"I would say the same." He looks down and his mouth forms a smirk. "One almost took out my eyes."

"It's not my fault that me being naked bothers you." I bring the cup of coffee to my lips.

"Nothing about you naked bothers me." He takes his own sip. "Quite the contrary, actually."

My head about whips around to stare at him, but I don't have a chance to say anything before his phone rings. He walks over to the jacket he tossed on the couch and pulls it out. "It's your brother."

"Don't fucking answer it," I tell him. "He'll probably be like, 'Hey, there's a break in the schedule, so we've added snowshoeing to it.'"

He laughs at me as he answers the phone and puts it on speaker. I narrow my eyes and glare right at him for not listening to me. "Hey," he greets, "you're on speakerphone and your sister is here."

"No, I'm not!" I shout. "I'm, in fact, not here. I'm a ghost."

"Oh good, I have the both of you so it can save me a phone call," he says and Nate puts the phone on the counter, and I hold my hands up like I'm about to strangle him. "Just a reminder that it's the day to do the last fitting."

"Last fitting?" I repeat. "I didn't do a first fitting."

"We know," Joshua replies. "We were wondering if you could maybe get there a bit early so she can work on yours first."

"Who is we?" I ask him. "I emailed her my measurements that I took with her on Zoom. It'll be fine."

"It's my wedding day," he snaps and I look up at Nate, who just raises his eyebrows.

"Yes, wedding day, not fucking wedding week," I retort. "I'll be there when I need to be there and not a minute before. I have things I'm doing."

"Yeah, like what?" he asks me.

"Like annoying Nate with my nipples," I declare, and he grabs the phone from the counter.

"No nipples have been seen on purpose," he denies into the phone. "I'll drive her there as soon as she gets dressed."

"No, he won't," I sing out as he disconnects the phone. "Fine, I'll just be lounging here." I walk over to the couch and put my knee into it before I sit down and cuddle in the corner. Whiskey comes up and joins me. "With my nipples, until fifteen minutes before we're due to be there."

"Should I make breakfast?" he asks me, leaning his elbows on the island.

"We would not say no to some pancakes and scrambled eggs." I pet Whiskey's head. "Would we?"

"So, you want pancakes and scrambled eggs."

"I mean, if you are making them for yourself"—I hold up my hands—"I won't say no."

"You could just say, 'Yes, Nate, that sounds great.'" He looks at me. "'I would love to have some pancakes and scrambled eggs.'"

"If you're making them, sure, I would like that very much."

"Were you always this much of a pain in my ass?" he asks me and I shrug.

"Pretty much." I turn back to look at him watching me. "I plan to be a pain in your ass every single day I'm here."

"Well, unlike bowling." He snorts. "You are killing it at that."

"Do you hear that, Whiskey?" I rub his head. "I'm a pain in his ass."

"Hey, at least now you're talking to me," he mumbles, and my head turns to watch his back as he takes the egg carton out of the fridge.

"What does that mean?" I ask him, the pit of my stomach now getting tight.

"It means exactly what I said it means." He puts the things on the counter.

"Are we talking in code?" I ask him, taking another

sip of my coffee. "Because I don't understand a thing you are saying."

"Really?" His eyebrows go up. "You have no idea?" The back of my neck starts to tingle. "None?"

"I have no idea." I stand up and head toward the kitchen. "Do you want to say, add anything?"

"Nope." He shakes his head, turning and walking to the stove and I just watch him. "I also have no eggs." He holds up the white container. "So how about we get dressed and I'll take you out for breakfast?"

"Are you going to fill me in on what I need to know?" I ask him and he's about to say something when the phone rings again, this time I see it's my mother.

"That would be for you," he says, pushing his phone my way. "I'm going to get changed."

I grab the phone and put it on speakerphone. "Super Sex Hotline, how may we assist you on the road to the best orgasms?"

My mother gasps at the same time Nate does, which makes me burst out laughing. "You are incredible," she hisses.

"I know." I smile as I walk past him with his phone in my hand. "I've been told. Many times." I look back at him and my eyebrows go up. "How can I help you this wonderful morning, Mom?"

"I just got off the phone with your brother," she answers, "and he says you're being unreasonable."

It's my turn to gasp. "Mom, he's becoming groomzilla," I say in my defense, "and he said I was bigger since he saw me last."

"He did not." Nate takes his side.

"No one is asking for you to intrude in my private conversation, Nate," I hiss at him before turning my attention back at my mother. "He said I needed extra time with the seamstress, what do you think that means?"

"I'm sure you misunderstood."

"Wow." I stomp up the steps. "I think I know what I heard."

"I'm coming to get you," she states. "I'll be there in fifteen minutes."

"No," I sing out, "Nate was going to take me for breakfast."

"I'll take you for breakfast. Nate, you can come with us."

"No worries, Denise. I have a bunch of things to do for the wedding anyway."

"Liar," I mouth to him, and he smirks. "Bye, Mom." I hang up the phone. "I hope you're happy."

"Why is this my fault?" He walks up the steps and stands in front of me. He holds out his hand and I hand him his phone. "It's your fault because you made me answer the phone."

"She knows where I live," he points out to me, "so she would have just shown up here."

"You are just full of excuses," I tell him. "Figures," I snip and walk to the bathroom.

"What the fuck does that mean?" he snaps at me.

I shrug my shoulders. "It means exactly what I said it means," I throw back in his face. "Now, as much as I would love to stand here and discuss whatever the fuck we are talking about, I have to get changed." I turn and head to the bathroom, shutting the door behind me and locking it. "He's not worth it," I mumble before I start the shower. "Just forget it. The time to talk about this was the day after, not now, after seven freaking years."

Merry Christmas
AND A HAPPY NEW YEAR

Ten

MISTLETOE

NATE

A CHRISTMAS CAROL is playing softly on the radio as I turn onto the gravel road that leads to the parking lot. Christmas trees line the wooden fence all the way to the open parking lot. Looking at the clock on the dashboard, I see I'm about one minute early and I was expecting there to be more people here already.

Turning into the first open parking spot, I put the truck in park before turning it off. My hand goes to the handle as I open the door and step out. The cold air hits right away; it's always cooler when we go north of the city. The sun shining in the sky is very much misleading as I grab my hunter-green jacket from the passenger seat, shrugging it on over my beige knitted sweater. I lean over to grab my beanie, putting it on the top of my head. Tucking my gloves in the pockets of my jacket, I snatch up my phone and tuck it in my back pocket of my jeans.

A gust of wind blows all around me as I head toward the log cabin. Garland lines the top of it with little twinkle red and white lights. Another wooden fence lines up with the entryway to the doors with rows of big Christmas trees. Some with lights on them. Some with red garland. Some completely bare.

I hear cars arriving behind me and I look over my shoulder to see at least ten more SUVs have just arrived. Turning around, I see Joshua hobble out of his SUV as Macy gets out of the passenger side, grabbing her bedazzled Bride hat. I look over at Joshua to see his black beanie has Groom written in white. When I make eye contact with him, I shake my head and all he does is smirk and then shrug his shoulders.

I left him two hours ago, after my suit fitting, and went to the office to make sure everything was okay and to check in with a couple of the animals that had surgery, promising to meet the wedding party here. The groom limps slowly with his bride beside him, holding her hand, and my eyes scan the crowd for Elizabeth.

Spotting her getting out of another car, I watch as her head tips back and she laughs at something someone said. Her blonde hair slips around her face as she puts on her black shades and walks into the parking lot greeting some of her family members, giving me a chance to take her in. She's changed from when she walked out of the house this morning to go for her dress fitting. Now she's wearing tight black leggings with a thick brown sweater. Her black vest opens at her chest, and she puts on a black knitted hat with a big pompom on the top that hangs back. Her boots go up to her calves with thick white socks sticking out.

"Hey." Joshua steps in front of me, blocking his sister out. "Long time no see."

"After the wedding," I mumble to him, "I don't want to see you for six to eight weeks."

He laughs and slaps me on the shoulder as the family now gathers around us. I look over seeing more of his uncles have arrived. All of them used to play for the NHL and they still practice at least twice a week. In the summer, most of them come down to help Zack with the arena and help with the on-ice training.

I walk up to Max and Matthew first and hold out my hand for them. "Hey," I say and they smile big at me. The two of them have always been a constant in our lives. Max might be the blood uncle, but if you tried to tell Matthew he wasn't their uncle, he would fight you until the bitter end.

"Hey yourself," Max says, slapping my shoulder. "Do me a favor." He leans in and whispers in my ear, "If you get married and do this"—he looks around—"I'm going to beat your ass."

I chuckle. "Trust me, if I get married"—I look down at my boots—"it'll be either really fucking small or we'll elope."

"I like that thought," Max says, looking over at Matthew, the running joke in the family since he eloped with Matthew's sister many, many years ago. To this day, Matthew is still bitter about it, even though they had a big wedding the year after, to Matthew it means nothing.

"Best thing I did was elope."

"Really?" Matthew retorts. "The best thing?"

"Yup," he replies, his smile going big. "Not only did I get to marry the love of my life…" He takes a deep inhale. "But I got to have one up on you."

Matthew glares at him. "That's still my sister."

"Yup," he agrees, "but she's my wife. Which I think trumps sister on the food chain."

I shake my head and walk toward Elizabeth, and I have no idea why I'm even going to her. I mean, I know why I'm going to her, I just don't like the fact I'm drawn to her anyway. This morning we traded jabs about that night, neither of us letting on that was what we were both talking about, but neither of us outright saying it. *It's been seven years, it's time to let it go,* I've been telling myself, but I don't know, something is not letting me move on. "Where is your jacket?" I ask her as I get closer to her. I can't see her eyes because of her glasses, but from the look on her face, she's glaring at me.

"It didn't go with my outfit." She uses both her hands to move up and down in front of her. "As long as my feet are warm, that's all I care about."

The sound of a whistle has us turning to look at the front. "Okay, if we can have everyone's attention." Joshua holds up his hand. "Thank you all for coming with us."

"Did we have a choice?" Elizabeth mumbles from beside me. "At this point I feel like I'm being held hostage."

I roll my lips and look down at my boots to stop

from laughing. "We are going to head in and meet with Sabrina, who will explain everything to us."

He turns and starts to walk toward the log cabin. "Explain things?" Elizabeth says to me as we walk behind everyone. "I thought we were coming, picking the tree, and then leaving."

"I don't think it's going to be that easy," I reply to her and she grips my arm.

"I will give you one thousand dollars to push me down"—she looks around—"and then I'll fake something."

"I'm not pushing you down," I tell her.

"Okay, fine, I'll push you down," she reconsiders. "I mean, you might be bigger than me, but I think I can take you."

I chuckle at her and then start to walk forward. "You really are no fun," she huffs out as she walks past me toward the log cabin.

"Someone is not in the Christmas spirit," I retort and she stops walking to turn and probably kick me in the balls, which will make me fall to the side.

"Oh look," one of the bridesmaids says, "they are under the mistletoe." We both look up and see it hanging on a clear fishing wire. "You guys have to kiss."

I look back at Elizabeth, who snaps at me, "Absolutely not." She actually pushes me away. "I'd rather have seven years of bad luck."

"I don't think it's an exact time frame." I walk past her. "Also, if a woman refuses to kiss under the mistletoe, it's believed she won't receive marriage proposals the following year."

"Who said that?" She folds her armd over her chest.

"It was said in Victorian times."

"How do you know that?" she asks me and I shrug.

"One of my techs mentioned it the other week."

"So someone else didn't want to kiss you." I hate that I can't see her eyes as she closes the distance between us. "Figures."

"She's one of my staff members," I tell her. "Even if she wanted a kiss, that would be a no."

"You can spin it whatever way you want to spin it. I'm going to go with she didn't want to kiss you."

I lean down now and go close to her ear. "If memory serves me right"—I can smell her soft perfume mixed with her berry shampoo—"you kissed me first." Her back goes straight as I step back away from her. To be honest, both of us lunged at the same time, but I'm not going to tell her that part if she doesn't remember.

She just stands there with her mouth hanging open. "If memory serves me, you kissed me back."

I smile at her brightly. "Damn fucking right I did." I smirk. "But it doesn't change the fact you kissed me first." I tap my finger on her nose.

She storms past me, and I can't help but chuckle to myself. "I guess it's one nothing for me."

She doesn't even hold the door for me and I catch it right before it's going to smash into my face. "Oops." She snickers. "My bad. My hand slipped."

"I'm sure it did," I state, standing in the back of the room, with everyone piled into the warm room.

There are Christmas trees decorated all around the room, next to each tree are racks and racks of ornaments. Each tree its own bright color. "If I can have everyone's attention." The woman holds up a stick. "We'd like to welcome you to Magical Winter Wonderland tree farm." She smiles. "It's our honor to have you here with us."

I look around and see a sitting area all the way in the back with a small counter and I read the menu, seeing they have a couple of baked goods and hot chocolate or hot apple cider. "We will take you all out to the field"—I turn back to her—"and you will get to choose the tree for your home." I hear conversations happening around the room. "You can either cut down your own tree, which we do recommend if you have done it before, or we can assist you."

The chatter starts once again and now Macy steps up. "If you see a tree and you already picked one out for home, let us know and we'll have it taken over to the reception area so we can take pictures with it."

We all start walking out of the cabin and head over to the side. "I'm cutting down the tree," Elizabeth declares from beside me.

"What?" I turn to her.

"You need a tree for your house," she points out, "and I'm assuming you will be getting one for your house. I will be cutting it down."

"You really think someone is going to give you a chainsaw to cut down a tree?" I turn to her. "Honestly, ask anyone if they would give you a chainsaw."

"I'm cutting my tree down," she huffs.

"To put in my house." I follow her as she treks it up the side mountain.

"You said make myself at home, did you not?" She stops next to a row of small trees. "This is me making myself at home."

"I could say no," I mention as she walks through a bunch of small trees. I see her parents over on the other side with Jack and Evie as they point out the biggest ones.

"You could," Elizabeth says, "or we can get two trees."

"Where would I put two trees?"

"I could put one in my room," she suggests, moving past the trees and going to the other section.

"You really are taking the *make yourself at home* saying literally."

"You betcha." She smiles at me. "Who do you think I talk to about getting the saw?"

"Elizabeth," I say her name, "there is no chainsaw, it's a handsaw."

"Okay, then who do I talk to about getting a handsaw?"

I roll my eyes. "Have you even picked out a tree yet?" I ask her and she looks around.

"I want to be prepared, Nate." She moves her foot, and she trips over a branch and falls flat on her face. The sunglasses fly off of her face as she uses her hands to stop the fall. I'm reaching out, but I'm not fast enough before she hits the ground.

I shake my head, making my way over to her, grabbing her glasses along the way. "How prepared are you now?"

She pushes up on her elbows.

"Wow." She turns on her back. "You aren't even going to fall down for me." She starts to get up and I hold out a hand for her. I'm thinking she's going to grab it, but instead she slaps it away.

"I don't need your help, Nate." She gets to her feet and dusts off the snow from her leg and her arm, her hands now turning red.

"Where are your gloves?" I ask her and then hold up a hand. "Let me guess, they didn't go with the outfit." I reach into my pocket and pull out my own gloves. "Here, I'll sacrifice frostbite for you."

She comes to me, standing toe to toe. "I'd rather suffer frostbite than accept anything from you."

"Well, if it makes you feel better," I say, leaning down closer to her face, not sure I should say what I want to say, but also not caring anymore. She's pushed every single one of my buttons since she paraded back into town. Not once even talking about that night to clear the air. If she doesn't care, I'm not going to. At least this is what I'm telling myself. "I would sacrifice myself and get naked with you if it meant keeping you warm." My words shock her, her mouth parting on a gasp. "Your glasses"—I hold them out to her—"wouldn't want you to trip."

Eleven

Christmas Tree Farm

Elizabeth

HE SMIRKS DOWN at me, his stupid face with stupid stubble and an even more stupid chin. "Well, if it makes you feel better…" He leans closer to me and I can smell his musky scent. My hand itches to grab his jacket and pull him closer to me, to see if the kiss I remembered vaguely is as good as I think it is. Or is it maybe going to be horrible and I won't want to kiss him anymore. "I would sacrifice myself and get naked with you if it meant keeping you warm." I have imagined a bunch of words coming out of his mouth. But I never in all my life imagined him saying that to me. His words leave me in shock, my mouth hanging open, while other parts of me tighten, and if he wasn't looking straight at me, I might even fucking shiver at his words. "Your glasses." His hand comes up to hold up my glasses. "Wouldn't want you to trip."

I snatch them out of his hand and hiss, "You better watch where you are going." I try not to sound like I'm panting from his words.

"Hey, you guys," Jack says, running to us, "have you found anything you like?"

"Does it look like we've found anything we like?" I ask him, putting my sunglasses on so I can stare at him without him actually knowing.

"Someone is grouchy today," he notes, trying not to laugh.

"Today?" Nate says, shaking his head. "How long has she been in town? She got grouchy probably the day before she landed." He puts his hands on his hips, his jacket unzipped, showing the beige knitted sweater under it. You can see how soft it is, and I find myself wanting to touch it.

"Long enough to be tired of being harassed every single morning about my nipples," I hiss at him, and Jack's eyes widen as he looks at Nate, who holds up his hands.

"Relax," he placates. "I haven't seen her nipples out in the open, but she wears thin shirts, so I see what I don't want to see."

I tilt my head to the side. "It's good to know you don't want to see them."

"That isn't what I said," he defends his words.

"This looks like fun," Evie interrupts, coming to stand next to Jack, "are you guys arguing over which tree you want?" She wraps her arms around Jack's waist.

"No, baby," Jack says softly, wrapping an arm around

her shoulders and pulling her to him before he then leans down to kiss her. "It's about Nate not wanting to see Elizabeth's nipples."

"Oh, will the two of you get a room already?" I urge, walking past them and over to the other displays of trees that are now in a row from smallest to biggest.

I walk down and in between the different rows, looking at the trees with him following me. "Why are you following me?" I look over my shoulder.

"I'm following you because we are going to be getting one tree," he tells me, "and we are going to agree on which one to get."

"And I'm going to be the one to cut it down," I declare, stopping at one that isn't too tall but is full, and I run my hand over the pine needles.

"If you think you can cut down a tree"—his tone is condescending—"then I will watch you cut down a tree."

"Oh, I'm going to cut it down all right," I assure, "and it's going to be this one."

"Really?" he asks, walking around it. "This is the one you like out of all of them?"

I look at the tree again, second-guessing my choice as he walks to the one beside it and then the one next to it. "You didn't even see them all." He looks around some more.

"What is wrong with this one?" I ask him and he comes back.

"Absolutely nothing, but I don't want you to argue with me later that we should have taken another one."

"No." I shake my head. "I want this one"—I point to

the tree—"and I want to cut it down." I look around and then spot a guy on a tractor with a red wagon behind it. I wave my hand in the air to flag him down and he comes over to us.

"Did you find the tree?" he asks, coming off the tractor and looking at the tree we are in front of. "This is a good one," he says, "lots of green needles."

"Yes." I admire the tree I chose. "This is the one," I tell him, "and I want to cut it down myself."

He smiles at me, his white hair shining in the sunlight. If his beard was longer, he could pass for a Santa. "The lady is cutting down her own tree?"

"I'm also a doctor," I inform him. "I did surgery rotation for a full six months."

"Because cutting into flesh is the same thing as cutting into wood?" Nate asks me and I take off my glasses so he can see my glare.

The man walks over to the wagon and I'm expecting him to come back with a chainsaw or something along that line. What I'm not expecting is for him to come to me with a metal saw with a wooden top and a green metal handle. "Here you go, girlie"—he hands me the saw—"have at it."

"Um," I say, grabbing the saw from him by the handle and looking down at it and then back at Nate, who is smirking at me, and I know that I'm not going to let him win. "Okay," I say, getting on my knees, then lying on my back to see the bottom of the tree. It's a lot thicker than I thought it would be.

Nate comes over and squats down beside me. "So

what are you thinking?" he asks me, and I can feel the wetness from the snow seeping into my black yoga pants.

"I'm thinking you shouldn't be poking the bear," I snap, "when the bear is holding a saw in her hand."

"Um," the guy says from behind Nate. "Not wanting to poke the bear"—he holds up his hand—"but I have a tarp in my wagon that we can put down so you aren't soaking wet."

"I will take the tarp," I agree, moving to a sitting position, which just makes my ass even wetter. As he walks over to the back of his tractor, he takes out a folded beige tarp. "Here you go, young lady." He hands me the tarp and I get up to grab it from him, putting the saw down on the ground and then unfolding the tarp.

"That is better," I state, looking down at the tarp and then getting on my knees and reaching over to grab the saw.

"Um," the guy starts again. "If you want, I have a pair of gloves," he offers to me, taking a pair of work gloves out of his back pocket.

"Thank you." I reach for the yellow gloves. "See? He's helpful, unlike you, who didn't even try to help."

"I offered you my gloves when you got here," Nate defends himself, then looks at the guy. "I offered her my gloves."

He stands back and tries to not laugh at him. "Okay." I put on the worn yellow gloves. "Here we go," I declare, getting on my stomach and then moving the bottom branches of the tree out of the way and they bounce back and smack me in the face. "Motherfucker," I swear at the sting of the branches making my face burn. I place the saw across the trunk of the tree and start moving it back and forth.

I move the saw back and forth for what feels like an eternity. A fucking eternity, and my breathing is coming in pants as I move it back and forth.

"If you want," Nate offers, "I can take over." I blow the hair out of my face. "Just saying, I could do my part."

"I'm fine," I assure, feeling the sweat rolling down my back from exertion and the cashmere sweater I'm wearing.

"Sometimes, the tree can bind the saw," he says as I huff out, and it feels like I'm running full steam ahead down a road that goes on forever.

"Well, how do we stop that?" I ask him, trying not to show how exhausted I am. "Are you going to give me another saw?"

"No." He chuckles. "It means the trunk is pressing into the blade."

"And how do we remedy this?" I ask, the saw stuck in the trunk.

"I'll hold the trunk and pull it back," he explains. "Usually it's the helper who does this."

I look at Nate, who is just watching me. "My helper is broken," I huff out as I continue cutting down the tree. "Where do I find another one?"

"I can hold it," Nate says to him and stands beside him as he holds the tree. The saw goes in easily now as I push through the rest, by the end of it my arms feel like they are on fire. The tree starts to fall to the side and I look up at the two men. "I told you I could do it." I drop the saw on the snow and then get up on my knees. "And you said I couldn't."

"No one said that," Nate refutes, trying not to smirk at me as he looks down at the tree with his hands on his hips.

"What you can do," the man says to us, "is cut the dead branches on the bottom. It will make putting it in its stand easier once you get home."

"Stand?" Nate asks. "It doesn't come with a stand?"

"No, sir"—he shakes his head—"but you can buy one inside."

"I have to do everything." I get up on my feet and hand him back his gloves. "Why don't you clean it up a little bit, and I'll go and buy the stand."

He reaches into his back pocket and pulls out his wallet. "Here." He tosses me his wallet and not just his card.

I catch his wallet in my hand as he walks over and bends down to take the saw. "What do you want me to do with this?"

"Pay for the things," he explains. "The PIN is my birthday."

"You know you aren't supposed to tell anyone your PIN," I remind him.

"You aren't anyone," he states, squatting down and sawing off the pieces of wood without breaking a sweat.

"Yeah, you got the easy part," I tell him and turn with a huff to start to walk back to the cabin.

"Hey," I say, walking in and seeing my parents there

with my aunts and uncle.

"Honey," my mother says, coming to me, "you have tree needles all over your hair." I pull the hat off of my head and shake it. "Did you fall into a tree?"

"No." I snort. "I was cutting down my tree."

She gasps, "What? There was a guy going around doing it for you."

"Yes, but I wanted to do it myself"—I dust myself off—"and I did."

"You were always so independent." She puts her hand on my cheek. "Never wanted me to do anything for you." She blinks away tears in her eyes. "So much so, you moved halfway across the world."

"Well, to be fair, that is where my job is," I remind her and she shakes her head.

"You can work anywhere and you know it." The words hit me to the core for the first time.

"I have to pay for the tree," I segue, my mind twirling around and around. I step up to the cash register and look at the woman. "I need a stand for my tree."

"They are all on that side." She points to the wall and I walk over to the side. I'm starting to pick one when I feel Nate beside me.

"What is taking you so long?" he huffs out and I see his jacket is now zipped.

"I was talking to my mother, and now I am deciding what kind of stand I want."

"Just take any one," he urges, picking up the first one that is on his side.

"What about decorations?" I ask him, looking around

at all of the trees decorated. "Do you have decorations?"

"I do," he says softly. "I have the ones from Grandma and Grandpa," he mentions the grandparents he moved in with after his parents were killed in a car accident when he was sixteen. They were coming home from an evening out when they were hit by a drunk driver. They died on impact and the driver died the day after. His grandfather passed away when he was eighteen and then his grandmother a year later. It's why he's so close to my family, they practically took him in when his parents died. He sometimes would be over at our house every single day. It would be a rare day when he wasn't having dinner with us. I think it was then I fell in love with Nate, but that was before he broke my heart.

"Do you have enough?" My voice gets soft, and he just nods his head.

"I have lots of ones from my childhood." He looks around. "But if you see something else you want. Just get it."

"No," I reply, smiling at him, "I think it'll be perfect."

"Did you pay?" he asks me and I shake my head, and he holds out his hand for his wallet.

"What were you doing this whole time while I was putting the tree in the truck?" His voice is tight, and the soft moment is gone. I know I should handle him with a little bit of care since it probably brought up sad memories for him. I can't even imagine what it must be like.

"You put the tree in the truck already?" I ask him, shocked.

"Yeah," he huffs out, "you did the easy work."

"Easy work?" I hiss out. "I will have you know that I about killed myself cutting down the fucking tree."

He hands the girl his credit card and she smiles at us. "You did that yourself." He points at me. "You could have let me help, but noooo, she had to do it herself." He looks around. "You know it's okay to not be the best at everything."

I fold my arms over my chest. "I'll let you know when I find something I'm not the best at." I grab the stand from the counter. "Thank you and have a blessed day."

Merry Christmas
AND A HAPPY NEW YEAR

Twelve

Nate

THE MINUTE SHE folds her arms over her chest, I know she's pissed. "I'll let you know when I find something I'm not the best at." She grabs the stand and turns back to smile at the clerk. "Thank you and have a blessed day," she says, looking directly in my eyes.

Oh yeah, I try not to laugh at her, she's past the pissed-off phase. She is in the I'm going to fuck shit up and then maybe I'll ask all the questions I should have asked before. I know pretty much everything about Elizabeth Morrow, and that's because I've been a part of her family my whole life. More so in my teen years when I felt lost and all I wanted was somewhere I could feel like myself. Somewhere I didn't have to fake being happy or like I was okay. My grandparents did the best they could, but they were also grieving, and I wanted to put very little stress on them. So, I spent the majority of my teenage years living with her family, so I pretty much know everything that sets her off. The downside to that is, I also know everything that makes her smile. "Thank you," I tell the girl behind the counter.

"You have your hands full with her." Her smile goes even bigger.

"Oh no, we aren't together." I shake my head, and my mouth also wants to say it's her choice, but instead I turn and see Elizabeth with Joshua and Jack. The three of them are posing for a picture. Elizabeth is in the middle with the two guys crowded over her as they smile at the camera. I know this picture will make its way on the wall above the mantel in the house by next month.

"Where is Nate?" Zack says, looking around and I hold up my hand. "Get in there." I stand next to Matthew.

"It's the kids." I point to them chuckling.

"You had your clothes in my laundry basket; you are considered one of my kids." He motions with his head, and I smirk and shake my head. Zack nudges my shoulder. "And you ate more food than my kids."

"That is not true," I refute, walking over to them and standing beside Jack, who puts his arm around my shoulders and slaps one.

"That's going in a frame," Denise declares. "Can we get the wives in there?" She looks around. "Soon-to-be wife anyway."

We rearrange the group and now I'm standing beside Elizabeth, and she looks up at me and smiles at me. The same smile she gave me that night. It was that smile that made me forget everything, and all I wanted was to make sure the smile stayed on her face the whole time. I shake my head and put my arm around her shoulders and pull her to my side, like I've done many times when we were younger. She looks down at our feet and then reaches around, putting her hand around my waist and the other around her brother.

"Smile for the camera," Denise says. "Everyone look here," she says and I look down at Elizabeth for a second when she looks up at me and I wink at her, making her smile even bigger. "Elizabeth, look over here." She calls her name, and she looks up at the camera. "This one is going to be blown up," Denise announces to everyone. "Okay, now, everyone inside," she says and then turns to hand the phone to one of the workers as the fifty or more people all crowd into the picture. Denise and Zack are in the middle as we crowd around them. I stand behind Elizabeth. One hand is on her shoulder, the other hand is hanging to the side when I have to squeeze in more, and her hand grabs my leg. Then, like it's always meant to be, I slide my hand in hers. Our fingers intertwine like they were made to be held together. We take three pictures and then everyone moves away, including us. Her hand slides out of mine and our fingers try to hold on to each other, but then our hands fall to our respective sides.

I'm sitting at the table with her father and uncles when she comes over to us and looks at me. "When are you thinking about leaving?"

"Answer right now," Matthew says under his breath, as he covers his mouth with his mug of hot chocolate.

"Now." I take his advice and stand up, grabbing my

jacket from the back of the chair. "I was waiting on you."

"Oh, dude." Zack shakes his head. "Just say sorry I kept you waiting."

"Okay, well, sorry I kept you waiting while I was waiting for you to finish," I state, knowing I can't let her win. But also knowing it'll probably piss her off.

"Well, I'm ready." She doesn't give me attitude, which should be my first sign to not poke the bear. "Bye, we'll see you all tomorrow, I guess, for another round of *Jumanji*."

"I think it's called *Groundhog Day* at this point," Matthew says. "I feel like I've been at this wedding for fifteen thousand years."

We laugh as we say goodbye to everyone, Joshua giving Uncle Matthew the stink eye. We walk out with my jacket under my arm and my hat in my hand. I take out the keys to my truck and unlock the doors.

I open the back door, tossing my jacket and hat in the back seat, as she gets into the passenger seat and rubs her hands together. I start the truck and turn up the heat. "Should we order pizza?" she asks me as I pull out of the parking lot and head down the path heading to the main road. The lights on the trees are all sparkling and it looks almost magical.

"We can," I reply, getting on the road and looking over at her as she is on her phone.

"It says it can be at your house in forty-five minutes," she says and then looks over at me. "Is that enough time?"

"Why don't you order it when we get home?" I look

back at the road. "We still have to unload the tree."

"Oh, that's right." She puts her phone away and for the whole ride she looks out the window.

We get home and then she reaches for the handle. "I'm going to order it now," she says, "I'm starving."

"That sounds good," I tell her and get out of the truck and walk up the steps to the front door. Pressing in the code, I then open it up and see Whiskey coming out with his tail wagging behind him.

"Are the cats not going to run out?" she asks me and I shake my head.

"They tried that once," I tell her, walking to the back of the truck. "Seems they are not cut out for living on the street. Baby Cat literally belly-crawled her way back in and Bean didn't like the grass under her feet." I open the back of the truck and see the tree is tied all the way around.

"Why does it look like it's sick?" she asks me, standing next to me and taking in her tree.

"We had to tie it all the way around for the drive home. Once you cut the rope, it'll open up again."

"It better," she mumbles to me.

"Don't you get a tree at home?" I ask her and she shakes her head.

"I do not. There is a tree in the staff lounge in the hospital and that is enough cheer for me to have."

"So you don't have one at home?" I question, shocked.

"I work the extra hours during the holidays"—she shrugs—"so it would be a waste of time to put up a tree."

"But it's Christmas," I retort, shocked as I pull the

tree closer to the edge.

"Yeah, so I've been told," she mumbles. "What do you want me to do?"

"I think I have it," I assure, trying to pick it up by the twine that's tied around it. I grasp it tightly and lift it over one shoulder.

"Just close the back of the truck." I motion with my chin to the tailgate as I walk across my lawn to the front door. The whole time I feel the pine needles falling down and know I'm going to have pine needles in my house for the next six fucking months. It's why I never get a real tree.

Whiskey backs up when he sees me walking up the steps, the cord feeling like it's cutting into my skin. "Out of the way, Whiskey." I give him the command and he runs inside the house. "Did you bring in the stand?" I look over my shoulder and she turns around and runs to the truck. "You had one job!" I shout at her what she would have shouted to me.

"Technically," she huffs out when she runs back into the house, following me, "I did my job by cutting down the motherfucking tree."

I can't help but laugh as I look at her when I get to the clearing. "Where do you want this motherfucking tree?" I ask her, knowing even if I chose someplace to put it, she will probably tell me I've chosen the wrong spot.

"Where do you usually put your motherfucking tree?" She giggles when she says it.

"Elizabeth," I say her name between clenched teeth, "the twine is going to cut through my flesh."

"Fine," she huffs. "Put it in that corner," she directs to the corner of the living room that faces the big window.

"You need to put down the stand," I hiss at her and she raises her hands nervously.

"Shit, shit, shit." She runs past me, taking the metal stand out of the box it came in. "Wait." She puts it down. "I have to put in the screws."

"By all means, take your time."

"You're rushing me," she throws over her shoulder as she tries to go as fast as she can. "Okay, put it in the hole."

"That's what she said," I mumble and she snorts.

"I led you right into that, didn't I?" she says as I turn the tree down.

"You're going to have to guide it in." I turn the tree down.

"That's what he said," she comes back with her own joke, and now I'm the one snorting at her.

"Walked into that one," I tease as I feel the tree being moved and I try to hang on. "Hurry."

"I'm going as fast as I can," she hisses at me. "There are five screws," she informs me, working around me. "Okay, let go." I let go and it starts to fall over to one side. "Shit," she hisses as she moves over to the side to make sure it's as tight as she can get it. "Okay, let go again."

I release my hand slowly and then wait for it to tumble, and it doesn't. "I did it!" she crows, lifting her hand in the air. "You're welcome." She smirks as she shrugs off her vest, and I walk over to let Whiskey out, who has been bouncing at the back door.

She sits on the couch as she unties her boots and pulls them off. "Okay," she says walking to put her boots at the front door, "let's do this." She heads into the kitchen and goes to the drawers as she looks for scissors. "Let's get her open."

"That's what he said also." I walk over to Whiskey's bowls and put some fresh water in one, then put in a cup of his kibble in the other before walking back over to the door to let him in.

He runs in and goes straight for his bowl as if he hasn't eaten for five days. "Are you ready?" she asks me and I look at her confused. "I'm about to let her loose."

"Can't wait," I say to her as she goes to the tree.

"Do I cut bottom and then work my way up?" she asks me and I shrug.

"From the top," I instruct her and she gets on her tippy-toes as she tries to reach the top of it. I lean on the counter, holding my chin in my hands, as I watch her try with all her might to cut the top rope.

"Do you need help with that?" I try not to laugh at her as she turns and glares at me.

"I think I can get it," she hisses at me as my eyes go from her hand trying to cut the rope to the way her sweater moves side to side, and then I see her ass. She has to be the sexiest woman I've ever been with, and she has no idea how sexy she is.

"Yeah, if you grow maybe a couple more inches," I goad, pushing off of the island and heading toward her. Pine needles have already started to fall and there is a trail from the front door to the corner. "Give me the scissors." I stand behind her and lean over her, fitting my front to her back. I put a hand on her hip, waiting for her to hand me the pair of scissors. "Thank you," I say, letting go of her and cutting the top.

"Don't do them all," she orders me and I look down at her, cutting one more to give her back the scissors.

She grabs the scissors from me and her head looks back as she stares into my eyes. "Thanks," she mumbles as she pushes her back into my chest.

"You're welcome," I say softly, our eyes are on each other as we both hold the scissors in our hands. My free hand wraps around her waist and I pull her more into me.

"Nate," she says my name in almost a whisper or a moan. I don't know, I'm too far gone to figure it out. Being here in my home with her and being so close to her, everything starts to fade away. The hurt I felt the morning after our night together. The hurt I felt when I heard she was leaving and didn't tell me. The hurt that she left without looking back. It's all faded into the back because now she's here and she's in my home.

"Elizabeth," I whisper as my head moves down and I'm almost about to kiss her. Almost seven years after our first kiss, I'm about to kiss her again; the thumping of my heart echoes in my ears. The room spins all around me and the only thing I can focus on is her. I lick my lips as I get closer and closer to her. I can taste it, and just when I'm about to kiss her, the doorbell rings, making Whiskey let out a bark.

She jumps in my arms and the hand that was on her

stomach now falls to the side. "That's the pizza," she says and turns in my arms. "I'll get it." She rushes away from me and out of the room, giving me a moment to get myself together.

I look up at the ceiling and close my eyes. "Don't be dumb," I tell myself. "She's leaving in less than two weeks." I rub my hands over my face. "Two weeks and she'll be gone again, and you'll be left alone...again."

Merry Christmas

AND A HAPPY NEW YEAR

Thirteen

Underneath the Tree

Elizabeth

I WALK AWAY from Nate, with my feet moving at the same time my heart feels like it's about to come out of my chest. I pull open the door and all I can do is blink at the pizza delivery man. "Elizabeth," he says my name as he balances the blue bag in his hand, keeping the pizza warm. I nod at him, my mouth suddenly dry. I'm also afraid if I speak, it'll come out in the squeaky voice I use when I'm very nervous. He unfolds the top of the bag and the steam from the hot pizza rushes out as he hands me the two pizza boxes, nods, then walks away. I shut the door with my foot and give myself a minute to calm down. I thought Nate was going to kiss me. Forget that, I knew he was going to kiss me. I also knew I should have pushed him away from me, but when it comes to Nate, I'm always doing things I shouldn't do.

I don't look at him as I walk to the counter and put

down the two boxes of pizza. "Food is here," I call out, like he doesn't know I just brought in the pizza. "Come and eat." I look over at him before walking to the sink and turning on the water to wash my hands.

"I'll cut the tree open after I eat," I tell him as I turn to grab two plates, trying to act like we didn't just almost kiss.

"Do you want a beer?" I ask him as I walk to the fridge and pull out two bottles before placing both on the counter next to each other. Nate walks to the sink to wash his hands before coming back. I open both pizza boxes. "I got cheese and the meat lovers."

"I don't need a plate," he tells me, grabbing a slice of meat lovers and eating it over the box.

I pull out one of the stools and sit down, grabbing a slice of cheese pizza, folding it, and then taking a bite before twisting open the bottle of beer. "I forget how much I miss pizza until I taste it here."

"There isn't a good pizza place back home?" he asks me as he takes another bite.

"It's just not the same," I say, taking another bite. "Where are the decorations for the tree?"

"In the garage. I usually keep them outside in the shed," he tells me, "but I knew I would have to put up the tree."

"Usually you have it up by now?" I ask him and he nods.

"But then I got so busy at work, knowing I would be taking off time for the wedding, so I just didn't get around to it."

"So, no regrets starting your own veterinary practice?" I ask as I take another bite.

"Not one," he confirms. "It was tough at the beginning, obviously, since you have to build it from the ground up. Find new clients, prove yourself and all that." He leans on the counter looking at me. "What about you, Elizabeth?" My body gets shivers when he says my name like that. "Do you like Australia?"

"I do," I admit, "it's home now." Even saying the words, I am not sure it is. It should be. I've been there long enough. But now it feels like one foot is in, one foot is out.

"Is it?" he asks me and I nod my head. "Are you with anyone?"

"I don't have time to date," I confess to him, then ask him the question I have not had the balls to ask him, nor have I heard anything about from any of my family members. "What about you?"

He shakes his head. "Not now, but I was with Britt for about three years," he shares, shocking me. "We even bought a house together."

I blink and the pizza falls from my hand onto the box. "I'm sorry what?"

"What, what?" he asks me.

"You were with someone for three years"—he nods—"and had a house together?" I repeat the words to make sure that I heard him correctly. "This house?" I point to the counter.

"No." He shakes his head. "I bought this after we broke up."

"Why did you break up?" I ask him, the pizza in my stomach feeling like it's going to curdle or something.

"She wanted the next step," he replies, standing up and taking a pull of his beer.

"You mean she wanted to get married?" I say, ignoring the pounding of my heart or the way this news is affecting me, it's getting harder and harder to breathe when it feels like my chest is caving in.

"Yeah."

"Well, obviously." I roll my eyes. "After three years, why didn't you propose?" Asking the question has the back of my neck tingling.

"I'm not really sure, something was just missing."

"Three years?" I repeat.

"Three years."

"Who broke up with who?" I ask him.

"She basically said if I wasn't thinking of marriage now, I would never be thinking of it," he states, looking at me. "So we had a come-to-Jesus moment, and I had to admit I didn't see us married. Not then and not in the future."

"You are so lucky," I tell him and his eyebrows pinch together. "If that was me and after three years you were like, it's never going to happen." I pfft. "I would burn your shit, all of it. You'd be living in your truck, naked."

"Why would I be naked?" He cocks a hip.

"Because, I burned all your shit. All of it. Down to, like, your condoms."

He throws his head back and laughs harder. "I'm not kidding with you, Nate."

"Oh, I'm fully aware that you are not kidding with me, Elizabeth." I swear every single time he says my name, my stomach gets butterflies.

"Where is she now?" I ask him, thinking she still lives around here and there is a chance I'll come face-to-face with her.

"Moved away closer to the city, shortly after I bought this house. She thought for some reason I would regret it."

"Did you?" I ask him, and I feel like I'm holding my breath. "Do you?"

"No." He shakes his head, taking another pull of his beer. "Not even a little bit. Besides, she got married a year after she left and now has a two-month-old baby."

"Girl or boy?" I ask him.

"No clue." He puts his bottle of beer down by his pizza box.

"That means you really don't care"—I grab my own beer bottle and take a pull—"because if you did, you would know every single detail about the other person."

"You didn't know I was with Britt?" He looks straight into my eyes when he asks me the question.

"I did not," I reply and he just nods his head, "but it's because—"

"It's fine," he says, tossing down his pizza crust. "I'm going to go and get the totes."

He starts to walk out of the room, and my chest is getting so tight it's getting hard to even swallow. "Nate." His name comes out shaky.

"It's fine, Elizabeth." He looks back and I can see

something in his eyes I've never seen before. The look haunts me and leaves me speechless. "I'll be back."

Whiskey walks with him to the garage and then comes back with him as he carries a blue Rubbermaid tote. "How many are there?" I ask him as he puts the first one down.

"Seven." My mouth opens in shock. "My mother really loved Christmas," he says, looking down at Whiskey, who pushes into his leg to get pet, as he avoids looking at me.

It takes him about thirty minutes to bring all the totes in, and I clean up the mess of the pizza boxes, putting it on the stove. "Do you have something to play music on?" I ask him once he places the last tote down and wipes his forehead with the back of his arm.

"Grab my phone." He motions with his chin toward the counter. "Open the music app, it's hooked up to the system."

I grab his phone and swipe up, it says face ID and then quickly asks me for the code once it sees I'm not him. "Is it your birthday?" I ask him and he shakes his head.

"I'll put it in," he offers, taking his phone from me and putting in his password. "There you go." He hands me the phone and I pull up the music app and the sound of bells starts filling the house. "Are you putting Christmas songs on?"

"I mean, we're doing a Christmas tree, might as well vomit Christmas all over the place." I smile at him as I grab the scissors as Kelly Clarkson's "Underneath the

Tree" starts to blare through the speakers. I raise my hands in the air as I sing the song, cutting the cords, and then seeing the tree come out. Every single time it flies open, I think a hundred pine needles fall from the tree.

"You need to put water in the holder," Nate shouts from behind me.

"What? Why?" I ask him.

"Elizabeth, it's a tree." He points to the tree. "It's like getting flowers, you have to add water to them or it'll turn brown or catch fire with the lights. I really like my house and I would like not to set it on fire."

He starts opening the totes as I walk over and grab the biggest glass he has and filling it with water. "How much water?" I ask him as I walk back and have to get on my knees to pour it into the stand.

"Until the top, I guess," he answers as he finds the lights and then comes over with the string of lights. "I'm going to need a stepladder." He puts the lights on the couch where Whiskey is now lying down, watching us. He walks out of the room and then Baby Cat comes into the room, gingerly looking around at the totes. He steps on a couple of pine needles and then flips his paw to get them off.

Nate comes back with a small white stepladder and goes to the tree. "Can you get the lights for me?" he asks and I walk over to the lights and then go back to give them to him. "We are going to have to move the tree away from the wall so I can get back there with the lights," he says as he gets down.

"I don't know if that's a good idea." I watch him grab

a hold of the tree in the middle as he moves it slowly toward us. "Fucking needles," he complains as we hear them falling. "I'll be sending you pictures in March, and I'll still be finding them all around my house."

I can't help but laugh, but then something else starts to creep in and I push it back. I've been home for maybe four days, and every day is one day closer to me leaving. Usually, I'm okay with it and I start feeling like this on the day that I leave. The dread starts to creep in, knowing that I'll be so far away again. "You okay?" he asks me, and I clear my throat, the lump was growing bigger and bigger as I think of heading back to the other side of the world.

"Yeah," I assure, shaking my head and fighting away the stinging of my eyes and the pinch in my nose. "I'm just... It's, you know, strange being home."

"Well, you don't do it often enough," he mentions as he walks around the tree with the lights. "Your parents miss you."

"Trust me, I get calls daily with a mandatory guilt trip." I smile at him, walking to the tree. "Pass me the lights from the back, we can tag team." We work in unison, putting on the lights, and we're at the end and he plugs it in, I can't help but smile at our hard work. "It's so pretty," I state, folding my hands together and putting my hands to my chin.

He stands by me as he takes it in. "Not bad. Now let's get this motherfucker decorated." I throw my head back and let out a laugh.

"Okay," I agree looking in the totes that are all open.

"Why don't we put your favorites in the front," I suggest, "and then the rest in the back where no one sees them." I walk from tote to tote, seeing all the special ornaments his parents picked out, and I'm sure he has memories with all of them. "Which ones are the most special?" I look in and see him reach a tray of ornaments.

"These," he says, holding one up and it's painted gold but in the front is a family with a mother, father, and son on a sled. "My mom made these herself," he explains, looking at them. "Every single year she would paint a couple more."

"Then those go right in the middle," I tell him, grabbing the one from his hand, "so you can see them."

He doesn't say anything as I hang the first one. "What do you think?" I ask him when I walk back to him as he looks at the tree.

"I like it." He looks down at me. "I like it a lot." I smile up at him. "I'd like it a lot more without the music, but now I'll forever have this memory."

"Put them on." I take the box from him. "Don't worry, I'll let you know if you aren't putting it on the right spot."

"I have no doubt you will," he replies, taking one out and arranging it, and each time he tells me a little story about the ornament.

It takes way longer than either of us thinks it will to finish decorating. When it's all done, it looks like a tree that is filled with love and memories and not the ones that look like they just came out of a catalog. "What do you think?" I ask him as I step back.

"I think this is the best tree I've ever had." He sits on

the couch next to Whiskey, rubbing his head.

"Good." I smile at him. "I'm going to go and get in the shower, then head to sleep."

He just looks at me and I'm about to walk out of the room when I stop. "Good night, Nate," I say, and he nods at me. I know I should just leave it at that. I know I should leave it alone, but something in me stops. "For the record," I start, wringing my hands together out of nerves, "I didn't know about you and Britt because I didn't want to ask about you, but not because I didn't want to know. I just couldn't." His mouth opens. "Just thought you should know."

Merry Christmas
AND A HAPPY NEW YEAR

Fourteen

You Make It Feel Like Christmas

Nate

December 18th

MY EYES FLUTTER open to the sound of Elizabeth's voice. "Did you sleep good?" Her voice is soft. "I'll let you out and then I'll fix your breakfast." I turn over on the bed and look out the window, seeing it's light outside. When I reach over to grab my phone from the bedside table, I see it's just after eight thirty.

I put my phone back on the bedside table before just staring off into the distance. Last night was a good one. One filled with lots of memories of my parents. Some I forgot about. Some I'd remembered so vividly it was like I was back with them again. It's never happened to me before. I would remember things time and time again, but I have never talked about the memories with someone. They just sat lingering in the black box in my mind, untouched, where I had put all my precious memories I've had in my life, including the night that I spent with her.

I sat on the couch I don't know for how much longer after she left me. Her words penetrated through and then brought up all these questions I wasn't sure I wanted the answers to. I had to let it go.

"Get out of there," I hear her hiss and look over at the open door, "if you break anything…" Her hiss is now a growl. "I will toss your ass outside." I flip the covers off me, getting out of bed. "Oh my God, what are you doing?" Her voice is frantic, and I walk out of my bedroom door and down the steps. "Get the fuck out of there." She is back to hissing. "I'm locking you out of my bedroom tonight."

I walk into the kitchen and look over at the tree, finding her standing there in tight-as-fuck black booty shorts. Her ass is filling them all out, and my cock—hard from waking up—is now hard for another fucking reason. "What is going on?" I watch her reaching into the tree, trying not to knock anything over.

"The fucking cat," she snaps, worry filling her face. "Baby fucking Cat is stuck in the fucking tree. Sleeping there like he lives there."

I scratch my head. "Tell him to come out." She moves away from the tree as I get closer to her. Baby Cat is literally lying across five branches just chilling, as if this tree is meant just for him.

"Just tell him to come out," she mocks my words, "like I didn't already try that. I don't think he'll listen to me." I put my hands on my hips. "He's not one to care about authority." She turns back to talk to him. "Find someplace else to sleep tonight." She points at him sleeping on the second-to-the-top row of branches.

"I think he just did." I try not to laugh at her glare as she turns and storms away. "If I were you," I lean in and whisper, "I'd get the fuck out of the tree. It's better to be in her bed than a fucking tree."

"What are you telling him?" she asks me as I hear the sound of the cupboards slamming shut. "You better be threatening him."

I shake my head and hear Whiskey at the door, his nails scratching to come in. I walk over to open the door as Elizabeth is busy in my kitchen. I haven't had a woman in my kitchen since Britt. I especially have never had a woman in this house. But seeing her there, it's strange to say that I don't see her anywhere else. I also don't see anyone else but her here with me.

"Good morning," I greet as Whiskey excitedly comes in bouncing on his paws around my legs as I pet his side. "You left me in bed the minute she got up, didn't you?" I look up to see Elizabeth bending over, putting his water bowl down. Her ass is right in my face practically. I groan and look back down at the dog. "I would too."

The smell of coffee is filling the room as she moves around the kitchen, taking out the mugs and then the milk. "What are the plans today?" she asks me and I shrug as I walk over to one of the stools and pull it out. "Let me get my phone."

She walks back over to the counter, picking it up, and

tapping the screen. "It says scavenger hunt." She puts her phone down and walks over to the coffee machine. "Like what the fuck is going on? Why can't he be like a normal person?" She pours coffee in both cups and then adds the milk. "Come down, meet a couple of the bridesmaids during a fitting." She turns and walks over, putting down a cup in front of me.

"Thanks," I mumble, picking it up while she walks over to the couch. Her mug is in her hand as she curls her feet under her and looks at the tree.

"Have a rehearsal dinner and then get married." She takes a sip of her coffee. "No, not Joshua. Joshua is like, what would annoy the fuck out of everyone? Let's do that." I snort.

"He knew how much it took for people to be away from their families during the holidays, so he wanted everyone to feel like they were family."

"We are fucking family." She turns her face to me. "Literally, everyone knows everyone."

"You know everyone?" I know she knows her family, but she doesn't know many of Macy's side of the family since she hasn't been here.

"I don't want to." She glares at me. "There is a difference. I don't do a lot of people." She holds the mug to her mouth and takes a small sip of the piping hot coffee.

I get up and walk over to the couch and sit down on the other side, watching the tree with the lights on. Baby Cat has slunk down, and his eyes are closed. "Good news." She looks over at me. Her hair is tied on top of her head and her face is free of makeup, and she's never looked more beautiful before. "There is this. The gingerbread house competition and then the joint bachelor/bachelorette party and then we are done."

"That's a lie." She sighs.

"No, he canceled the snowman building since there is no snow."

"That's not what I meant. You left out the rehearsal dinner and the wedding."

I chuckle and hold my coffee in my hands tighter when I see Whiskey come toward us and jump on the couch in between us. "Well, those two were a given and always going to be on the list." He turns in a circle and then plops down, putting his face on Elizabeth's legs, and I've never been more jealous of my dog in my life. "So I take it, when it's your turn to get married"—the coffee now feels like it's curdling in my stomach—"you won't do the two-weeks-of-getting-to-know-each-other kind of thing."

"No," she snaps. "It will be maybe a rehearsal dinner. I don't think I'll have a big bridal party like Macy. A maid of honor, maybe one bridesmaid, and then the rest will be invited. The wedding is really between two people and not five hundred."

"You might want to never say that to your parents," I warn her. "Maybe your uncle Max will agree with you, but he's about the only one who will."

She chuckles. "What about you?" She puts her hand on the back of the couch and then leans her temple on her closed fist. "How do you see your wedding?"

"I really couldn't care less, as long as I get to marry the girl I love," I admit to her. "If she shows up, I'm already winning." She tosses her head back and laughs and when she looks back at me her eyes are twinkling. "It could be just the two of us, or she can have whoever she wants there, I really don't care."

"Would you say your own vows or do the generic 'I take you as my wife' sort of thing?"

"Again, it would be what she wants. I could do both. If we decide to do the generic"—I take a sip of my coffee, trying to get the image of her being my bride out of my head—"I would write her a letter with my vows to her." Her mouth opens up in shock.

"That is so nice." It comes out in almost a whisper.

"Why are you so shocked with everything I say? It's like you don't know me." I finish my coffee and get up from the couch, not sure I want to continue having this conversation because, eventually, I'm going to stop being scared and ask her why the fuck she left me after our night together. "I'm going to shower and then get ready, we have to be at the reception hall at eleven."

"Great," she mumbles and follows me up. "Are you not going to get the cat out of the tree?"

I look over and shake my head. "If he's comfortable sleeping there, who am I to say different?"

She picks up my mug and takes it to the kitchen as I walk away from her, listening to her in the kitchen telling my cat he's going to be very, very sorry if he doesn't get his ass out of the tree.

An hour later I'm walking down the stairs, tucking

my phone in the back pocket of my jeans, and see her at the bottom of the steps putting on her boots. She looks over her shoulder at me. "I'm almost done." She turns back around and puts on the second boot.

I sit on the step behind her. "Take your time." She's wearing a dark-gray turtleneck today and I just know it's silky soft cashmere I'd love nothing more than to grasp between my fingers.

She gets up and I see she's wearing another pair of black leggings, and the oversized sweater is tucked in in the front. "It's cold out," she mumbles, walking over to grab her black jacket.

"You should have worn that jacket yesterday when we were plucking trees."

"Didn't we go over this yesterday? It didn't go with my outfit." She rolls her eyes. "Besides, I was sweating balls by the time I started to saw that motherfucking tree down." I chuckle as I walk to the front door and put on my black boots. "I'm going to go and let Whiskey out one more time," she tells me before calling my dog, who I look up to see walking out of her room. Great, another one that gets to sleep in her bed. It's literally everyone else in this house in her bed except me. "We're going to do a stupid activity for your uncle Joshua," I hear her speaking to Whiskey. "I'm going to need you to eat one of his shoes the next time he comes over. Maybe nip him in the ass. I'll leave it up to you to do whatever it is you feel that you should do. Just know it will be okay by us. You might get extra treats." The smile fills my face even more as I put on my short puffy jacket. When she comes back into the room, Whiskey is following her again. "I unplugged the lights on the tree," she says as she pets Whiskey, and we walk out of the house together. She walks ahead of me as I press the lock button on the door and meet her in my truck.

"It smells crispy"—she rubs her hands together—"which means I'm going to hate every single second of today."

"Crispy?"

"Yeah, like cool and crisp," she says as if that makes any more sense than before, "it's going to be even colder than yesterday I think."

"Great." I pull out of the driveway and head toward the reception area. The parking lot has about ten cars as I get out first and then meet Elizabeth around the back of the truck.

"Listen," she plots, "why don't we get a clue and then leave, and they can come and try and find us?" The laughter rips through me. "Now that's a scavenger hunt." I look up at the big venue that is a red barn, but now has a big wreath in the middle of it, on top of the doors, and then garland hangs on both sides. "We'll be at, like, the spa or something, and if they find us, they win."

"If you get Joshua to go along with it, count me in," I say as we walk side by side to the front doors. I pull one open, but not before she glares at me. "It's not me who organized this."

She steps in before me and the warm heat hits you right away. The bridal party is literally spread out everywhere. "Shit, you're here," Jack says, coming toward us, "I owe

Evie twenty bucks.”

“What? Why?” Elizabeth asks, confused.

“I thought for sure you would bail,” he says to her.

She turns to look up at me. “I should have stayed home and let Jack win. Do you see what you did? Now he’s sad.”

She’s about to say something when Belinda comes over to us. “Hey,” she says, smiling at me, “can I have a minute?”

“You can have more than a minute,” Elizabeth replies, and anyone who knows her knows the tone is not friendly. She pushes Jack when he tries to say something.

I watch her walk away from me before turning my attention back to Belinda. “What’s up?”

“I got the pictures for the speech,” she says and I cringe. “I’m guessing you didn’t look yet.”

“I’ll do that tonight,” I assure her. “I’ll add it to my calendar to remind me.” I take the phone out of my pocket and then hear Joshua calling everyone over.

Belinda goes back to her group of friends and then I stand beside Elizabeth, who looks at me and then back at Joshua. “Okay, you are going to need a partner for this,” he says and I look at Elizabeth as I tuck my phone away.

Everyone walks to someone else and Elizabeth and I are the ones left together. “Guess it’s me and you.”

“Don’t you want to team up with the maid of honor?” she asks. “It should be like partners walking down the aisle.”

“Pretty sure her husband would say no to that,” I reply, and Elizabeth looks over at Belinda, who is now hugging said husband. "Yeah, she's married. Gregory is a great guy. He works night shift most times, which is why we haven't seen him around."

"Well, I'm not going to be your sloppy seconds." She looks over at Jack and Evie. "Evie and I will be partners and you and Jack can be partners."

"But," Jack whines, "we were going to find a corner and make out the whole time."

"You act like the two of you don't wake up together," Elizabeth huffs. "You can be without her."

"Okay, there are six pit stops with clues," Joshua continues, "and each pit stop has a different clue for your number." He walks around with a bowl with folded papers in it. "Pick your number and that will be your clue envelope."

"What do we win?" Jack asks.

"You win," Macy answers, "the trophy." She holds up a dollar store little trophy. "And the right to say you are the winners."

"Yeah, no," I hear Elizabeth mumble from beside me and I have to stop from laughing.

"It'll be so much fun," Macy squeals as Jack picks a paper from the bowl.

"You're a fucking tool and I hate you," Jack declares with a smile on his face to Joshua, who closes his eyes and nods, "and I'm going to break your foot for real."

"What number are we?" I ask Jack, who looks at the paper.

"Seven," he says, handing me the paper.

I look over at Elizabeth, who is looking around. "You

sure you don't want to be on my team?" I ask her. "We can let these two make out with each other."

"Evie said she's over Jack and his stupid make-out sessions anyway," she snarks, making Jack laugh.

"She's more in love with me now than ever before," he states winking at Evie, who just blushes at him. The two of them are quite literally the most annoying in-love couple you've ever met.

"Are we ready?" Joshua asks.

Everyone but the four of us mumble, "Yes."

"Get set," he says. "First clue is at the table." He points over to it. "And go." Everyone but the four of us rush to the table. "Last place team has to come and help us do the seating chart," he announces, and the four of us spring into action. "Good luck."

Fifteen

DECK THE HALLS

ELIZABETH

December 19th

"**D**ID YOU JUST get the text?" I ask as I walk into the kitchen the next morning and see Nate sitting on the couch with a bucket of pictures beside him.

"No, what text?" He looks up as he flips the stack of pictures in his hands.

"From Joshua," I tell him and he shakes his head. "Apparently, it's a two-for-one day," I announce, going over to the kitchen to grab a cup of coffee, "so we can have a free day tomorrow."

"What the fuck does that mean?" he asks me, his head turning to me and I see his hair is sticking up on the side. He's wearing another pair of fucking gym shorts that hang softly on his hips, and I wonder if I pull them down, if he'll be naked under them. The thought alone makes parts of me tingle.

"It means today is the gingerbread competition, which"—I walk to the fridge—"I'm going to win." He rolls his eyes. "Then it's the ice hockey game tonight."

"Did you forget who won yesterday?" he asks and then points to the stupid trophy that is sitting on top of his counter.

"Seriously?" I lean against the counter. "You going to say you won fair and square?"

"Fucking right," he declares as he looks through the pictures in his hands and puts the stack to the side and grabs another one from the basket.

"You hip-checked me," I point out to him.

"It's not my fault that you were in my way."

"I was standing up reading my clue," I gasp.

"And also, in my way."

"And what about when you took our clue with you by 'accident'?" I mention the last clue they took with them so we wouldn't catch up to them. The minute Joshua threatened us with helping do the seating chart, it was like you thought we were in *The Amazing Race* and were going to win one million dollars as the prize.

"We didn't take it." He rolls his eyes. "It accidentally fell on the floor and was pushed under a table."

"You should have been disqualified." I point to him.

"But we won, so it's neither here nor there," he gloats, and I walk over to the couch and sit down in the spot where I've sat every single morning, "and we got a trophy for it."

"At least yours survived." I snicker. "Jack's ended up

crushed under Evie's shoe."

"I did not see that coming." He laughs also. "She fucking pummeled that thing as if she was King Kong." We both laugh.

"I wonder if she let him in the house?" I ask. "I can't believe she left him at the venue and said 'Find your own ride home.'"

"I can't believe he chased Joshua around the fucking venue saying he ruined his day." I laugh so long I have tears in my eyes.

"I thought Jack was going to deck him," Nate says, "and I think he might have if your father hadn't walked in to see what was happening."

"Right time, right place," I say. He suddenly stops what he's doing and looks over at me. My heart races when I remember when I said those words to him, and I quickly look away. "Needless to say, someone was in trouble and for once it wasn't me."

"You kicked me," he hisses out, not touching on the remark from before or maybe he doesn't remember. But with the way he looked at me, I know he does.

"I did not." I shake my head. "I accidently fell forward with my leg connecting to your shin. It was as much of an accident as the clue ending up under a table." I shrug. "Anyway, what the heck are you doing?"

"I told Belinda I would get a couple of pictures of Joshua in high school and some of us growing up."

"I haven't seen a real picture in forever," I mention, leaning over and grabbing the stack. "Everything is all digital these days."

"You know what is making a comeback?" he asks, as I flip through the pictures. "Those disposable cameras." I gawk at him. "I know someone who works with me always brings it with her. We were at a team dinner the other day, and we all posed for a picture and she took out this square thing from her purse. It had the flash and everything."

"But then how do you know if the picture is good or not?" I ask him and he shrugs.

"You find out like in the old days when it's printed."

"Oh my gosh." I turn one of the pictures over. "Is this prom?"

"I think it was semi-formal," he replies. I look back at the picture of both of them in suits, standing side by side. My eyes go to just Nate, who was always hot, even back then. But it was different, he was just Joshua's best friend back then. He was also one of the people I could have counted on just like Joshua and Jack.

"That hockey flow." I laugh at their long hair.

"Don't knock that haircut," he retorts, "it's making a comeback too."

"So is the mullet, who would have thought?" I mumble as we look through pictures. He finds one of the two of us, sitting side by side, our hair wet from the pool with towels on our laps, his arm around my neck, hanging. "I'm keeping this one." I show it to him.

"No, you aren't." He snatches it from me. "It's mine, go find your own."

"Where?" I get up.

"Where do you think I got these from?" He holds up

the pictures. "Your parents."

"You're so annoying." I grab my cup. "I'm going to get dressed to slay the day."

"You do that. I'm going to sit here and watch my trophy." He smirks at me. I slap it off the counter and watch it fall to the floor.

It rolls over twice and just lies there. "Oops"—I put one hand in front of my mouth—"my bad."

I walk upstairs and head for the shower. "We have to be there at eleven!" he screams up at me.

"Worry about yourself," I tell him before walking into the bathroom and finishing my coffee as I wait for the water to warm up.

"IF I NEVER see this venue again," I say to Nate as I get out of his truck, "it'll still be too soon."

He laughs at me as I look over at him with his white sneakers today. His light blue jeans are just right with their fit and show off his package and his ass, as if they were made for him and only him. The white hem of his T-shirt is sticking out below his light gray-and-black long-sleeved sweater. The front of his black puffer jacket is open, showing you his outfit. His hair is pushed back, and you can see where his fingers pushed through it. It's annoying how hot he is with no effort at all.

He holds open the door for me and I step into the room and see rectangular tables set up all around. Two chairs are on each side with small bowls in the middle of the tables.

"There he is," Joshua greets, walking to us, "the winner of the scavenger hunt."

"I think you mean the cheater of the scavenger hunt," I correct him as he slaps his shoulder, trying not to laugh.

"It's all hearsay." Joshua sticks up for him and I look around to see Evie is here talking to my mother, with Jack holding her fist in his hand.

We make our way to them. "Morning," I say to the group and Jack side-eyes me, "how is everyone?"

"Great," Evie grumbles, "just peachy." She tries to get her hand away from Jack, who just smirks at her. "Let me go."

He releases her hand but it's only to wrap his arm around her waist and pull her to him. "Never," he vows, looking into her eyes and I roll my eyes when I see softness come into her expression. "I'll never let you go."

"He's just the sweetest," my mother coos as Jack kisses Evie softly and then turns back to smile at Mom.

"He just made me throw up a little in my mouth," I tell her. "And that one"—I point to Joshua—"he's lucky I got here before he told me about all these fucking events, or I wouldn't have come. If anything happens to him, my defense is going to be that he lured me here under false pretenses."

"Don't say that," she hisses at me.

"Mom, I feel like by the time he gets married, no one is going to give a shit," I tell her as everyone but her laughs. "Also, I'm eloping and not telling anyone."

"Don't you dare take that away from me," she warns, putting her hand to her chest like I just told her I would never talk to her again for the rest of my life.

"Relax there," I console her, "you have had two out of three, that's like sixty-six percent. You are still winning."

"Wait until I tell your father." She storms away from me to find my father.

"We should grab a table," Evie says to us, and we walk over to a table. I pull out a chair and expect Evie to sit next to me, but instead Nate pulls out the chair beside me. He shrugs off his jacket and puts it on the back of his chair, and I do the same thing with the vest I'm wearing.

I look down at the place setting in front of me, seeing two sides of what will be the gingerbread house with two holes for the windows and two rectangular solid pieces that are for the roof. There are two other pieces for the front and back of the house, with a hole in each of them. Then there are four smaller pieces that we could use for doors maybe, not sure. In the middle of the table are two tin gingerbread-shaped trays, with all the fixings you would need to help decorate it. Around the gingerbread trays are more decoration in round tins.

"Lay off your mother." I hear my father beside my table. "She's under enough stress at the moment, she doesn't need more."

"I didn't do anything to her." I hold my hand to my chest like she just did. "I just told her I'm not going to give her grandchildren." He gasps. "Kidding, I said I was going to elope, isn't that better?"

"Why are you this way?"

"I have been asking myself that question since she moved into my house," Nate interjects and I glare at him.

"Trust me," I hiss at him, "your house is the last place I would want to live." I look back at Jack. "I'm coming to your house and sleeping on the couch."

"Enough, you two," my father hisses to us. "You two could never get along."

"That's not true," I defend myself and at the same time Nate. "Also he started it."

"Well, you finish it." He turns and storms away.

"This is so much fun. We should do this more often," I retort, turning to glare at Nate, who casually puts his arm around my chair, and I move it so he doesn't touch me.

He chuckles as the wedding planner walks around the room explaining how the rules work. "It's a fucking gingerbread house, how many rules can there be?" Jack grumbles.

"We will set a timer for one hour," the wedding planner shouts in the room, and I look around to see everyone sitting down and ready to get this over with. "We have four people who will be the judges of all of this," she says and I look down at my pieces. "We start in three, two, and one."

I grab the icing bag and put some on the side of the house and then slowly put the sides together. "She has a surgical hand," Jack says of me. "That's not fair."

"Just focus on your own, loser," I tell him as I take an empty plate and grab the circular red-and-white mint candies and then decide I'm going to cut four small pieces and make it the chimney. I lay a long line of icing on the top of the roof and then put white-and-red small gumballs in a line. Then I do the same thing on the side but instead of the small gumballs I use the round candies. I'm so in the zone, I don't pay attention to anything around me. So I don't feel Nate get up and lean over to get something. I look up and it all happens in slow motion. The round tin in his hand slips out and falls right onto my house, I gasp, "Nate." I push away from the table and his eyes are big, the sound of gumballs falling off the table and hitting the floor.

"Elizabeth," he says my name, "I swear I didn't mean it."

"Oh my God," I hear Evie say in a whisper, but it's very faint because all I can hear is the echoing of my heart thrumming in my ears. And then a soft buzzing or maybe it's a loud buzzing.

"It was an accident," he tries to defend himself, but the anger rolls off of me and I move toward his house and grip the roof in my hands, crushing it.

"Elizabeth," he says my name again but I'm too far gone. I take my hand and press down on the sides of the house. Jack and Evie push away from the table as I slide his house off of the table and it falls with one of the gingerbread trays. The sound of clanking fills the room and then I hear gasps coming from around the room.

"Oh my God," my mother shrieks, "what did you do?"

"What did I do?" I point to myself, my hand full of icing. "What did I do? Look at what he did." I point to my crushed house. "He ruined my house."

"You two," she hisses at us, "go and clean yourselves up." She points to the side where the bathroom is.

"But, Mom," I whine, sounding like a teenager all over again.

"Now." She uses her mother voice, and I glare at him and storm off to the side where the sign for the toilet is.

I push open the door and walk to the side, grabbing a paper towel, and wipe off the icing from my hand before I turn the water on. I add soap to my hand and the door slams open from behind me, and I look into the mirror and see him coming in, a scowl on his face.

"Seriously," he hisses, and I shake the water off my hands and turn it off before grabbing the paper towel and wiping them dry before turning around and facing him.

"Seriously," I hiss back at him, "you did that on purpose." I step closer to him, making me toe to toe with him.

"Why the fuck would I do that on purpose?" He looks down at me, his eyes narrow.

"Because you suck." I push his chest back. "Because I was going to win." I push him again. "Because you want to piss me off." I'm about to push him again when he grabs my wrists in his hands and then turns me, so my back is against the door. He drops my hands but only to grab my hips, and then his mouth is on mine. One of my hands flies to his jaw while the other cups the back of his head. His tongue slides into my mouth and I tilt my head to the side as the hand holding his jaw now wraps around his shoulder. He picks me up and my legs wrap around his waist. The kiss is hungry and wild, both of us trying to take it even deeper. I know nothing good can come from this. I also know I will throat punch anyone who comes in and tries to stop us.

Sixteen

MY ONLY WISH (THIS YEAR)

NATE

I WRAP ONE arm around her waist, picking her up off her feet as she wraps her legs around my waist. As the other arm moves up her back to grab the back of her head, as I try to take over the kiss. She pushes herself deeper into me as her hand that's on my jaw moves to the back of my head. We hold each other the same way as I kiss her or she kisses me. Either way, I kiss her like it's either the last kiss I'll ever have or it's the last kiss I'll ever give her.

I'm about to press her deeper into the door when I feel someone pushing on it. "Hello." I hear Jack's voice. "I think one killed the other and pushed them against the door."

I let her go but I don't move back from the door until it's being pushed again. "Are you okay in there?"

"No," Elizabeth throws over her shoulder, "we are not

okay."

"Unwrap your legs from my waist," I whisper, even though I don't want her to. I feel her uncling herself from me.

"Ugh," she gulps as she stands on her feet and then lifts her hand to wipe my lips. "Do you want to lie on the floor and play dead, or do you want me to do it?"

"Why is anyone playing dead?" I ask her and she points over her shoulder toward the door with her thumb.

"What other excuse are we going to use?" She barely gets the words out before she's pushed forward and Jack squeezes in.

"What the fuck is going on here?" he asks me, and I get so nervous that my mouth is moving before I even know what I'm saying.

"She's blocking me in and refusing to let me leave." She gasps out.

"I was not." She looks over at Jack, who stands in between us, looking at her, then at me.

"She wouldn't move until I admit that I ruined her house on purpose," I fabricate, and she just shakes her head side to side, her mouth literally hanging open. "She blocked me from leaving and threatened to kick me if I got closer to her."

"Oh, I'm going to kick something all right," she threatens me, coming to charge at me but Jack catches her and pulls her away from me. "Let me go."

"Calm down," he snaps. "Now the two of you are going to go out there and be civil." He lets her go and she shrugs away his hand. "Or else the next time, I'm going to let Mom have a go at both of you, and you do not want that."

"Make sure he stays far away from me." She side-eyes me and I want to tell her she's fucking dreaming if she thinks I'm going to stay away from her after that kiss we just shared. I plan on kissing her a lot more, but before that, we really need to clear the fucking air and she's going to tell me why she left me that morning. She storms away from me, pulling open the door, and I think she growls as she walks out.

"Listen," Jack starts, "I'm not saying she was right."

"I didn't do it on purpose." I put my hands on my hips. "It literally slipped out of my hands."

"Well, we all know Elizabeth can be a bit—"

"Of a hothead," I fill in for him and he grins.

"I was going to say competitive."

"She's that too," I mumble. "I'll stay clear of her," I tell him and he smirks.

"I'd also sleep with one eye open if I was you." He looks down and laughs. "Remember what she did to me when she found out I was the one cutting her dolls' hair when I tried to convince her we had ghosts in the house." I can't help but laugh at the memory. "It took forever for my hair to grow back." He turns and walks out of the bathroom.

"How did she even put the wax strips on your legs without you waking up?" I ask him as we walk back toward the hall and the noise.

"She's like one of those cat burglars that you don't hear or see until it happens. I went to bed and thought

I felt something, but I was too dead asleep to open my eyes, and when I did in the morning, she had taken my mother's wax strips and placed six of them on my legs. Six."

"Oh, I remember," I tell him, "I was the one who had to pry them off of you, don't forget."

"You and fucking Joshua did it with huge smiles on your faces." He pushes my shoulder, and when I walk into the room, my eyes roam the room looking for her.

She's next to Evie as the two of them are working on Evie's house. The mess that was my house and then her house is now cleaned up. "You can help with mine," Jack offers, "that way if I lose, I can just blame you." He slaps my shoulder and walks around me as I watch Elizabeth's face full of concentration as she does the roof.

"We come in peace," Jack announces, holding up his hands, "and so does he."

"You"—Evie points to me—"keep your mitts on that side of the table."

"It was an accident," I again try to defend myself.

"I'll show you an accident," Elizabeth mumbles, her eyes never looking up from what she is doing.

The end of the hour comes very quickly, and when I step away, I look over at Elizabeth and Evie's and then at our house. "Dude." I lean in to Jack.

"Yeah, we're not winning this," he agrees with me.

"THAT JUDGE NEEDS to get his eyes checked," Elizabeth

hisses out as we walk out of the venue and head toward my truck. "How the fuck did we come in second place?"

I look over at her. "She was an eight-year-old little girl."

She rolls her eyes. "Exactly, her gingerbread house was shit and everyone knew it." She looks over at me. "Her house looked like it was covered in blobs of icing."

"I believe she called it a snowball fight," I correct her.

"Whatever." She opens her side of the truck. "She probably paid off the judge."

"He was the cook for the caterer," I point out to her.

"Wow," she deadpans, "it's like you didn't even want to win."

I chuckle as I get into the cab of the truck and start it. "If it's any consolation"—I look over at her—"yours was way better than that eight-year-old's."

"I know," she replies.

"I also think you handled it with grace and dignity. The parents were not at all offended when you mumbled out that it was rigged."

"I think it *was* rigged. Did you see the way she smirked at me?" She turns her back to the truck door. "She knew exactly what she was doing." She reaches for the seat belt. "I think she even made her lower lip quiver."

I make my way over the arena, pulling into the parking lot and then grabbing my bag out of the back seat. "I didn't bring my skates," she says as I toss my bag over my shoulder.

"Pretty sure your dad has everything you need," I assure as we walk in, and she looks around to see all the changes they made over the years. The walls are now covered with pictures from everyone in the family who has practiced here and has made their way into the NHL.

The first one on the side is of Cooper Stone, who came here one year to rehab and fell head over heels in love with the owner, Parker. Matthew was fifteen and Allison was five. Needless to say, the minute Cooper came into their lives, their father started retreating, and coming around for visits. He even stopped taking Allison when it was his week to get her. Matthew had long since given up on him, but Allison was ten years younger than him. You would never know if you saw them together that they weren't his kids. Especially Matthew who, from what everyone says, is a caveman when it comes to his wife. He apparently learned it all from Cooper.

"Dad," she says once she sees Zack walking out of one of the dressing rooms. Jack, Joshua, and I have spent more time here than we did at home when we were growing up. Jack had what it took to make it to the NHL, but when it came down to it, he wanted to follow in Denise's footsteps and help people, instead of becoming a doctor, he focused on medical research. Joshua had a taste of it, but now he's working behind the scenes as a sports analyst. "Where are my things?"

"In the locker room where they always are." She nods at him and I follow her and get into my skates beside her. She heads out to the ice before me, grabbing her helmet and gloves.

She spent her younger years playing hockey, stopping when she turned thirteen and decided she hated it.

But Zack still made her come to the rink every single Saturday and Sunday and help the younger kids learn how to skate. She grabs a hockey stick off the side of the wall, making sure she likes it, turning it to the side, and then skates out onto the ice. She goes in a circle before skating to the puck and moving her stick side to side.

People start to trickle on the ice as I grab my own stick and skate onto the ice. I'm gliding on when the puck hits my skate. "Oops." I look over to see her.

"What is your problem?" I ask her and she shrugs and looks at me.

"Me?" She points to herself as she skates around me and then backward. "I don't have a problem. What's your problem?"

"My problem," I start, skating away from her, also backward, "she's about this high"—I motion with my hand to her exact height—"has blondish hair and green eyes." She tries not to smile.

She stops skating and I stop in front of her. "My eyes are blue green."

I look down at her. "I know exactly what color your eyes are, Elizabeth," I assure, and it's like it's just the two of us on the ice and not the twenty or so who have now started skating around us. "When you are really happy, they turn like a light green." She doesn't say a word. "When you get angry, they are more blue than green. When you are mischievous, the bottom of your eyes are a light blue and the top of your eyes are almost a golden. When you are really fucking happy about something, they're a darkish blue in the middle and then they get a greenish, almost gray around that. But what I love the most, is the dark blue that is on the inside is also on the outside ring. It's fascinating and also the color I always try and make sure you have."

I can see her chest rising and falling, but before she can say anything, the sound of a whistle blows and the two of us look over to the side. "Okay, we're going to do a couple of pickup games," Zack says, skating onto the ice. "The teams are posted."

We play hockey for two hours, and by the end of it, I need a shower so bad. "You stink," Elizabeth declares from beside me.

"Why do you automatically assume it's me?" I ask her as I untie my skate. "It could be you." I pull off my skate and she doesn't say another word to me as we get dressed and then get in the truck to head home.

They are having a pizza party at Zack and Denise's house in two hours. When we pull up to the house, I get out and grab my bag before walking up the steps to her waiting at the door. "If you would give me the code, I could have been inside and put Whiskey out already."

I put the code in, and she walks in after me. "I got the dog," I tell her, dumping my bag and kicking off my boots before heading to the back of the house and letting Whiskey out.

"I'm going to take a shower," she yells toward the kitchen, and five minutes after letting Whiskey back in, I'm also stepping into the shower.

I get out, grabbing a pair of shorts and a T-shirt before going downstairs. I don't expect to find her sitting on one of the stools drinking a beer, her hair piled up on top of her head. She's wearing a black shirt that goes off her shoulder, and it looks like it goes down to her mid-thigh, her legs are bare and one is crossed over the other. "I'm not going for pizza," she declares and I walk over to the fridge and grab my own bottle of beer. "I already called my mother and told her you were icing your pride because you lost the hockey game."

"It's a team sport, I didn't lose the game, the team lost."

"You know what I heard from that sentence?" she asks me, and puts down the beer. "You lost and I didn't, that is the only thing I heard."

I lean against the counter in front of her, twisting the cap open, tossing it on the counter beside me. "Why did you leave?" The second the words are out of my mouth, her eyes fly up to mine.

"What are you talking about?" she asks me, her hands wrapping around her beer.

"You know exactly what I'm talking about, Elizabeth. Why did you fucking leave?" I knew we would be having this conversation, I just didn't know it would be happening now. Even though, after all the years I've had to think about how I would have this conversation, it never started out like it just did.

"I didn't leave."

"Okay, fine." I take a pull of my beer. "I guess we can't discuss this like two mature adults."

"Why did you ignore me?" Her question shocks the shit out of me and all I can do is stare at her. "That day you came over to the house and you totally fucking ignored me. Didn't even look at me."

"You left my bed and didn't even have the decency to fucking wake me up and say goodbye." My voice rises. "Hey, last night was good. Even if you didn't want to continue it"—I stare at her—"you could have at least told me instead of just leaving."

"I didn't fucking leave." She slaps the counter.

"I woke up and you were gone."

"You thought I left?" she says, shocked that I would come to this conclusion.

"I woke up and you were gone. If that doesn't scream up and gone, I don't know what will."

"Yeah," she agrees, "not to leave, dumbass. I wanted to make you breakfast in bed and you didn't have anything in the fridge, so I went out to grab a couple of bagels from your favorite bagel store." My head rears back as if she hit me. "And then when I got back, you were gone. I thought you went out to work out or something. I stayed there until noon and then left." Her voice goes soft. "Then I saw you that night and you ignored me, wouldn't even look my way. I thought you regretted it but didn't want to tell me."

"Are you crazy?" I shake my head, admitting to her what I've admitted to myself over the years. "It was, hands down, the single best night of my life."

Merry Christmas

AND A HAPPY NEW YEAR

Seventeen

The Greatest Gift of All

Elizabeth

I SIT ON the stool in front of him, my body shaking with anger and then more anger. My hands bunch into fists on the cold counter. "Are you crazy?" He shakes his head and then I hear the words I think I've waited seven years to hear. "It was, hands down, the single best night of my life."

I look down at the bottle of beer and close my eyes as I try to calm the racing of my heart. The minute he came down and asked me about that night, I knew this was going to be it. I would be the one who would bare my soul and then he would shatter it, just like he did seven years ago with the silence. I thought for sure I would be the one to throw it in his face, but I was not expecting what he said. "Why didn't you just talk to me?" The question comes out as a whisper and only when it's finally out do I look up at him.

"Why didn't you?" he throws the question back into my court.

"For one"—I place my open palms on the counter and push up—"I was embarrassed." My voice rises as I continue to talk, "We had just had sex and, let's be honest, I wasn't that experienced, and I don't know—" I throw up my hands because I've never placed the blame on myself. I've had the what-if conversations, but it usually was what if I hadn't left. Or what if I never kissed him back. It was never what if I would have forced him to talk to me. "I don't know," I say more calmly.

"How would you have felt if you woke up after our night and I wasn't there?" I swallow down at his question as the back of my neck starts to feel heated.

I move my hand to cup it. "It's not about what I did, it's about what you did."

"God, you are so stubborn," he hisses at me. "Answer the fucking question, Elizabeth." His voice is tight. "What would you have done if you woke up and I was gone? You looked around and all of my things, gone." His eyes bore into mine. "If you had the best night of your life and you got up and looked around, and I was gone." My chest gets tight as he continues to speak, "You call my name twice, but all that is there is silence." Breathing is getting harder and harder as he continues, "You sit back down on the bed and wonder, did I dream it? Was it another dream where I finally got to kiss you?" The lump in my throat forms now. "But you can still vaguely smell my cologne…" He trails off. "What would you have done?" He doesn't wait for me to answer, instead he answers for me, "You would have set my house on fire."

I look up to the ceiling because he is not lying, I would have done that. "But then you show up at my house and you think I'm going to talk to you. I'm going to pull you aside or get you alone so you can talk to me. I thought maybe you were regretting it. So I braced myself for the talk. Braced myself for the words. Braced myself, knowing it would never be the same between us. But instead of all of that, I got silence."

"Nate," I say his name and he just shakes his head.

"No, Elizabeth," he says, looking to the side and all I can do is stare at him, "do you know what that did to me?"

"Yes." I push away from the counter and get off the stool. "I know what that did to you because I felt the same way. I was hurt." I put both hands on the counter stretched out by my sides. "Fuck, why do you think I fucking went all the way across the fucking world?" I shout at him and now it's his turn to look at me shocked. "Yeah, that's right. You think I wanted to do my semester in Australia?" I don't wait for him to answer me, just like he didn't wait for me. "No, I didn't, but I did it because I knew if I stayed here, and we just pretended that night had never happened, I would have been crushed and so broken-hearted, I don't think I would have survived. The pain was that deep."

"Elizabeth," he says my name the same way I said his, but now the ball is in my court and I'm not going to let him get away with it.

"No, Nate." Unlike him, I stare into his eyes so he can

see the hurt. "Do you know what that did to me?" I walk around the island, our eyes on each other. "Do you have any idea what that did to me?"

"Yes," he replies in a whisper, "because I felt it too."

I stand in front of him. "I'm sorry," I say the two words I vowed I would never say to him. Hearing how he was just as hurt as me, I say them. I raise my hand, seeing it shake a little, feeling it in my soul as I place it gingerly in the middle of his chest. I feel his heart beating quickly, in time with mine. "I'm so sorry."

"Not as much as I am." His voice is as broken as I feel. "Not nearly as much as I am." He puts his hand on top of mine. His head shakes and I move my hand around his neck. He licks his lips as I get up on my tippy-toes, finally letting myself touch him more. I run my hand through his hair and down the back of his shirt.

Neither of us says a word as I press myself into him, wrap both arms around his neck, and kiss his jaw softly before he bends his head, his forehead on mine. I take a deep breath in, then he closes the gap and kisses me. This kiss is unlike the one in the bathroom. It's sweet and soft, and his tongue slides in with mine for just a minute before he lets me go. His nose is against mine as my hand leaves his neck to cup his cheek. Our eyes lock on to each other, as our hands roam.

I can't stop touching him. I don't want to stop touching him. I turn my head to the side, kissing him again, this time his hands move from beside him and go to my back. I let go of his lips and this time he takes a deep breath in as my hands move from his neck to the side of his face.

"You," he says right before he kisses me again, and the softness is gone, "you fucking drive me insane." This kiss is full of need. Full of lust. Full of anger and frustration that for the past seven years we've both been thinking the other person was wrong. His hands move from my back up my sides as his tongue fights with mine. One of his hands moves down to cup my ass while the other wraps around the back of my neck.

The kiss deepens as he pulls me up. My legs wrap around his waist as he turns and walks out of the room, the sleep shirt I am wearing moves up to the tops of my thighs. My mouth is on his as he climbs the stairs to his bedroom. He walks into his bedroom and sits on the bed. My knees go to the sides of his hips, straddling him, as I move my head to the side and deepen the kiss. His hands move my long sleep shirt up and then his hand palms my ass, my booty shorts so thin I can feel the heat from his hand. I let go of his lips and his mouth moves down to my neck as his hands slide up my back and then down again to my ass, squeezing it and then back up again. My own hands move from the side of his neck down his arms and up again.

"Seven fucking years," he mumbles as I slide my tongue into his mouth. Our hands are frantic with the need to touch the other person. Bunching his shirt in my hands, I pull it up over his head, tossing it to the side before I kiss him again. This time I need more, so I rotate my hips on his covered cock and our mouths swallow our moans.

His hands trail from my ass to my back as he pulls

the shirt up and over my head, leaving me with just my black thong on. His mouth bends to take one nipple in his mouth. My back arches as he bites it, then kisses the middle of my chest moving to suck my other nipple as my hand holds the back of his neck. His eyes come up to mine as he lets my nipple go. "Seven fucking years, Elizabeth," he pants breathlessly.

"I know," I reply, moving my hips back and forth on his hard cock. My mouth waters to taste him again. My pussy is dripping, practically begging to have it slam into me. My hand itches to touch it. I place my hand behind me on his knee, putting the other one on his shoulder and move faster now. "Dreamed about this," I admit to him in my haze of arousal as he grips one ass cheek and then his other hand holds on to the back of my neck. "Need you." I arch my back when both of his hands move to grip my tits in them. He pinches my nipples between two of his fingers before squeezing them in his closed fist. My head moves to the side as he devours me. The kiss is so much better than I have ever imagined. The kiss I'll be forever remembering from this moment. The kiss that will probably be the one I'll compare every other kiss to for the rest of my life. I push his chest as he falls onto his back and I lie down on him.

My hips lift, giving me access to his cock as I reach between us and palm it. His hands rub the side of my thighs. "Need you too," he groans. I get off and kneel beside him before I push his shorts down over his cock. I don't even wait for it to be completely free before he's in my mouth. I grip the base of his cock and let my mouth meet my hand before moving back up, working him with my mouth and my hand. "Fuck," he hisses out, lifting his hips to fuck my mouth at the same time pushing the shorts off of his hips. "Going to hit the back of your throat." He grips my hair in his fist, not letting me move but instead fucking my mouth. My other hand moves between my legs and into my panties, sliding one finger into me. I moan wanting it to be his fingers and not mine. "Where is your other hand?" he growls, his hips not missing a beat as he slams his cock into my mouth as deep as I'll take him, even pushing it more and more.

"Dirty fucking girl." He moves his hand and meets mine. "Going to help me finger-fuck you while you take my cock?" I don't answer him with words, I just nod my head. Two of his fingers slide through my slit and into me with one of mine. "You don't get to make yourself come." He pushes my head down. "I get to make you come when you are in this bed." His fingers move at the same rhythm as his hips, my own hips moving to get him to go faster, to get that first orgasm out of me. It's lingering there on the surface, my body waiting to explode.

"First time I come," he says, "it's not going to be in your mouth." He pulls my mouth off of him. "It's going to be in your pussy." His fingers slip out of me and then I watch him bring them to his mouth and he sucks them in. "Going to eat that pussy for hours, but first I'm going to need you to slide your pussy down my cock." He holds his cock up for me. "Let me see you swallow me."

I'm so gone for him, I swing my leg and move my

thong to the side, ready to slide down his cock. Not slow, nothing about this is going to be slow. "I need you to make me come." He grips my hips, his fingertips pressing so hard. "You're so big." I pause for just a second, adjusting to having him in me.

He helps move me up and down his cock, my hands moving behind me on his knees. He fists the side of my thong in his hand and in one move it snaps apart. "Want to see your pussy with my cock in it."

"Then watch," I urge as I move until the tip of his cock is about to come out of me as I slam down.

"Nothing better." He licks his thumb. "I thought there was nothing better than seeing my cock in your mouth." He rubs my clit up and down. "I was wrong." My nipples tighten at the same time my stomach does. "Watching your pussy take my cock is much better." He rubs my clit faster. "You are so close. Pussy is getting tighter and tighter."

"I'm there," I hiss out and close my eyes. Then I feel his hand move away from my ass and the sting of his hand moves through me and I open my eyes again. "I want your eyes on me when you come."

"Okay," I pant out, "just—"

"I'm going to make you come on my cock," he tells me. "Then I'm putting you on your back and I'm going to fuck you like I have wanted to fuck you for the last seven years." His hand moves back, and he slaps my ass again. "And you're going to take what I give you."

I'm about to close my eyes when I feel his hand again. "Don't close those fucking eyes," he barks at me.

"Waited seven fucking years to see those eyes again." He thrusts up hard. "Don't fucking close them."

I don't close them. I stare into his and I jump off that cliff. The orgasm roars through me, my pussy pulsing over his cock, with one word on my lips and one word only, his name, "Nate."

Eighteen

NATE

SHE PANTS MY name as she lets go, pussy gripping my cock so tight it's a wonder I don't come in her. I watch her eyes go half-mast, and I think about slapping her ass again, but instead I pinch both her nipples. Her eyes fly open as she watches me. I wrap one of my arms around her waist pulling her up to a sitting potion. My cock goes deeper into her as my head comes down to take her nipple into my mouth. Her pussy contracts on my cock. With both arms wrapped around her as I move her up and down on my cock, her hand goes to my knee and, I swear, I don't think I've ever been so hard in my life.

She continues riding me, one of my hands moving to cup the back of her head, my mouth devouring hers. Her tongue slides into my mouth, the kiss needy as she picks up speed. She lets my mouth go to breathe out my name again. "Nate," she sighs. My cock twitches in her as I suck her neck. She turns her face, and her lips fall on mine again. "Nate," she says in a whisper when my mouth leaves hers.

"Do you know how many times I thought about his moment?" I hiss as my arm tightens around her waist as I get up and turn with her legs wrapped around me. "How many nights you were asleep across from me and all I wanted was to have you right here." Putting a foot in the middle of the bed, and then bending to my knee, placing her on her back in the middle of my bed. Her legs are on the sides of my hips as I touch her face, burying my cock to the hilt inside of her. Feeling the heat of her pussy. "Been dreaming of this moment for seven years." I pull out of her and then slide back in. "Seven fucking years," I repeat in a hiss as I pull back out. "Waited to see those eyes." I bend to kiss the middle of her heaving chest and move my head to her other nipple. "Eyes that haunted me." I move my lips lower, my cock slipping out of her. I grab her tits in my hands, playing with her nipples. "Hated myself for always thinking about you." I move up to kiss her lips, her hands going to the sides of my face. "But couldn't help it."

I move my lips down, licking her nipple on my way down to her stomach. "Nate," she moans my name. "God." She arches her back when I nip her side. "It's always been you," she says as I move up and grip the backs of her thighs and push her legs back. "Always been you I come back to in my mind." She gets on her elbows as my tongue slides into her pussy, and her taste on my tongue is what heaven must fucking taste like. All of her is what dying and going to heaven feels like. Her hand runs through my hair as my tongue moves from her pussy to her clit, flicking it with the tip of my tongue and then sliding two fingers into her. "Nate," she moans as my fingers move and I suck her clit. I wait for her to almost come before I slide my fingers out of her and lick up and down her slit, moving my mouth side to side when I get to her clit. "I'm going to—"

"No, you're not," I counter, moving over her now, gripping my cock in my hand. "Going to fuck you now."

"Yes, please," she pants out, "fill me up." My mouth slams onto hers as she sucks my tongue like she would suck my cock. "Fuck me like you wanted to all these years," she urges.

I rub my cock up and down her slit. "If I do that," I tell her, sliding in, "I'll break you in two."

She smirks. "Don't make promises your cock can't keep." She moves her legs back and tilts her hips, making me sink deeper in her.

My hands grip the mattress, and I give it to her. I pull out and slam into her over and over again, each thrust as hard as I can. She contracts on my cock each time, until I can't take it anymore. I fuck her faster than I ever did before. Harder than I did all those years ago, but she pushes me each time.

"Is that all you've got?" She lifts her hips. "All these years," she pushes, "and that's all you've got." She moans out the last word as she comes on my cock. Her pussy gushing with wetness.

I get back on my knees and throw her legs over my shoulders. "My turn," I grit between clenched teeth, "you get to decide though."

"Hard," she states as I grip her side and slam her onto my cock.

"Pussy or mouth?" I ask her. "Where do you want my cum."

"Where do you want me to take it?" She barely can get the words out, her eyes rolling to the back of her head as I slam into her over and over again.

It happens so fast, I don't even have a chance to decide. "Fuck," I hiss out when my balls tighten and my cum shoots into her. "Pussy this time," I say between clenched teeth, "mouth next time." I fuck her until I have nothing else to give. Her legs fall down from my shoulders onto the bed beside my hips.

I collapse on top of her, her arms and limbs wrapping me up as I turn on my side. "Well"—I move her hair from the side of her face—"that was some way to have a conversation." She giggles as she buries her face into my neck. "I think we both used our mouths with perfection."

"I think so," I agree, "but just to make sure, I'm going to have to fuck your mouth again one more time."

"As long as it ends with you fucking my brains out." She moves her leg over my hip, then she gasps, "We didn't use protection."

My head snaps up. "Oh shit." I look at her and then down at our naked bodies. "Fuck, I didn't even—"

"I," she starts to say, "it's been a while."

"Same," I tell her.

"I hope these sheets are clean," she says and I laugh.

"This is the first time I've had sex in this bed and in this house. That is with another person. I've had sex with myself daily, twice daily since you've been here."

"You've never had sex on this bed?" I slide out of her and turn to get off the bed.

"No." I shake my head, looking down at her on her side, holding her head up with her fist. "Bought this bed and moved into the house, I don't know, it just never was—"

"The last time I had sex was three years ago," she confides to me and I hold out my hand for her as she takes it and moves off the bed to stand in front of me.

"So, we're both clean," I tell her. "Are you on—"

"Of course, I'm on the pill."

"Then we're good." With her hand in mine, I pull her closer to me. "Time to take a shower and then get something to eat."

"How about we eat and then shower?" She tilts her head to the side, the hair that was piled on to the top of her head now sideways, half of it hanging out. "We can order pizza."

"Okay, I'll go get cleaned up," I tell her. "Then I'll order you pizza."

"Or"—she smirks—"you order pizza and then we both get cleaned up."

"Or you get the shower started and I'll come and join you after I order the pizza."

She gets on her tippy-toes and kisses my neck. "You got it."

I walk out of the bedroom and head downstairs, grabbing my phone from my jacket pocket and pulling up the app to order pizza, but instead opting for a couple of burgers. Besides, it is what will take the most amount of time to get here. I place the order and see I have forty-seven minutes before the food should arrive.

Walking back up the steps, I walk into the room, heading straight to the bathroom. The sound of the shower fills the room, and I can see the door is steamed over from the heat. Opening the shower door, I catch her sitting on the bench facing me. Her hair is wet and hanging down around her shoulders, droplets of water coating her body. My eyes trail from hers down to her one leg that's propped up on the bench, but what my eyes are fixated on is her fingers moving in and out of her.

"Started without you." She moves her fingers out of her and then moves her hand up to her clit where she rubs it side to side and then back again into her. "Hope you don't mind," she says and I step into the shower and walk to her. "This bench is the perfect height," she notes, gripping my cock that is at half-mast, "for you to fuck my face." The water cascades around me, as her mouth swallows my cock.

My head falls back as I take in her hot mouth around my cock, my hips moving on their own as my hand comes up to hold her head. She stops sucking my cock and I look back down at her. "It's better when you watch me swallow your cock." She winks at me. "See how far I can take you down my throat." She moves her hand down the shaft as she tries to take it all in her mouth.

"You going to make me hit the back of your throat?" I ask her as she nods her head. "Elizabeth," I groan her name when she sucks as deep as she can and then lets my cock go to suck one of my balls in her mouth. I step away from her, my cock in my hand. "I'm close," I tell her, "and I want to paint your tits with it." She squeezes her tits, and I let go of my cock, stepping close to her. "Play with my cock," I tell her as she grips my cock with her hand, while keeping the other inside herself. Both my hands come up to play with her nipples and she moans as soon as I roll them between my two fingers. "How many fingers you have inside you?"

"Two," she says, her hands moving in sync, "and I'm close."

"How close?" I ask her and she moans when I pinch her nipples harder than before.

"Now," she declares and she moves her hands frantically and it's all I need for me to follow her. She feels my cock jerk in her hand and she aims my release for her tits. She lets me go when she's squeezed every drop from me. "That was"—she stands and then quickly sits back down—"one way to do it." She tries again, this time pushing me out of the way so she can wash my cum off of her. "Next time"—she looks over her shoulder, grabbing my body wash—"your mouth better be on mine.'"

I hug her and bend my head to kiss her. My tongue sliding in with hers, and twenty minutes later we're both getting out of the shower. The burgers are the perfect decision, and that night when I slide into bed, she is right there beside me.

I don't know what time I open my eyes, but the minute I do I hear the sound of the beep coming from the front door. I look toward the bedroom door, wondering if I'm hearing things. There are two people who know the code to the front door and both those people are the men in her life. One is her brother and the other is her father, neither of them I think would be cool with her walking out of my bedroom.

"What is that noise?" she mumbles from beside me, her back to me, the sheet and cover up to her neck hiding her nakedness.

The door opens and I fly out of bed. "Hello," Joshua's voice shouts from the front door.

Elizabeth is out of my bed in a nanosecond, and she looks over at me. "Oh my God," she mouths, searching through the covers for the pajamas she wore to bed but quickly rid herself of as soon as I felt them.

"Is anyone up?" Joshua asks up the steps as I grab the pair of basketball shorts from the floor at the same time she is shimmying her panties on and then her tank top. "Hey, Whiskey." I hear the sound of the thumping of Whiskey's tail on the wall and I know Joshua is rubbing his neck.

"I'm going to go out," I mouth the words with no sounds, "get him in the kitchen."

She finally finds her shorts and holds up a thumb to me, as I walk out of the room, thinking this is not the way I wanted to wake up this morning. "Hey," I say when I get to the top of the stairs and I walk down to Joshua.

"What's up?" I run my hands through my hair.

"Not much, on my way over to my parents' and thought I would swing by and check that you two didn't kill each other." He laughs and I pretend laugh with him. She did almost kill me, I'm about to tell him, but it was with her mouth and not her hands.

"Yeah," I mumble, "I think she's still sleeping." I walk away from the door, and when I get to the kitchen, I look over to see that he's followed me. "Do you want a coffee?" I ask him and he nods as he walks over to the door and opens it for Whiskey.

"I have to head to my parents," he looks at his watch, "But I'll have one quick. I also want to remind you two that we have to get going though, it's the joint bachelor and bachelorette party tonight."

"Ugh," I hear and turn to see Elizabeth has put on a pair of pants and a big shirt, definitely not what she's been wearing these last couple of days. "I've about fucking had it with this wedding shit," she complains, walking to the stool and pulling it out sitting on it, she looks at me. "Good morning."

I look at her as if I didn't wake up with her, and I can't help the smile that fills my face when I say, "It is a good morning."

Nineteen

PLEASE SANTA PLEASE.

ELIZABETH

December 20th

I SIT IN the kitchen on a stool, trying not to show that my heart is about to beat out of my chest. "It is a good morning." He smiles at me, and I quickly look to Joshua to see if he's noticed the difference in his tone. But he's so consumed with Whiskey that he doesn't really notice it. He also doesn't notice the twinkle in Nate's eyes, something that comes out when he's really fucking happy. We didn't see it a lot when we were growing up, but when we did, it was a gift that none of us knew he was giving.

"But is it?" I counter and he folds his arms over his chest.

"Oh, trust me, it is." He smirks. "Best morning I've had in quite a while."

"Then you should get out more," I practically hiss at him.

"Well, I see you two are making peace." Joshua chuckles as he comes over and sits on the stool beside me.

"Yup," Nate confirms at the same time I say, "Hardly."

"I don't know about that, pretty sure we buried the hatchet yesterday."

His eyes stare into mine as Joshua throws his head back and laughs. "Yeah, nothing says let's bury the hatchet like her smashing your gingerbread house to smithereens."

"That's true," he agrees with him, "but when we got home, we had a chat. Used our mouths." My mouth opens in a gasp. "Said a couple of things, and boom, hatchet buried deep."

"Aren't you making coffee?" I ask him. "You can do that instead of using that mouth and making sure the hatchet doesn't get unburied." I raise my eyebrows at him.

"Okay, you two," Joshua intervenes, "I need your help." We both look over at Joshua. "Besides the fact I'm going to need you two to stop fucking with each other." He points to me and then to Nate. "Any other time I would find it amusing, but I want my wedding to go off without the two of you going at each other."

"What do you need?" we both say at the same time.

"See," Nate says, "we're in sync."

"Okay, Macy's brother is coming in to surprise her for the wedding," he explains, his voice filled with animation. "It's a big deal for her."

"I would hope so," I say, "I came all the way from Australia. So that is a big deal also."

"Well, he's in the military and on leave," he fills me in. "The two of them are thick as thieves and talk and text all the time. He didn't think he would be able to get leave, but he finally got permission and he's flying in for the wedding and flying out the day after."

"Okay, fine, he has a better excuse than I did." I roll my eyes as Nate snorts at my comment.

"I'm going to need you guys to pick him up at the airport and keep him here, and then bring him to the party tonight."

"Why do we both have to do that?" I ask. "I think Nate can do this on his own."

"He can but," Joshua says, "I'm asking you both to do it."

"Anything for you," Nate agrees looking over at me, and I just roll my eyes.

The smile on Joshua's face is from ear to ear. "She's going to freak out that Gavin is in town. Besides us getting married on Christmas, this is the next best thing to happen."

"I'm just saying this for the record right now"—I point at him—"if you ever get divorced and then remarried, I'm not coming." Joshua laughs and continues smiling. "I'm not kidding with you, Joshua, this is crazy."

"I know," he agrees, "but Macy's dream was to have a winter wedding."

"You can have a winter wedding without it being two

fucking weeks long."

"It's not two weeks long." He rolls his eyes.

"I've been here for a week and for a fucking week I've done nothing but attend your wedding events."

"I don't know about that." Nate puts a mug of coffee in front of me, and I make a mistake of taking a sip of the coffee while he continues his words. "I've seen you do other things besides wedding stuff."

I choke on the coffee and swallow it, coughing as I look at him leaning against the back counter and bringing his own mug to his lips, trying to hide the smirk he has. "Are you okay?" Joshua asks me as he rubs my back.

"Yeah," I say between coughs as I glare at Nate, "I'm fine."

"Good," he says, getting up off the stool. "Now I'm going to go and get to my parents' house. Macy is supposed to be meeting me there and she thinks I'm stopping for donuts. So I have to do that as well."

"So, you are starting off your marriage with a lie." I clear my throat and blink my eyes that are filled with tears from all the coughing I've just done. "I mean, if that is how you want to start things, I think it's good. She might not."

"I'm not lying to her," he defends himself, "I'm surprising her."

"Okay, if you say so," I tell him as he reaches in his back pocket for his phone.

"I'm sending you his flight information," he mentions to Nate.

"Do you want us to make a sign?" I ask him. "Like

'welcome back from prison'?"

Joshua's face gets tight as Nate starts to chuckle. "I'm not even kidding with you right now."

"What? It's funny. He might think it's hilarious." I hold up both my hands. "But if you want to be a Debbie Downer, we'll just make a sign with just his name."

"Or just show up and find him."

"What is this, Where's Waldo?" I take a sip of my coffee and then he turns his phone to me, showing me a picture of Macy and her brother. "Memorized," I assure, "but what if he looks different?" He shakes his head. "Listen, he could come with a shaved head."

Joshua gives up talking to me and then turns straight to Nate. "Are you going to be okay?"

"I got you," he reassures him, and he nods his head.

"See you guys later," Joshua says, "and don't text me either in case Macy sees it."

"You know who says those words?" I ask him as he's about to walk out the room. "The guy who is cheating on his wife."

"If I ever get remarried," he retorts to me, "you aren't invited."

"Aww." I close my hand in a fist and put it under my eye. "Sad panda."

"Later," he says, walking out of the room, and I wait for the door to slam shut before turning back to look at Nate.

"What the fuck is wrong with you?" I ask him and he smiles at me. The smile that leaves my knees weak and gets certain parts of me riled up.

"I don't know what you mean." I walk to stand right in front of him, the island between us.

"You know exactly what I'm talking about."

He holds his mug with one hand while his other hand is outstretched beside him. "We should talk about what happened last night."

"And this morning," he reminds me. "If we discuss it, we should discuss it all, don't you think? Look at what happened the last time we didn't talk about things." He brings his mug to his mouth. "We spent seven years pissed at each other for no reason."

"I don't think we should do what we are doing," I start and just watch his face. "I mean, I'm leaving sooner rather than later."

"I know." His voice is soft.

"It'll just become harder and harder if we continue this and then I leave." The knot starts to form in my stomach. "Not to say that last night"—he's about to correct me—"and this morning wasn't good."

"Wasn't good?" He grins. "You have to admit it was better than good."

"Fine, it's was great," I admit to him. "You learned a lot in seven years." I say the words and it shouldn't bother me that he was with someone else, but I'm fucking bothered by it. "Needless to say, it wouldn't be smart for us to continue this."

"I agree, but I've learned that I don't like to do the smartest things."

"Like kiss me?" I don't know why my feelings are hurt by this.

"No," he quickly states, "kissing you was definitely smart." He brings the cup to his mouth. "If I hadn't kissed you, we would have never cleared the air."

"This is very true." I can admit he's right on that. "But then you didn't have to kiss me again and then drag me to your room."

"You kissed me the second time," he counters, "and I didn't drag you to my room." He cocks his hip. "I carried you willingly."

"Potato, pa-tah-to." That's the only thing I can counter with. "Either way, we need to just move forward and it'll be good we are doing it without trying to kill each other."

"I agree," he says. "So from now on, it's going to be strictly platonic between the two of us." I nod because I don't know how my voice will sound if I speak to agree with him. "Good. I'm off to take a shower." He grabs his mug. "A cold, cold shower," he mumbles and I can't help but laugh as he walks up the steps.

"Don't go after him," I have to tell myself. "Nothing good is going to come if you go after him." I lean back on the stool and take a sip of my coffee. "Don't do it," I tell myself. "Don't you fucking do it." I look over at Whiskey. "I really want to go and take a shower with your dad," I tell the dog, who is lying on his side unimpressed with the heart-to-heart conversation I'm having with him. "Do you think I should go after him?" He doesn't even lift his head. "Yeah, I don't think I should either." I look over when something catches my eye from the side. Baby Cat saunters into the room, his eyes look like he just got up as he looks at me with a "where were you last night?"

face. "Did you miss me?" I chuckle at him, stopping and sitting down, looking out the window. "Sorry to break it to you, buddy, but you having the whole bed for yourself was a one-night thing."

I get up, putting my mug in the sink and rinsing it out before walking upstairs, and hearing his shower still going. I wrestle with it for about two full minutes before I groan and head toward my own shower.

"DO YOU REMEMBER what he looks like?" I lean over to Nate and ask him as we stand at the bottom of the escalator waiting for Macy's brother. The airport is jam-fucking-packed with last-minute travelers. If I thought the airport was crowded when I was traveling here, I was dead wrong.

"You think I looked at the picture?" He looks over at me. "I was watching you the whole time."

My stomach should not flutter at those words, and I literally have nothing else to say to that, so I just look forward, watching people come down. "So this is what it feels like," I mumble as I look around to see people celebrating with their loved ones.

"What what feels like?" He looks down at me.

"Well, for one, what it feels like when someone remembers to pick you up at the airport and the other"—I point over to the luggage carousel that has people picking up their luggage—"to have their luggage waiting for them. It's a privilege."

"You act like they didn't find your bag." He snorts.

"Do I have the bag?" I ask him. "They said they located it but where is it? Why isn't it here with me?" I shake my head. "They said it would be a couple of days," I snap back at him, "and it's been a couple of days since and no bag."

I look toward the escalator, scanning the arrivals. "I think that's him." I point to the guy wearing jeans, a white T-shirt with a black jacket, and a buzz cut.

His eyes scan the area, and when he sees the two of us, he holds up his hand. "It's him."

"I'm holding a sign with his name," he reminds me. "I hope he can read."

"Hey," he says when he comes closer and his smile beams, "you must be Elizabeth." I'm expecting him to hold out his hand to shake mine, but instead he takes me for a big bear hug. "I would recognize you anywhere."

"Um," I say looking over at Nate, who looks like he's about to rip off this guy's arm, "thanks?"

"I have to say"—he steps away and gives me a megawatt smile, as he gives me a scan from head to toe—"you look even better in person than you do in pictures."

"No, she doesn't," Nate snaps, and I gasp while he holds out his hand. "I'm Nate."

"Hey"—he shakes his hand—"thanks for coming to get me."

"Are we waiting for a bag?" Nate asks him and he shakes his head.

"Got everything I need here." He shrugs his shoulder

for the backpack. "Joshua said he'd hook me up."

"Let's go," Nate urges and he makes it so he's walking in between me and Gavin as we make our way to the truck.

"You can sit in the front," I tell Gavin. "It has more leg room."

"That's very generous of you," he replies to me, his brown eyes now a chestnut color.

"No, it's not," Nate grumbles, unlocking the door and I almost burst out laughing.

He turns to laugh at Nate, thinking he's joking, before he turns and opens the back door of the truck to me. "After you, my kind lady," he says and I smile at him.

"Well, look at that," I say to him and then look over to a scowling Nate, "chivalry isn't dead after all." I shrug one shoulder. "Welcome home, Gavin, and thank you for your service."

Merry Christmas

Twenty

SNOWMAN

NATE

I WATCH GAVIN openly flirt with Elizabeth, and if I didn't love Joshua and the Morrow family as much as I do, I think I would throat punch him. "After you, my kind lady," he says to her, and she smiles back at him. The pit of my stomach tightens when she does it.

"Well, look at that," she replies to him and then turns to me as I glare at her, "chivalry isn't dead after all." She shrugs one shoulder at him. "Welcome home, Gavin, and thank you for your service."

"That's a bit of a stretch," I state, getting into the truck, "we don't even know what he does in the military."

"I would tell you," Gavin says, getting in and tucking his backpack by his feet before reaching for his seat belt, "but it's classified."

"Oh," Elizabeth says from behind me, and I look over my shoulder as I start the truck, "that sounds important."

"I'm pretty sure that's the common answer for anyone who is in the military and has clearance." I pull out of the parking spot.

"That's not necessarily true," Elizabeth says, "if he was on tour, he would be able to talk about it."

"She's beautiful and smart," he tosses over his shoulder, and I think he even winks at her. "That, my friend, is a lethal combination."

"I'm not your friend," I remark, looking out the window as I merge into the lane onto the highway.

The phone rings as soon as I pull into the driveway and turn off the truck. "Hello." I put the phone to my ear.

"Hey," Joshua says, his voice in a whisper, "did you get the package?"

"If you are asking if I picked up your brother-in-law," I start, looking over at Gavin, who gets out of the truck and holds the back door open for Elizabeth as they exchange a couple words; words that make her laugh out loud and pretend she's bashful, "that would be yes."

"Oh good. I have my father bringing over clothes for him to wear tonight."

"Great," I say, slamming the door and trying to ignore the sound of the two of them talking. "How about he goes home with your father also?"

Joshua laughs at me. "What? Why?"

"No reason," I say as he holds out his hand for Elizabeth.

"Wouldn't want you to fall and injure yourself."

"We wouldn't want that now," Elizabeth replies, staring up at him, "would we?"

"We most certain would not." He tucks her hand around his bicep, walking up the stairs.

"They're not slippery," I tell them, "nor are they wet." I look around. "So the chances she's going to fall are slim to none."

"We can never be too safe." Gavin grins at her.

"Yeah, how long do you want me to keep him here?" I punch in the code for the door and then open in.

Whiskey hears the door from wherever he is in the house and comes trotting over to us. He smells me and then his tail wags even faster when he sees Elizabeth and just as fast when he sees Gavin. "Traitor," I mumble. "Let's go outside," I snap my command and he turns his attention back to me and follows me to the back door. "So why can't he leave with your father?"

"He'll be bored out of his skull with my father. The two of you have a lot in common," Joshua explains, and I turn to see Elizabeth showing him around and offering him something to drink.

"I don't think I have anything in common with him. I don't even know what he does." I turn around and my voice is low.

"He's in top-secret communication, something or another." I roll my eyes at his description of Gavin's job. "Either way, take good care of him, and I'll see you guys in a couple of hours."

"You know what would be fun? Why don't you bring Macy here and we can surprise her now?" He chuckles at my idea. "You know what, after your wedding, I don't want to see you for a month," I grit between my clenched teeth.

"Okay, well, I'm going to go upstairs and get ready for tonight," Elizabeth announces. "Or, you know what, you've been traveling all day—"

"Or maybe he just took an hour flight," I cut in. "We don't really know where he came from."

He points to me and chuckles. "You trying to get me to tell you my secrets?"

"Couldn't care less." I put my hands on my hips. "But if you want to tell us your secrets..."

"Took an AMC flight overnight and landed this morning, then got on a flight from Delaware."

"So you say." I hold up my hands. "No one can tell if you are lying or not, so we just have to pretend that is what you did. But you could have also just flown in from Virginia."

"I guess we will never know." He perches himself on the stool.

"Well, anyway," Elizabeth interrupts, "you should take a shower before I do."

"I couldn't," he tells her. "It's not right, you should go first."

"Or you can take a shower in my bathroom," I tell Elizabeth, "and then you can shower at the same time."

"That sounds good," Elizabeth agrees. "Do you want to follow me and I'll show you where the bathroom is?"

"That would be amazing."

"I don't think you need to show him where it is," I counter. "It's the second door on the right." He nods at me, picking up his backpack and walking away.

"What is your problem?" Elizabeth asks me. "You are being so rude."

"I'm being rude?" I put my hand to my chest. "I'm not the one pretending I'm the President of the United States with some top-secret bullshit. Who the fuck are we going to tell?"

She rolls her lips. "I'm going to get in the shower and then get ready."

She turns and walks away. "Remember the house rules," I call to her retreating back and she turns to look at me, "no nipples in the common area. Must be fully covered."

"I'll make sure to knock on Gavin's door to tell him the house rules." She turns and walks away from me. I'm about to chase after her when Whiskey scratches at the back door and the doorbell rings.

I get Whiskey and Elizabeth gets the front door. "Hey," I hear her say, "what are you doing here?"

"Delivering this." I peek my head around the corner and see Zack with a black bag. "This is for the mystery guest."

"Dad, she's not here, you don't have to talk in code," Elizabeth chides. "He's upstairs in the shower."

"Okay, well, can you give him this?" He hands it to her.

"I'll give it to him." I snatch it from her. "He's in the shower right now, but I'll put it at his door."

"Someone is uptight," Zack states. "Four days to go and we'll be over all this wedding talk."

"One can hope," Elizabeth retorts, getting on her

tippy-toes to hug her father, "but I have to go and get ready now."

I watch her walk away from her father as she tries to grab the bag out of my hand, and I give her a look that says *try me*. "So hostile," she says as she struts up the steps and goes into the spare bedroom.

"Have fun tonight," Zack says, "but not too much fun, we have family lunch tomorrow."

"Good God, is this ever going to end?" I ask him and he chuckles.

"Soon." He pulls open the door, slamming it behind him.

"Not soon enough," I mumble, looking up to see Elizabeth come out of her room with a bag in her hand and walk into my room. "Not soon enough."

"Elizabeth!" I shout her name up the steps. "We've got to go."

"You can't rush perfection," she shouts back at me and I look up at the ceiling. I'm standing at the front door with Gavin, who is wearing black tailored pants and a black button-down shirt. I, on the other hand, went for black pants and a taupe sweater that has five buttons down the front, two of them left open. I can hear her heels clicking on the floor as she comes into view.

Gavin whistles from behind me. "You definitely can't rush perfection," he praises and I watch her walk down the steps. My mouth is watering when I see her outfit. Her white oversized knitted sweater falls off of one shoulder, the front is tucked into her black miniskirt that molds her body. But that isn't what gets my mouth watering, it's the black thigh-high boots that show you just a hint of her thigh between the top of the boots and the hem of the skirt. Her hair is wavy and draped over one shoulder. "You look—"

"She knows what she looks like," I mumble. "We have to get going."

I open the door and hold it open for her and she steps out, followed by Gavin who, make no mistake about it, is checking out her ass.

He holds the door open for her and then his hand so she can step up into the cab of the truck, her skirt rising more, and I grit my teeth as my cock comes alive and stays that way throughout the drive to the restaurant where the joint party is being held. We can hear music already playing and I swear Joshua is going to owe me big-time for this.

"Here we go," I say and pull open the door. He steps in, and I think ten seconds later, I hear the sound of Macy screaming his name. I step in beside Elizabeth and her perfume hits me right away, as she looks up at me and gives me one of her smiles. It's not the same smile she's been giving Gavin. It's a different one, this one is more of a smirk and then a smile. Just for me.

Gavin turns Macy in his arms as she quietly cries, then puts her down. "I can't believe this." She puts her hands to her mouth and then looks over at Joshua. "You did this, didn't you?"

"I might have," he admits to her, and she walks to him, hugging his waist.

"He did help," Gavin says, "but it was your sister-in-law who came to get me."

"I guess me driving wasn't a factor in all of this," I mumble and she looks up at me again. I know we shouldn't go down this road with each other. I know the best thing I can do for myself it to just let it go. I know all of this, yet the only thing I can think of is getting her back into my bed.

"Thank you, guys, so much"—Macy comes to us—"for bringing him here and taking good care of him."

"The pleasure was all ours," I say with a smile and Elizabeth looks down at the floor and then back up again. She gives her a hug and then walks away from us. "I need a drink," she says and walks away from me and toward a couple of her cousins.

"Thanks, man." Joshua comes to stand beside me. "I owe you big."

"That you fucking do," I agree.

"Let's get something to eat." He slaps my stomach as he walks away and goes to gather everyone to sit down.

The meal is quick and I'm sitting next to Joshua and Macy, along with Jack and Evie. Elizabeth at the far end of the table with Gavin as the two of them do a shot. She slams the shot onto the table and throws her head back and laughs at whatever he said. I take my phone out of my pocket and text her. I got her number two days ago when we both went to try on our outfits for the wedding.

Me: You look beautiful when you laugh.

She must feel the phone vibrate on the table as she turns it over and looks down, and then I can see her smile. The phone then buzzes in my hand, and I can't help but bark out a laugh when I read her response.

Elizabeth: I know

Me: Meet me near the bathroom.

Gavin is talking to her and her cousin, along with a couple of other bridesmaids. Her eyes come to mine before she looks down and answers me.

Elizabeth: For?

Me: You'll have to find out.

Elizabeth: I mean, you aren't saying anything to get me there.

She looks up at me and I can see the twinkle in her eye from her spot down the table.

Me: What good is it to tell you when I can show you?

Elizabeth: It better be worth my time.

I push away from the table. "I'll be back," I mumble to the group, but no one notices me as I walk to the back where the bathroom is. I take a look around and spot the maintenance closet.

Then I hear her boots coming my way. "Well?" She folds her arms over her chest. "You got me here." She looks around. "What do you have to show me?"

I slip my hand in hers and pull her with me into the closet. A soft light is on overhead and there are racks of cleaning and paper supplies. She turns around at the same time I close the door and push her back against it. "You look beautiful," I tell her, stepping into her space.

"Yeah." Her voice is breathless as I step even closer

to her, and she puts one hand on my chest. "You look hot," she compliments with a smile as she tilts her head to the side. "Really fucking hot."

"I know we said we shouldn't do this," I mumble as I tilt my head the other way, my lips getting closer and closer to her, "but I just can't stay away from you." I rub my nose with hers. "I don't want to stay away from you."

I don't know who moves first, but my lips are on hers and her hand on my chest is now snaking up to the back of my neck. The kiss is frantic as she moves away from me. "Waited for you in the shower," she informs me. "Was playing with myself"—my cock strains to get out—"hoping you'd come in and take over." She grips my hand and pulls it up. "Tried to get there but it just wasn't good enough." She takes my forefinger and my middle finger into her mouth, sucking them like she would suck my cock. "Need you to make me come," she pleads, dropping my hand and then gripping her skirt at her hips and shimmying it up. "No one has made me come like you have," she admits and I look down to see her skirt is now around her waist. "Nate"—she arches her back, grabbing my wrist—"please, make me come."

I move my wrist out of her hand, rubbing it down the front of her panties. "I'll make you come"—she shivers—"but when we get home, I want you on your knees"—she nods—"and in my bed."

"Yes," she hisses as I move her panties to the side and tease her entrance with my fingers. Her mouth opens and hovers over mine. "Yes," she pants out, waiting for it, "I need—"

"Don't tell me what my pussy needs," I hiss at her, "I know what you need." I ram two fingers in her and she moans out. "It's going to be fast," I tell her as I slide my fingers in and out of her, then bury them to my knuckles and curl them into her G-spot. Her legs open to give me more access. "I wish I could bend you over and fuck you silly." She writhes against the door, the sound of her heavy breathing filling the room. "Come in your pussy." I can tell she's close, her pussy gets wetter on my fingers. "Have me leaking out of you all night." My cock struggles to get out and into her.

"Yes," she moans, "God yes." I cover her mouth with mine as soon as she comes, swallowing down her moan. Her juices drip down my knuckles to my wrist as she spasms around them.

Only when she rests her head back against the door, and her orgasm tapers off, do I slip my fingers out of her. Bringing my fingers to my mouth, I wink at her. "I told you it would be worth your time."

Twenty-One

Elizabeth

December 21ˢᵗ

I GRIP THE sheets in my hands, my elbows moving back and forth as he fucks me from behind. I woke up with Nate's head buried in between my legs, which then led to him sliding into me and then, when I was fully awake, treating me to my third orgasm of the morning. "Nate," I moan his name and his hold on my hips tightens each time.

"Yeah, baby," he answers, not stopping his rhythm.

"I'm close," I tell him, even though he knows. It's like he has an owner's manual for my body. He works me like no one else has ever worked me before. The sex is always good, and just when I think it won't get better, he basically says, *hold my beer* and makes it feel like I'm floating in the atmosphere.

"I know, baby." He slams into me one last time and that is what sends me flying over the edge and crashing into the abyss. I fuck him back, riding out my orgasm. "Fuck, I don't know if I can hold back." "Then don't." I look over my shoulder at him as he pulls out of me and places his cock between my ass cheeks as he grips it and shoots his cum on my lower back. I arch my back as he slaps my ass and I smile.

"Don't tease me with that ass," he warns and moves away from me, and I collapse on the middle of his bed. Where I said I would never go again. But last night, after the closet, we walked back out and I couldn't stay away from him. The soft touches no one saw. The looks he would give me over the table. It was all too much. When he parked in his driveway and we walked in, he put his hand around my waist and then I walked straight to his room where I got on my knees. "I don't think I can move."

"Well." He smacks my ass lightly and then kisses the back of my neck. "I have to go let Whiskey out, and I can bring you a coffee."

"That sounds like a plan," I tell him as he grabs his shorts before going to the bathroom to clean up. He walks out with a white cloth in his hand as he wipes my back.

"How chivalrous of you," I tease, and he glares. "You were jealous."

"I wasn't jealous," he denies. "Do you want coffee or do you not want coffee?" He wipes my lower back.

"I would like coffee," I answer and then flip over when he's done, "but I'll come with you. You can make the coffee and I can feed Whiskey and let him out." Getting out of bed, I slip on one of his discarded T-shirts from the chair in the corner.

I follow him out of the room and come face-to-face with Bean, who's decided to come out of hiding to witness my walk of shame, and Baby Cat. "Your cats are very judgmental," I tell him as they stare at me and I stare back at them. "Don't tell me you've never slept in his bed before." I walk down the steps as I follow him as he waits for me at the bottom of the steps.

"Someone is jealous." He swats my ass, and I don't get to answer him because Whiskey comes down the hallway, stretching and then wagging his tail.

"First, I am not jealous of cats," I refute, looking up the steps to see the cats now sitting at the top of the stairs side by side, "and you *were* jealous of Gavin." He stops walking and turns around. "Don't even try to deny it. You were grouchy the minute he started flirting with me, and if looks could kill, he would be dead." I walk to him and tap the tip of his nose with my finger. "Don't even try to deny it."

"The guy is probably a con man and pretends he's in the military, so no one asks any questions." He taps my nose and then turns and walks toward the kitchen.

I shake my head and walk into the kitchen, going to the back door while he makes the coffee, and filling Whiskey's bowls with water and food. I sit down on the stool and watch him. He places one cup in front of me and stands exactly where he did yesterday morning. "We need to talk about—" I start saying and he holds up his hand.

"We're two adults who enjoy each other's company," he starts and then smirks. "Listen, Elizabeth, I know the deal and so do you." I don't say anything, I just nod my head. I mean, realistically, he's saying what I want him to say. However, saying we are just two adults who enjoy each other's company, and nothing more, stings like a motherfucker. "So while you are here, we can do what we are doing."

"I leave after New Year's Day." My heartbeat starts to speed up while I say it, and I bring the cup of coffee to my lips, taking a small sip.

"How about we just…" He looks down at his coffee not sure how to word the next part.

"Fuck each other's brains out while I'm here?" I fill in the part for him when he takes too long to think of the words.

"Fuck each other's brains out while you're here." He chuckles. "It'll be our little secret."

"Just like before, except now we know the terms." I trail off. "I won't think you hate me."

He looks me in the eyes. "I could never hate you, Elizabeth," he assures, picking up his cup. "Be annoyed with you? Most definitely, but hate?" He shakes his head. "Never."

I gasp, "How could little old me annoy you?" I lean back on the stool and tuck one of my feet under me. "I'm perfect."

"That you are," he agrees. "That you are."

HE PULLS UP to my parents' house and I look around to see there are double the cars that were here the last time. "It's safe to say"—I look over at him—"the family has descended."

"This isn't even all of them." He puts the truck in park and then turns over to look at me. "The majority are only getting here for the rehearsal dinner."

"Smart people," I grumble as I reach for the door handle. "I should have done that."

"If you had," he chirps as he opens his own door, "then I wouldn't be able to bang your brains out."

I don't know why, but hearing him say the words makes me laugh in a way I haven't in a while. Like throw my head back and just laugh. "That is very true."

I get out and walk side by side with him up the front steps and open the door. The noise hits us right away, along with the smell of food. "I'm starving," he remarks kicking off his boots and adding them to the mammoth collection that is now at the front door. There are boots and sneakers, both male and female, along with kids' shoes tossed in every single direction.

"You should have eaten something." I look over at him and he grins.

"I did." He looks around to make sure no one is listening. "Twice."

"Oh, there you two are," I hear over my shoulder and

see my father walking into the room. He's dressed in track pants and a T-shirt that has the rink name across it in a teal-blue color. "Guess what?"

"The wedding is off, and Christmas is now cancelled for all eternity." I hold my hands together and smile. The joke going over his head as he glares at me.

"That is not funny."

"Depends who you ask." I shrug my shoulder. "If it's not, then I give up."

"Your luggage was delivered this morning," He announces and I gasp, turning in a circle to see if I see it anywhere.

"Did you guys accept it or did you give it away like you did my room?"

My father laughs. "So dramatic." He hugs me with my arms pinned to my side. "It's in the living room." He kisses the top of my head. "I can put it in the truck for you."

"I've got it," Nate offers, walking to the living room and grabbing my black suitcase.

"Be careful with that luggage," I tell him, "it's precious cargo."

"It's a suitcase," Nate answers back.

"Yeah, with my things in it and I'm precious, so it's precious fucking cargo, Nate."

"Got it." He nods and opens the door to put my luggage in the back of his truck.

"Come and say hello to your cousins." My father puts his arm around me as we step into the kitchen that looks like it's packed with over forty people, if not more.

"Why is it that it always seems like we multiply?" I ask him and he laughs.

"You guys keep growing up and adding babies into the mix," he answers, right as my cousin Zoey's sons race past me.

"If you guys break anything in this house"—Zoey follows them—"it will be a huge time-out for both of you and…" She puts her hands on her hips, using her best mother voice. "I'll take the money out of your piggy banks." They look at her with big eyes. "Yeah, I said it and I mean it. Go find your father." They turn around and take off running, zigzagging through the throngs of people.

"Hey," she greets, coming to me and giving me a hug. "I was looking everywhere for you." I give her a hug.

"Well, you couldn't find me because my parents tossed me out on the streets." I side-eye my father, who just rolls his eyes and walks away from me. "When did you get in?"

"Late last night," she replies. "Nash had a meeting in Dallas, so we stopped there for a couple of days and then came up here." She mentions her husband who she eloped with a week after she started working for him. They never even went out on a date, and the next thing you know, they were married. She actually took off from New York after her long-term boyfriend wouldn't commit to her, and then she found Nash, who refused to let her go.

"How's California treating you?" I ask her as we make our way over to the side where a couple of round tables are set up. The dining room that used to hold our dining room table has now been cleared out and in its place are five round tables with chairs.

"It's great," she says, "I love it. What about you? How is the land down under treating you?"

"It's good," I reply, but for the first time since I moved there, I am not missing it.

"I don't know how you do it," she says, putting her hand on mine. "My parents live about a four-hour plane ride from me, and I don't know if I would be able to be across the world from them and everyone else, for that matter." I smile at her. "Do you miss home sometimes?"

"It was hard at the beginning, for sure," I admit to her, "and every single time I came here and then went home, it would be really hard to get back into the swing of things. I miss it here more times than not. Especially when everyone gets together and all I can see is pictures," I share and look over when Nate walks back into the room. His eyes roam around the room until he finds me.

He moves around people to get to the side of my table. "Bag is in the car," he reports and then walks with a smile to Zoey. "Hey there."

"Hey yourself." She tilts her head back and he bends to kiss her cheek. "You look good."

"No, he doesn't," I say, shaking my head and making them laugh.

"The two of you"—she gets up, shaking her head—"always oil and water. I have to check to make sure my kids are not swinging from the chandeliers," she says, walking away and I look over at Nate.

"I'm the oil, you're the water." He just shakes his head.

"Whatever you say, Elizabeth." The look in his eyes is flirty. "Whatever you say." He turns back and walks toward the crowd of people, going to say hello to everyone, while I sit here and try not to think about how it's going to feel not only leaving him, but leaving my family again.

Twenty-Two

SANTA, CAN'T YOU HEAR ME

NATE

I PICK UP a plate at the end of the long makeshift buffet table that has been set up in the kitchen. There are people literally everywhere, and Denise and Zack could not be happier. The whole family is like this. It's like the more the merrier but on steroids. "Hey," I hear from behind me and look over to see Gavin. "What's going on?"

I grab the serving spoon and scoop some eggs onto my plate. "Not much," I reply. "What about you?"

"Exhausted," he admits as I walk to the next tray of breakfast sausage.

"Jet lag." I try to be polite with him.

He smirks and then grins. "Something like that," he says, looking around. "Let's just say, I didn't get much sleep last night."

"Good to know." I move to the pancakes and grab a couple. "Take care," I say, grabbing two slices of bacon and then taking off before he says anything more to me.

I look around at all the full tables and see Elizabeth sitting with a bunch of her girl cousins, and I smile when I hear her laugh. Smiling because she's getting to spend time with her family. Making a mental note to ask her if she misses them when she's not here. I make my way over to the table where Jack is sitting with Matthew, Max, and Zack, pulling out a chair and sitting down. "I'm starving," I declare, making the staple Stone breakfast taco, where you put the scrambled eggs, sausage, and bacon in the pancake, and then dip it in the syrup.

"I'm taking it that Elizabeth didn't cook you breakfast." Jack snickers while he takes his own bite of food.

"I don't know about you," Matthew offers, "I would not eat anything from someone who wanted me dead."

"She doesn't want me dead." I look at the guys, who just give me a confused look.

"She's wanted you dead for the past, I don't know, ten years."

"No, she hasn't," Zack adds. "The two of them used to fight just like Jack and Joshua." He defends me. "She would get under his skin at times, and he would get under hers, but she never really wanted to kill him."

"Pretty sure when he used to eat her food that was in the fridge, she wanted to kill him." Jack laughs. "Once he took the last ice cream sandwich that she tried to hide, and she took all of his shoes and threw them in the pool after she poured honey in them."

I shake my head, remembering the memory. "Yes, and

she also put it in my skates, and I didn't check before I put my feet into them."

"I remember that," Jack says. "The floor in the locker room was sticky for a fucking month."

"Don't remind me," Zack states. "We also had an infestation of ants after that."

I can't help but look over at her. The two of us have so many stories over the years, some good, some bad, some so great it fills your soul so full like it's about to explode. Then the worst was after our night together. The only other time I had felt that type of pain and sadness was when I lost my parents and then my grandparents.

The phone rings from my back pocket, and when I pull it out, I see it's the office calling. "Hello."

"Hey, Nate," Chloe, my vet tech, says, "I know you aren't on call and are on vacation but—"

"What's up?" I ask her.

"Priscillia got food poisoning last night and Bruno," she mentions the vet who is taking over for me and the dog one of my first clients has, "has come in with a blockage in his—"

"What did he eat?" I ask her.

"A pair of panties," she replies, trying not to laugh.

"I'll be there in a bit," I tell her and disconnect. "I have to go in. My replacement got food poisoning." I finish my taco and push away from the table. "I have to go and tell Elizabeth."

"I can take her back to your house," Jack offers, "or she can come home with us."

"I'll just tell her," I say, grabbing my plate and taking

it to the kitchen, putting it in the sink before I turn and walk toward Elizabeth, who is still sitting with her cousins.

I walk to her and her eyes fly up to meet mine. "Hey," I greet, nodding to all of them. "I just got a call and I have to go into work. One of my dogs got into some personal items and has eaten a pair of underwear," I tell her. "Jack said he can take you back to my house or you can wait here."

"Or," she suggests, "why don't I come with you?"

"To my work?" I ask her, shocked that she would come with me instead of staying with her family.

"Yeah." She gets up and looks at the girls. "I'm a doctor. I'm pretty sure it's almost the same thing in the operating room."

I shake my head as she moves quickly to say goodbye to her parents and then meets me by the door. "You don't have to come with me."

"Are you kidding?" she replies, putting on her boots. "This is a much-needed escape. They were talking about doing some sort of wedding prep, and I'm not about that life."

"What wedding prep?" I ask her as I put my own boots on.

"Something about welcome bags and party favors." She grabs her jacket. "All I know is I'm not making anyone a welcome bag when I was kicked out of my own house."

"You know, technically, it's not your room anymore," I remind her as I shrug my jacket on and she just glares at me.

"Wow, someone is choosing violence before he has to perform surgery. I would hate to, I don't know, break a finger or something."

"Noted," I deadpan, opening the door for her and waiting for her to walk out. "See? Chivalry."

She rolls her eyes at me as she follows me to the truck. "Do you want me to open the door for you?" I ask her as she reaches for the handle.

"A gentleman would have just done it and not asked," she throws over her shoulder, getting in the truck.

I get into the truck and start it as she rubs her hands together. "You cold?"

"It's not as cold as it was yesterday," she replies and I look out to see little snowflakes falling as I take off toward my clinic.

I pull into the parking lot and head to the back where I park. Two other cars are in the parking lot, one Chloe's and the other Benny's, who is the receptionist and vet tech intern. I get out of the truck and meet Elizabeth at the back, the snow coming down a little bit heavier now. "Wow, so this is where the magic happens?" She looks around, seeing the brown one-story building with green roof.

"You should know, the magic happens in my bedroom," I tease, and when she snorts, I wink at her. She pushes my shoulder, and I grab her hand, walking to the brown door, pulling it open, and stepping inside. In the small space there are four pairs of boots, along with five pairs of inside shoes. I shrug off my jacket and hang it on an available hook, while I kick off my boots and slip into my work Crocs.

Elizabeth stomps her shoes and then rubs them on the carpet. "Are there slippers I could wear?" I point to my second set of Crocs as she kicks her boot off and then slides into them. Her feet look like they are being swallowed by them. I open the white door and step into what I call, command central. There are two long stainless steel tables in the middle of the room and a long counter desk in front of the tables. All around the room are counter spaces to work on and drawers under them where we store all medications and supplies we keep locked up.

"Hey," I greet, and Chloe looks up at me, a big smile filling her face.

"Hey yourself," she says and the smile on her face fades as she sees Elizabeth behind me. "Um." She tries to cover up the fade and then gives me the same smile.

"Chloe," I say to her, "this is Elizabeth. Joshua's sister."

"Oh," she replies and she quickly now changes the smile back to the one she gave me when I walked in. "Hi." She walks over to Elizabeth and extends her hand. "It's so nice to finally meet you."

"It's nice to meet you." Elizabeth holds out her hand and smiles at her.

"So," Chloe asks, "how is the wedding prep coming along?"

"It's almost over," I answer, walking over to where we keep the charts. "What do we have?" I pick up Bruno's chart.

"Mr. Milioti said he started acting funny this morning and then started throwing up, so he brought him in. X-ray shows there is something." Chloe comes to stand next to me. "He's blocked right there." She points to the scan. "Because of where it's sitting, we can't give him any meds."

"I'm going to have to go in and remove them," I state and then look to Elizabeth. "It should take me about an hour."

"I'm good," she assures, looking around and then going over to the six crates we have piled up with two cats in them. "Hi," she coos to the cats and sticks her hand in. One of them swats at her. "I like you the best," she tells the cat. "Zero fucks to give, I get it."

I walk to my office. "Want to see my office?" I ask her and she follows me in and then shuts the door. Only when it's closed do I push her against the door and do what I've been wanting to do for the last hour. I hold her chin in my hand and my lips touch hers. Her mouth opens and her tongue slides out to meet mine. Her hands grip my sides, pulling me closer to her. The hand at her chin now slides into her hair as I turn my head to the side and the kiss deepens.

"Is this why you want me to see your office?" She smiles up at me after I let go of the kiss.

"No," I deny and then kick off my Crocs and then peel off my pants.

"I'm not having sex with you in your office with your staff members right outside this door." She folds her arms over her chest. "Especially since Chloe is for sure in love with you."

I stop midway to taking off my sweater. "She's my technician," I say softly.

"So, people don't fall in love with people they work with?" she asks me and my eyebrows go up.

"Did you ever fall in love with someone you work or worked with?" I don't even know why that statement bothers me, but it does.

"No"—she shakes her head—"because I know not to shit where I eat."

I peel the sweater over my head and toss it to the side. Her eyes get heavy with lust as she gives me an up-and-down look. "You are going to have to wait," I tell her as I put a clean pair of scrubs on, "until later."

"I think I can contain myself." She holds up two hands. "Do I have to change to come in the room with you?"

"You really want to come in the room with me?"

"Well, yeah." She crosses her arms at the hem of her own sweater and pulls it up and over her head, leaving her with black leggings and a black lace bra. I lick my lips. "You're going to have to wait"—she points at me, peeling her leggings over her hips and down her legs—"until later."

"Fine," I huff, my cock half-mast as she reaches on the shelf for a pair of scrubs. My hand comes out to roam over her ass. "But after"—I slap it softly—"it's all mine."

She gets changed into the scrubs and has to roll the top of the pants twice and then use an elastic band to bunch them at the side.

We walk out of the office and Chloe sees the both of us in scrubs and just turns her head the other way. *Shit*, I think to myself, *Elizabeth might be right about this one. I have never once given her any notion that it would be more between us.* I make a mental note to stay strictly even more professional with her.

"Is Bruno ready?" I ask her and she nods her head.

Two hours later, we are both dressed again and walking out of the vet clinic. Bruno was just waking up and the nighttime tech is going to be on duty all night long, making sure he's okay. The minute I open the door, I see that not only is it still snowing, but there has been an accumulation of the snow. "Shit," I swear. "This might be a storm." The wind picks up as the snow blows into my face. "Get in the truck," I tell her, opening my door and starting it before taking the snow brush out of my back seat. My fingers feel like they are frozen by the time I get back into the truck.

"My father just called, said they are expecting six inches of snow over the next twenty-four hours."

"Oh fuck." I look at her.

"Macy's having a minor meltdown, and my uncle Matthew is on the phone trying to make sure we get a couple of chartered planes on standby."

"Shit, we should hit up the grocery story now that we're out. It might be a day before the roads are clear."

I pull out and it takes me thirty-five minutes to drive the fifteen minutes to the grocery store. The two of us fill the basket with all sorts of things. We get home and the steps are covered in snow. "Go open the door," I tell her as we get out and I reach into the back to grab the bags.

"I don't know the code," she tosses over her shoulder.

I close my eyes, knowing I'm going to have to give it to her. "It's one, two, two, three, eighteen." The minute I say the numbers, she looks over at me.

"What?" I pretend I don't know what is going on.

"That," she says, standing on the second step, "that's the night we—"

I nod my head, not sure I want to have this conversation in the middle of the steps.

"We should get in there," I tell her, avoiding looking at her as I pass her on the steps. "Whiskey has been in all day."

Merry Christmas
AND A HAPPY NEW YEAR

Twenty-Three

ELIZABETH

I LISTEN TO him give me the code and then look over at him, not sure I've heard him right. "Did you say, one, two, two, three, eighteen?"

"What?" He pretends like he doesn't know what is going on.

"That," I say, my head spinning, "that's the night we—"

He stands there on the second step nodding his head, the snow falling all around him, his feet buried in the snow as he holds the bags in his hands. "Whiskey," he repeats what he said before, "it's been a long day."

"Nate," I say his name and he just walks up the steps and moves me away from the door. I watch him touch the keypad that turns blue, and then he punches in the numbers he told me and the sound of the lock turning open fills the silent front stoop. He struggles with the bags in his hands to open the door, and when he does, Whiskey is right there jumping on him.

"Back," he orders him and he moves backward, giving him a chance to dump the bags. "Can you put him out?" he asks me. "I'm going to shovel the steps."

"Yeah," I reply softly as he walks past me and heads to the garage door. I watch him as I try to calm down the way my heart is hammering in my chest. I watch him until I feel my hand being moved and Whiskey shoving his nose to smell me. The sound of his tail hitting the door makes me look down at him.

"Do you want to go out?" I ask him and then he barks as he backs up again into the house. "Okay, let me get out of these boots," I tell him, stomping my feet as I step inside and take off my jacket and my boots. "There you go," I say, opening the back door and watching him sprint out. I turn and go to refill his bowl of water and then his food, before walking back to the front and picking up the bags of groceries Nate dumped before going out to shovel. I take them back into the kitchen and start unloading them, stopping to let Whiskey in, who goes directly for his food bowl.

I walk to the Christmas tree, plugging in the lights and seeing the tree light up the room as I make it back to the kitchen, leaving the ingredients out for the dinner we said we would make. The front door opens and then slams shut. Whiskey takes off like his life depends on it. The sound of his tail hitting the wall every time it wags makes me smile as I hear Nate chuckle. "Okay, okay," he says. "Did you play in the snow?" he asks him, and then

I hear his footsteps coming down the hall. "It's coming down even harder out there."

"I think we should hurry and make dinner before we lose power," I suggest and he nods his head, walking to the sink and turning on the water to wash his hands.

"Just got off the phone with Joshua, the power is out at your parents' and also at the hotel. They have the generator going, but the panic is starting to set in that the food might be ruined for the wedding if the caterer doesn't have a generator."

I gasp. "I'm not going to say this is a sign"—I put my hands on the counter—"but I'm not *not* saying it." He chuckles. "Nate," I call his name and he looks over at me, and for the first time in my life, looking at him makes breathing hard. For the first time in my life, I accept the fact Nate has been the man I've secretly been in love with. For the first time in my life, I have no idea what the fuck I'm doing. Not. One. Fucking. Clue.

"Elizabeth, why don't we cook and then we can discuss it when we eat."

"Okay," I reply giving in to him. "Do you still want me to make my chicken with pasta?"

"Yes." He shakes the water from his hand before grabbing the towel to dry his hands. "What can I do to help?"

"You can butterfly the chicken." I point to the breast. "I'll get the spices I need for it." I walk over to the side and open the little cabinet next to the fridge and grab paprika, garlic powder, onion flakes, and dried thyme. "How do you have all these spices?" I ask him, taking the jars out and walking over to the other side of the island.

"Your mother gave me one of those spice racks that turn," he explains as he takes out the cutting board and then a knife, "and then came over one day and decided that it didn't look nice, so she stored the bottles and threw away the spinny thing."

I chuckle. "That sounds nothing like my mother." I walk over to the drawer I know he keeps his utensils in, grabbing a small bowl and mixing the spices.

"Okay, the chicken is done." He looks at the cutting board and I walk over to inspect them.

"Not bad for a vet." I wink at him, and he laughs. "We are going to need twelve cloves of garlic."

He walks over to the fridge and opens it, taking the little jar from the fridge. "Crushed?"

"No, roughly chopped," I tell him as I pinch the spices in between my hand and coat the chicken with it. "Do you cook for yourself often?"

"Often enough." He pulls the garlic bulbs loose. "I like to eat, so usually I cook maybe three times a week and then I have leftovers for at least two to three of those, and then there is always a pizza night."

"Is it even a week if there is no pizza?" I look over at him as I turn the chicken over and season the other side of it. I walk over to the drawer beside the stove and take out a deep pan, putting it on the stove and then starting it.

"Do you cook often?" he asks me and I nod my head.

"I do. I have this thing where I get into bed and I go down the rabbit hole to all these one-pot recipes online.

Where is the olive oil?"

"Where we've always kept it," he replies and I open the small cabinet by the stove where we used to keep the oils and vinegar. "I got used to doing things like your mom."

"So, it followed you to your own house?" I ask him as I drizzle a little bit of the olive oil in the pan. "I want to say I don't do the same at my house, but I do." I laugh as he roughly chops the garlic. "My kitchen is the exact replica of where all the cooking stuff is at home."

He laughs at me. "Why do you think you can find things so easily in this kitchen?" he asks me. "Everything is the same."

"I tried to move things around," I admit to him, holding my hand above the pan to see if it's hot enough. "You know, because I'm stubborn and would always fight about how placement was done in the kitchen."

"Of course." He shakes his head. "I remember once when you had a huge fight with her about the mugs not being right above the coffee machine but in the small cupboard on the side."

I laugh at the memory. "And it took me a whole week defiantly fighting about how right I was, yet every single time I went to the other cabinet." I put the chicken in the pan. "It really sucks when your mother is right." I look over at him. "Remember the mug you got me for my birthday that year?"

"How could I forget?" He ducks his head to the side. "This is what I had to do to avoid you throwing it at my head."

"It was a reflex, it wasn't my fault," I defend myself.

"How was it a reflex.? He pushes the garlic to the side. "You literally took it out of the box, read it, and threw it at me."

"And why did I throw it at you?" I ask him and he just smirks. "It said 'Mom was right about everything, and so is Nate.'"

"I paid extra for that." He points the knife at me. "It had our faces on the other side."

"I got scared," I joke with him as I set a timer for four minutes. "I need you to dice an onion."

He walks over to the fridge and gets an onion from the drawer. "You got me back." He looks over at me and I look down into the pan, trying not to laugh at what I did to him. "Here, Nate," he mimics my voice, "my mother bought these swim trunks for you and wants you to try them on."

"She technically bought it for you since I had to use her credit card to buy them." I look over at him, seeing the glimmer in his eyes at the same time.

"Then you said she wanted to know how they felt in the water." I look over at him. "And then stupid old me, I got into the water and then what happened, Elizabeth?"

"I don't—" I start to say and he glares at me. "I gave you a towel, didn't I?"

"I was naked in the pool in the middle of the afternoon, and your grandparents were over," he hisses at me. "You gave me a dissolvable bathing suit."

"Nate," I say his name as I flip the chicken over, "that's what you do when you have a crush on someone."

"You had a crush on me?" he asks me and I have to look away.

"It was working its way up." I can't help the laugh that comes through me. "It was definitely there not long after," I confirm. "It might have even started when I saw you come out of the pool." I shrug. "We'll never know." I go and get a plate, putting the chicken on it and then looking at him. "Plus, I think you broke my heart not long after when I caught you making out with Taylor at the side of the house."

"You were fifteen," he shrieks, "your father would have killed me."

"Whatever, you were four years older than me, it's not that big of a deal."

"Twenty-six and twenty-two is not that big of a deal. Thirty and twenty-six, not that big of a deal. Fifteen and nineteen, very much a big deal."

I add in some butter and then fry up the onions and then the garlic. Adding in the veggie stock that we bought and then the cream, making it thicken a bit, before I add the pasta. "Now we wait eight minutes or until the pasta is done." He nods at me, walking to wash his hands and wipe down the counter where he was cutting the stuff.

"Do you want some wine?" he asks me, looking over his shoulder at me as he dries his hands.

"I would love some." I wait for him to turn around before walking to him and gripping his hips in my hands. "And I'd like to make out with you more."

He grins as he grabs my hips and lifts me up on the counter, my legs opening for him to stand in between them. His head slants to the side. "Have I told you you're beautiful today?" he asks me and I put my hands flat on his chest, feeling the way his heart beats under them. Our hearts beating in sync, it's something I've never done with another person in my life. But him. Always with him. Always with Nate.

"You have not." I smile up at him as my hands go up his chest to lock around his neck at the same time the lights flicker a couple of times. "I need it to hold off for another ten minutes, max." I look over at the stove, seeing the pasta boiling. "After that, it can go off."

"The stove is gas," he reminds me, "but we might be eating by candlelight."

"That sounds romantic." I smile at him and he bends to kiss me.

"Then let me start looking for those candles." He starts to turn away but I pull him back.

"I'm really fucking sorry I didn't force you to talk to me back then."

"I'm fucking sorry I thought you left me," he says softly. "But you have to know, Elizabeth"—he pushes the hair back away from my face—"that that night…" He holds one side of my face in the palm of his hand, and I press deeper into it. His thumb rubs my cheek back and forth. "It was, hands down, one of the best nights I've had in my life." His eyes stare into mine. "It was as if everything that was happening or had happened all led to you." The words sear my soul as if you lit a fire, heated a branding tool, and marked my heart with his name on it. "The morning after, not seeing you there. It broke my heart." The lump starts to get bigger in my throat. "It doesn't matter now."

"But it does," I quickly add, "it matters now, just as it did back there. The only thing is, we can't change what happened back then, but we can change things going ahead."

He smirks. "Elizabeth, you live halfway around the world." The smile is sad, his voice low. "There is no going ahead."

Even though I know he's not trying to hurt me, it still does. "I know that," I reply, heaviness now forming in my chest. "What I meant is"—my fingers go to the back of his hair—"going forward, we both know that night meant something to both of us."

He nods. "Wrong time, wrong place."

"No," I say, breathlessly, "right person, wrong time." He kisses me softly as the lights flicker again.

"I'm going to go and search for candles before we are really without lights."

"Okay," I say softly as he turns to walk out of the room. One of my hands falls to my side as I put the other one against the pain in my chest. "Right person, wrong time," I mumble. "With you it's always going to be the right person."

Twenty-Four

NATE

"THAT WAS…" I put down my fork on the empty plate. "The best meal I've had—"

"If you say ever, I'm going to know you are lying." She looks over at me, her face illuminated from the two candles in the middle of the table, as well as the tree that is also lit in the corner. Even though the lights are still flickering on and off, I decided that we would eat by candlelight. Especially when her face lit up as I walked back into the kitchen with four candles in my hand.

So, while I set up the table with the candles, she plated the pasta with the chicken. Bringing it over, she put the bigger plate in front of me, as I got us both some wine. "I was going to say that was the best meal I've had in a while."

She picks up her glass of wine and it dangles in her hand side to side. "Good save." She brings it to her lips and takes a sip. "Very good save." The smile she gives me makes everything in me come to life.

"You know what we should do?" I pick up my own glass of wine and finish it. "We should play a game."

"Oh?" She puts down her empty wineglass. "I like this already."

"Of course you would." I pick up the bottle of wine and fill her glass, emptying the bottle. "Unless you lose, then there'll be hell to pay."

"I can lose a game and be a good sport," she counters and I snort.

"Tell me when that happened." I push away from the table. "I need a date and time."

"I don't know the exact date or time," she backpedals, picking up her glass of wine. "But the four of us were having a Connect Four tournament."

My mouth hangs open when she brings up the memory. "You're kidding, right?"

"It slipped out of my hands," she defends herself. "Joshua put his face in front of me and—" She tries to hide the smile with the glass.

"And you picked up the Connect Four tower and bopped him on the head with it," I remind her, and she looks to the corner of the room trying her hardest not to laugh. "He got five stiches at his hairline."

"He was lucky I didn't stab it in his eyeball," she retorts. "He was taunting me the whole night. I win! I win! I win!" she mimics what she thinks his voice sounded like. "Loser." She even uses her finger in an L on her forehead. "He taunted me. I had no choice but to defend my honor."

"Your parents forbade us to play any more games ever. They threw out all the games."

"And again, whose fault was that?" She waits for me to answer her, and when I take half a second longer than she wants me to take, she answers, "It was Joshua's fault. It's always Joshua's fault for pushing my buttons."

"Elizabeth." I stop beside her chair to take her plate, and she looks up at me, and all I can do is bend my head and kiss her lips. "The minute you are going to lose, something comes over you."

"I don't like to lose," she admits softly, her hand coming up to cup my cheek.

"Well, the good news is, the game we are going to play"—I turn and walk back into the kitchen, putting the plates in the sink—"there are no winners or losers."

Her face goes into a grimace. "I already don't like it. There is always a winner and a loser."

"This one, we can all be winners," I clarify and she fake vomits.

"That's like everyone should get a trophy, which sucks." She shakes her head. "If I win, I win. I want to be the only one with a trophy. Not have everyone else with a trophy so they don't cry."

"Wow." I try not to laugh at her. "Let's not have you be in charge of the children at the wedding."

She pffts but takes a sip of wine. "What can I do to help speed this game playing and me winning along?"

"You can go and sit on the couch and look at the beautiful tree and wait for me." I point to the Christmas tree in the corner, which lights up the room. I clean up the kitchen but she puts her glass on the table and comes over to help me. "I thought I told you to go and sit on the couch."

"Nate," she says my name and her tone is playful, "the only time I want to follow your orders"—she looks up at me—"is when you tell me to get on top or when you tell me face down, ass up."

My cock immediately gets hard at her words. "Good to know." Those are the only lame words I can say. I can't even follow that up with my own dirty talk because I'll forget all about cleaning the kitchen and throw her over my shoulder.

"There"—she points to my face—"right there, what were you just thinking?"

"Why?" I ask her.

"Your eyes changed, and the softness was gone out of your face." She takes the pot from the stove and then looks for a Tupperware to store the rest of the pasta in.

"I'm not telling you my deep personal thoughts." I rinse off the plates and put them in the dishwasher.

"It was about me"—she chuckles—"and sex."

"How do you know that?" I ask her.

"You had almost the same look on your face as when you jumped into the shower with me." She looks over at me as she stores the leftovers in my fridge.

"I guess you'll just have to wonder what it was about," I mumble not ready to give in to her and admit she was right.

She's wiping down the counters while I'm rinsing the

sink. "Okay, now that we're done, let's play."

"We need another bottle of wine," I tell her, walking over to the cabinet and taking a bottle out, "unless you want to do something else."

"Wine is good." She takes her glass and my glass off the table and walks to the couch. "It's still coming down out there pretty hard."

"Yeah." I open the bottle and toss the cork on the counter before walking over to her and pouring some in her glass and some in mine. "Okay, so let's play Never Have I Ever."

I sit beside her on the couch, turning my upper body to face her while she sits in the corner, her legs curled under her. "If you have done what the other person has never done, you take a sip of wine."

"Got it," she says with a smirk. "I'm so going to win."

"I'm hoping that we fuck on the couch so we can both win."

She throws her head back and lets out a laugh, and for the life of me, I can't tell you a better sound I've heard in my life. Actually, scratch that, the way she says my name when I slide into her. That's the best fucking sound, but her laughter is an easy second. "Okay, who goes first?" she asks with a twinkle in her eye. "Are we doing spicy Never Have I Ever?"

"We can," I say, willing to give her anything to keep her smiling like that. "We can also take a drink and then strip a piece of clothing off."

"Now this is a game," she cheers. "Who is going first?"

"You can go first."

"Okay." She looks to the side thinking. "Never have I ever gone skinny-dipping." She smirks at me.

"I'm not drinking," I tell her and she laughs. "That was unintentional skinny-dipping."

"Ummm," she clarifies, "I wasn't talking about that time." She points at me. "I was talking about when we went on vacation one summer, and the guys thought it would be a good idea to go streaking down the beach and then into the water."

"Fuck," I swear when I think back. "Fine, I have, so I will drink." I take a sip of wine. "You've never gone skinny-dipping?"

"No!" she gasps out. "My biggest fear is one, someone steals my clothes and I have to end up walking around naked, and two, it's so dark and that is where danger lies. You have to take something off." She points at me and I hand her my glass as I pull off my shirt.

"Okay, my turn," I declare, taking back my glass and tossing her my shirt as she lays it on her lap. "Never have I ever faked an orgasm."

She gasps again. "That's not fair." I wink at her and she tilts her head, and I know now it's on. She takes a sip of her wine and then I point at her, my finger going up and down, waiting to see what she is going to take off. She hands me her glass the same way I handed her mine, and she takes off the sweater she is wearing, leaving her in black tights and a black sports bra. "Your turn," I say with glee that I at least won one question.

"Never have I ever hooked up with one of my friends'

siblings." I look up at the ceiling and I can't help but laugh at her. "You can just chug the whole glass now," she tells me and I take a sip before I put my glass down on the table and get up, peeling off my pants and tossing them to her, leaving me in boxers and my socks. "Looks like I'm going to win."

I pick up my glass. "Never have I ever used a dating app for the sole purpose of hooking up with someone." I point at her.

She slaps the couch. "That is not fair." The words come out of her as a hiss. "How else was I supposed to meet someone when I went to an all-girls summer camp?"

"Not my problem." I smile big at her. "I'll take your pants."

She scoffs at me, "Like hell you will." She takes a sip of her wine and then throws me her sports bra. "If your nipples can be out, so can mine. My turn." She taps her glass as she thinks. "Never have I ever ghosted someone after sex."

"Yes, you have." I point to her. "You ghosted me."

"That was not me ghosting you," she denies. "This game is so dumb."

"It's dumb because you're playing to win and not for fun," I tell her. "Okay, my turn. Never have I ever had multiple orgasms in a row."

"Motherfucker," she hisses at me, finishing the glass of wine in her hands, "that's cheating." She puts the glass down and peels off her pants, leaving her in just her lace thong. "I hope you are happy with yourself." She tosses the pants at my face, and I catch them.

"You're naked on my couch." I smirk at her. "I'm very happy with myself." She fills up her glass again.

"Never have I ever used a sex toy with a partner," she states, thinking she is going to win this round.

"I have never," I admit to her and her eyes about come out of her sockets.

"You were in a relationship, and you never did that?"

"No." I shake my head. "I knew she had a vibrator, but if she wanted me to see her use it, she would have told me."

"That's…" She shakes her head. "That's on the top of my list for my next relationship," she shares and the food I ate at dinner feels like it's going to come up.

"What is your longest relationship?" I ask her and I don't know why I am asking her; I don't really want to know.

"Six months," she answers and then shrugs. "I'm just too focused on my job to have time to do both."

"That sounds—" I try to think of the polite words to say.

"It sounds sad." She laughs at her own assessment of it. "I don't know why I never took the step to get serious with someone. Maybe I knew that if I did, I would be sort of stuck there."

"Has it ever felt like home to you?" I ask her and she thinks about the question.

"At times," she admits to me, "then at times it sort of feels like I am just there biding my time."

"You have a whole life there."

"I do." She takes a sip of her wine. "I have a house there. I have friends there. I have a job there."

"But you have no family there." My chest tightens for her. I don't have any family left, but I have the Morrows, and they are as much my family as my blood family.

"But I have no family there." Her voice trails. "I never thought of it that way."

"You're welcome," I say and she laughs. "Also, I think I win."

"Is that so?" She puts down her glass in the middle of the table and then comes over to me, grabbing my glass and putting it with hers, before she comes back to me and I turn to face her. She puts one knee on the couch beside one hip and then does the same with the other, straddling me. "Are you sure about that?"

She puts her hands on my shoulders as I grip her hips. "Oh, yeah." I try not to smile as I run my hands up her bare back. "I definitely win."

She puts her forehead on mine. "Now you have to make it up to me." She tilts her head to the side.

"Oh, trust me," I assure softly, "I'm planning on spending all night making it up to you." I chuckle but it's silenced when her mouth is on mine. I wrap my arm around her waist and turn her so her back is to the couch. "I might as well start making it up to you now"—her hair is fanning all over my couch—"by giving you those multiple orgasms in a row."

Twenty-Five

MAKE IT TO CHRISTMAS

ELIZABETH

December 23rd
Rehearsal dinner

I SLIDE OUT of bed, going to the bathroom and seeing Nate on his back sleeping. One arm is thrown over his head, the other on his stomach. The bedding covers one of my favorite parts of him.

A couple of minutes later, I'm walking out of the bathroom, and I see him still sleeping. I walk to his side of the bed, taking him in. The most handsome man I've ever seen, but it's more than just a handsome face. He's the kindest person I've ever had the privilege of knowing. He would literally give you the shirt off his back. Now that I think about it, I was wrong for ever thinking otherwise.

I slowly flip the covers off him, seeing him naked.

His one leg is cocked to the side, almost in the middle of the bed. I softly put one knee on the bed and then follow with the other. Making my way to him, my hands grip his cock and his eyes flutter open. "Morning," I mumble to him right before I take his half-hardened cock in my mouth. He groans as I grip his base.

His hand that was on his chest is now buried in my hair. "Fuck," he groans, his hips thrusting up a bit so he can get deeper in my throat. His cock, now fully erect, is filling my mouth halfway. "That's it." His voice is rough with sleep. He pushes my head down on his cock as he lifts his hips, going to the back of my throat. My fist and my mouth work him at the same time with his own little thrusts up. "Get up here," he orders between clenched teeth. He rolls to the side, his tongue slipping into my mouth before he holds his cock up. "All yours."

I move my leg over him, gripping him in my hand, and positioning him right under me before I slide down his cock. His hands go to my hips, as my hands go beside his head on the pillow. "It's so good," I moan as I move up and down his cock.

His head moves up off the pillow to catch one of my nipples that are moving over his mouth. He sucks one nipple in his mouth before moving to the other one. The only sound in the room is of us breathing as I ride his cock, his hips moving up to meet mine when I slide down. "More." I close my eyes, taking in the feeling of his cock in me and his mouth biting my nipple. I grip the pillow by his head. "More." I slam down on him as hard as I can.

"Want me to give you more?" he asks, and all I can do is moan as he wraps an arm around my waist, and in the blink of an eye, his cock is buried to the hilt inside me as he flips me to my back. "I'll give you more," he hisses between clenched teeth, pulling out of me and then slamming into me.

"Harder." I pull my legs back to get him to go as deep as he can, and does he ever. He slams into me over and over again, pushing me to the brink of orgasm.

His forehead is on mine. "I'm almost there," he says. I arch my back as I open my eyes, right before I jump off that cliff and everything inside me shivers. "There it is," he hisses as my legs wrap around his waist. He plants himself all the way in me and buries his face in my neck. "Fuck." I wrap all my limbs around him as he collapses on me.

"That we just did," I joke, silently laughing as he gives me soft kisses.

"Good morning," he mumbles before he slides out of me and falls to the side on his back. "Now that is a good fucking wake-up call."

I turn on my side. "Figured I should return the favor since that is how I woke up yesterday morning." He looks over at me, his eyes a light green and so warm, all you need is for him to look at you and you know you'll be okay. He'll settle all the insecurities you might have.

"Thank you for that," he says.

I get up on my elbow and look out the window. "I think it stopped snowing."

"I should hope so"—he gets up off the bed—"it

snowed all day yesterday." He walks toward the bathroom as I watch his ass disappear. Then I get off the bed, searching the floor for the pj's I started to wear to bed but got ripped off me as soon as the lights went off.

I grab the shorts and tank top before walking to the door and opening it. Whiskey is sitting outside the door, looking up at me with a look that says, "it's about time" and "how could you lock me out of the room?" "Good morning, boy," I say as he gets up and circles around my legs and then steps into the room looking for Nate, who is in the bathroom. He hears the water running but then looks at me when I say, "Want to go outside?"

I walk down the step with him following beside me as I turn and head toward the back door. The snow is piled up in the back and you can see exactly where Whiskey played yesterday while we tried to shovel him a path. He couldn't care less and kept jumping into the snow and then back again.

Letting him out and starting the coffee, I head over to the living room to turn on the lights on the tree. Something I did also when I got up yesterday. Snow was still falling when we woke up yesterday and all day long. The message to everyone was if you could stay in, stay in, so we did. We made breakfast and then lounged on the couch to watch a movie, which ended up with us having sex. We lounged around all day long, either having sex or laughing when we would remember old stories about each other.

By midafternoon the snow had trickled off and everyone was going to gather at my parents' house, but we opted to just stay in. It felt like neither of us wanted to let the outside into this thing that was going on between us.

I'm making the coffees when I hear him coming down the steps. I feel him before I have a chance to look over my shoulder at him. One hand is by my side, the other hand sliding against my stomach, he buries his face in my neck as he pulls me against his chest. "Just in time to let in Whiskey." I move my head to the side, giving him access to my neck.

"Got it." I watch him over my shoulder, going to the back door and letting him in.

"Good morning," I hear him tell Whiskey and then hear the sound of him tapping his side. "Go get your grub," he adds. "I'm going to check the front." He walks to the front. "Snowplows finally passed," he announces as he walks into the kitchen, "which means we can finally get out of here."

I don't know why it bothers me when he says that, but it does. "Great." I turn around and hand him his cup of coffee before sitting on the stool I've sat in ever since the first morning. "Do you want to make breakfast today?" I ask him and he leans against the counter.

"I could eat." He shrugs. "What's your favorite breakfast meal?"

"I don't really eat breakfast." I take a sip of my coffee. "I get off at eight a.m., and by the time I get home it's middle of the morning and I'm exhausted, so I usually just heat up some leftover food from the morning before." I laugh. "I sometimes grab a breakfast bar."

"Well, let's pretend you worked a normal nine-to-five job," he says. I don't know why I have this need to get up and go to him and have this conversation with my arms around his waist and my head against his chest.

"Okay, let's pretend." I smile at him. "I would probably have some pancakes and scrambled eggs, maybe some breakfast sausage."

"Done," he states, walking over to the fridge. "We have everything that we need to make it."

"I'll help," I offer and he shakes his head.

"You made dinner the past two nights." He looks over his shoulder, grabbing the ingredients. "Let me make you breakfast."

"I won't say no to that." I watch him mix up the pancake batter before putting the breakfast sausage in the little toaster over he has to the side.

"Have you ever thought of working regular daytime hours?" he asks me as he makes the pancakes.

"I did," I admit to him, "but I felt when I would work during the day, I was missing out on things that happened at home." He looks at me. "I know it's crazy. It wasn't like I could just be here at the drop of a hat." The feeling of dread hits me like I just hit a brick wall. "But at least I could be in the moment. I would sleep when you guys would sleep so I felt I was semi-involved."

"Have you thought of maybe, perhaps, that you want to just come back home?" he asks me and I shake my head.

"No," I say honestly and shrug, "I have a life there."

"But do you?" he asks me. "Because everything

you've said to me since you've been here is that you miss home. I mean, not in those words, but everything. The way you live your life, it's like you live there but you want to live here."

"I can't just move home," I declare.

"Why not?" He asks me the question I've never been asked. So many people have just said move home, and when I said I couldn't, they would just drop it. But not Nate. Nate is the one who would always ask me the questions that everyone else was either scared to ask or didn't care to ask.

"Because," I answer him and he just laughs.

"Solid answer." He turns back. "So you have thought of moving back home?"

I'm thinking about what to say to that. "I mean, all the time, but what would I do?"

"You're a doctor, you can work anywhere," he points out. "You can even work with your mother or Jack."

"But then it's like I'm giving up." My heart hammers in my chest.

"What the hell are you fucking talking about?" He looks at me as he flips the pancakes. "How is you coming home and working with your mother, you giving up?" He shakes his head. "It's not like you didn't go to med school and your mother just gave you a job. You literally are a doctor."

"Yeah, but it'll be me taking a handout," I tell him. "Look at you."

"What about me?" he questions, putting the pancakes on the plate and doing three more.

"You built a whole fucking vet clinic," I say, my voice going higher. "No one did that but you."

"Are you nuts?" He looks at me. "My grandparents left me a shitload of money and so did my parents." I roll my eyes. "If it wasn't for them, you think I would be able to have my own clinic?"

"Yes," I answer wholeheartedly. "You would have still had the clinic, you just would have been in debt for a bit longer."

He snorts. "I worked sixteen hours a day for four years straight. Took any animal I could. Did house calls. You name it, I did it. The same way you did it. You didn't just wake up and get the shift you wanted or the department you wanted." I have this tightness in my chest when I think of all the struggles he had and not knowing or being there for him. The last seven years have been lost to us and it's half my fault.

"Yeah, but it's still different," I refute, letting his words settle, "you did it by yourself."

"No one does anything by themselves, Elizabeth," he says my name and finishes breakfast. "At least not if they don't have to. My parents, my grandparents, your parents, they all helped." I look at him and I'm about to say something to him when the front door opens.

"You really need to start locking the front door after you come inside," I remind him as we both look to the side to see who is going to be coming in.

"I smell food," Joshua says and I put my head back and groan.

"For thirty-six hours," I say, looking at him, "I forgot

all about you and this wedding of yours."

"Well, happy to break it to you, but there are only a couple days left." He pulls out the stool and sits down. "There is the rehearsal dinner tomorrow and then the wedding."

"Put a finger down if you are counting down the hours until I never have to hear about this fucking wedding again?" I deadpan and hold up my middle finger. "It's me."

He laughs. "I have to say the snowstorm was a blessing in disguise." He looks at us. "Don't say anything to Macy but I'm so done with all of this, I just want to be married already."

I slap the counter. "I'm telling everyone," I tell him. "I'm getting a billboard in Times Square. I'm getting one of those planes that fly overhead with a long whatever it's called. I'm putting an article in the newspaper." The two of them laugh at me.

"Anyway, I'm here to talk about Christmas." The minute the words leave his mouth, Nate and I groan. "Relax, it's nothing big."

"I just changed my flight," I tell them. "I'm leaving Christmas morning at six a.m." I try not to smile but the look on both their faces, I can't help myself. "Kidding, I'm kidding," I say. When I look back at Nate, a new look fills his face, and it's not a look I've ever seen before. I hate it.

Twenty-Six

NATE

"I JUST CHANGED my flight." I hear her say the words and everything inside me stills, everything. "I'm leaving Christmas morning at six a.m." I stare at her, the sound of my heart pounding in my chest, echoing into my ears, as she tries to hide her smile. "Kidding, I'm kidding." It's like all the air inside of me is sucked out and all I can do is look at her. My heart studders as if someone is sitting on my chest.

I turn around to make the scrambled eggs. "Mom and Dad would kill you if you left on Christmas Day," Joshua informs her and I close my eyes, trying to get a hold of myself.

"You think they are going to do anything Christmas Day after your wedding is the night before?"

"I think they mentioned they would be doing Christmas dinner at the house. But from what I gather, most of the family will be taking off that day."

"Well, yeah, they only have a couple days off," Elizabeth says. "I think I heard some of them have to travel on the twenty-sixth."

"For whoever is left here"—Joshua moves to the coffee machine to make his own coffee—"they are doing a dinner." He pours a mug and leans against the counter. "So I'll count you two in."

"Negative," Elizabeth denies before me. "I'll be nursing the biggest hangover I've ever had in my whole life." I look over my shoulder at her. "I plan on drinking as much as humanly possible." She looks at me and the smile on her face settles me. "Don't worry, I plan to sleep on the bathroom floor anyway."

"Well, I'm not telling them that," he scoffs. "You can tell them that. They might take away the Christmas presents they got for you."

"Fuck." She slaps the counter. "I didn't buy anyone anything," she hisses. "This is all your fault." She points to Joshua. "I was so distracted by all the wedding stuff, I forgot presents."

"If you want," I offer as I pour the eggs in the pan and start to stir them, "we can hit up the mall, and then there is the Christmas market."

"Yes," she agrees. "We can go to the market and get everyone Christmas stuff"—she looks at Joshua—"so they can maybe hate Christmas as much as I do."

I snort. "You are going to waste money, so they hate Christmas?"

"I didn't say it was a good plan. I just said it was a

plan."

"Well, we love Christmas stuff," Joshua reminds.

"Who said I'm getting you anything?" She fights back and he finishes his coffee before putting the mug in the sink, rolling his eyes.

"Okay, I'm out, I will see you guys tonight."

Elizabeth groans, "Do I really have to practice walking down the aisle if I'm not the one getting married?"

"Yes," he confirms. "You're lucky I talked her out of doing a flash mob."

"No." Elizabeth shakes her head. "You're lucky," she growls at him as he walks to her and kisses her head.

"Love you the most," he says and she pushes him away.

"You're a lying liar who lies," she hisses at him. "You better make sure no one objects at this wedding, or I'll fight all of you."

"Don't put that shit in the universe." He puts his hands on his hips.

"I'm not putting anything in the universe," she defends herself as I plate the eggs and then walk over to grab the sausage. "If you fucked up by cheating on her and the woman is coming to claim you, how is it my fault?"

"I'm not cheating on her." He puts his hands on his head. "Can you not even say that as a joke?"

Her eyes go big and I can see her fucking with him. "If there is already doubt, this marriage is doomed from the beginning." His face goes ashen.

"Elizabeth," I say her name and she bursts out laughing.

"I'm just fucking with you. I know you would never cheat on her because if you did and I found out, I would tell Mom, and then she would have Dad kick your ass. Then Jack would kick your ass." She tilts her head to the side. "Then I would definitely shank you."

"Noted." He gives me a chin up and walks out of the house. She pushes away from the counter and gets off, running down the hall after him.

"Where are you going?" I look down the hall to see her coming back into the kitchen.

"I locked the door"—she gets back on her stool—"so no one else comes in here." I laugh at her. "Imagine if you were doing me on the counter and Joshua just walked in."

"That would be pretty hard to explain." I chuckle and sit next to her. "Definitely can't be like, 'it's not what it looks like.'" I chuckle with her. "Do you really want to hit up the Christmas market?" I cut a piece of sausage.

She nods her head. "I do, and now I have an extra gift to buy." She looks at me and I laugh.

"I know a couple things you could give me off the top of my head."

"I've already done most of those things," she jokes, "unless we get a whole box of toys and really have a party."

"I wonder if there are any Christmas sex toys?" I ask her and her eyes go big as she takes out her phone. "What are you doing?"

"I'm looking up sex toys for Christmas." She looks over at me. "Once I was in Paris and there was a vibrator shaped like the Eiffel Tower." I open my mouth in shock. "It came in different colors also." She types something is her phone. "Okay, here are a couple of things." She takes a bite of her breakfast. "You ready?"

"I'm not sure anyone is ready for this," I admit to her, "but here we are."

"Okay, stocking stuffers, anal plugs."

I look over at her. "I could do that."

"Could you?" she asks me.

"I mean, it'd be hot knowing you were sitting in front of me with a plug."

She laughs. "I was thinking the same. Sitting down to have Christmas dinner and seeing you wince." I laugh.

"Okay, so that's out." I shovel more food in my mouth. "What's next?"

"Santa's sex position coupons," she reads and I nod my head in agreement. "Twelve sex games of Christmas."

"We are like one day out, so we'll have to do triple every day."

"That goes on the maybe list, then." She takes another bite. "Under-the-mistletoe-sex dice."

I laugh at her. "I don't even know what that means."

"Well, it says Keep Christmas Slutty." She laughs. "It's a roll of the dice that says suck dick, fuck like dogs, grind genitals, or fuck like rabbits."

"We already do all of that."

"True that. Ohhh I should get this for the bridesmaids." She turns the phone so I can see. "Reindeer or Santa nipple pasties."

I snort and move my finger up, swiping the screen.

"That's it," I say, "a candy cane vibrator." She turns to look at it. "Add to cart." I shake my head. "I'll surprise you."

"Please do. I wonder if they sell boxers that have the mistletoe right on the dick area."

"Ohh"—she points at me—"I'm going to get that for my dad and Jack, just to make them feel really uncomfortable."

"Your mother would die." I can't help but laugh. "Or she might thank you."

"Eeew," she says, "I'm done eating. I don't want to think my parents still do that."

"They've been together for a long time, I'm going to say they have a healthy sex life."

"Nate," she hisses my name, "I'm going to need you to shut the fuck up right now."

I can't help but laugh at her. "I'm going to take a shower and get ready for the day."

"But I cooked," I remind her as she walks out of the kitchen. "Who cooked doesn't clean."

"You should have thought about that before you opened your mouth," she quips.

I did not do the dishes, instead I joined her in the shower. I did the dishes while she fixed her hair. An hour later we are walking out of the house, I slide my hand in hers as we walk toward the truck. "It's a nice day." She lets my hand go to get in.

"You think the snow is going to be melted by the time the wedding comes?" she asks me when I get into the truck.

"Not sure." I start the truck. "But my guess is Macy is going to make us take pictures outside."

"Great." She looks out the window as I make it to the Christmas market. I pull into the parking lot, shocked that it's full. It takes a full twenty minutes before I find a parking space.

Getting out, she meets me in the back of the truck, and I bend to kiss her lips. She smiles at me as she lifts her hand to wipe off the lip gloss. I turn and slide my hand in hers as we walk toward the little huts that have been set up. There are rows and rows of huts set up like a little village, all around the lot.

A big Christmas tree is in the middle of the square with children running after each other. "Where do you want to start?" I ask her and she shrugs.

"I'm not sure, why don't we start here?" She looks up at me. "Then work our way down the aisles."

"Sure," I agree. "Just tell me when you want to stop."

"You'll know. I'll be yanking you." She holds up our hands, our fingers loosely holding on to each other.

We pass a candle shop first and she pulls me into it. The scent of pine hits right away when I see wreaths hanging at the sides, as well as over the wooden top that is hanging overhead to stop the rain or snow from ruining them. "These are so pretty." She picks up one of the candles in a mason jar. The top of the candle has a string of red and white around it, with holly hanging from it. "It smells like cinnamon," she mentions, taking a whiff of it and holding it to my nose. "They are so good," she says, taking another one that smells like cranberry and orange. "This would smell so good in the house."

"So, buy it," I urge and she nods her head. We walk out with a bag of three candles. I grab the bag from her as we walk to the next shop. This one is all full of knickknacks and she just walks past it until she gets to the shop where they have homemade hanging stockings.

"Ohh look." She points to one of the socks that has a caramel cat on it with a Santa hat. "We have to get this." She looks at me. "And this one for Whiskey," she says of one that has Woof written down the front, a Santa face in the OO's. "We need one for Baby Cat and Bean also."

She looks through them and then a woman comes over. "Can I help you?"

"You wouldn't have one with a gray cat, would you?" she asks her and the lady shakes her head.

"Just take one that has a cat on it," I tell her and she glares at me. "You know he's not going to know, right?"

"We're going to fill it with cat toys," she informs me.

"Elizabeth," I reply, trying not to laugh, "cats don't really play with toys." She looks at me like I just told her Santa isn't real and she's eight. "They chase things when they want to chase things." The glare turns into a deep look of death. "I'll shut up now."

"That would be wise," she agrees. "We'll take these three," she tells the woman, "and I'll take this one." She picks up one that has a Grinch on it. "Which one best suits you?" she asks me. "Here, you can either have a reindeer or a snowman."

"Why don't you surprise me?" I tell her and she shoos me away. I turn and head away as she picks a stocking for me. I see her smiling at the woman and then walking to me, practically skipping. "I got one for each of us." She holds up the bag. "We can hang them and fill them with little treats."

"Like the anal plug?" I ask her and she throws her head back and laughs. I reach around to hug her neck, pulling her close to me. The smile on her face is from ear to ear and it dawns on me that in a little over a week from now, she'll be gone. I don't say anything else, instead I let her go and she walks over to the other hut, and I try to contain the crushing of my heart. I knew the score going in, knew it wasn't going to end well. I had just hoped it wouldn't hurt.

I. Was. Wrong.

Twenty-Seven

Elizabeth

"Are you almost ready?" I look up from the side of the bed as I tie the strap around my ankle. The smile fills my face instantly as he stands there in front of me wearing a black suit with a white shirt. The top of his button-down shirt open, showing you a hint of his neck and the top of his chest. His hair is combed to the side, but the top of it falls onto the front of his forehead. His greenish-blue eyes are more gray than anything. "Wow," he says when he sees me, "you look stunning."

"You haven't even seen my dress yet," I point out to him as I move to the other ankle, doing the strap, and all of a sudden, he's squatting down in front of me. His hands move to replace mine as he buckles my shoe.

"Is that too tight?" he asks me and all I can do is shake my head side to side. The lump in my throat has come out of nowhere. No one has ever done something like this for me before. Sure, sometimes my mother has helped me out, but for a man to do it, it just stuns me. Especially this man. The man who I've loved for longer than I've hated him. The man who maybe I've just been comparing everyone to. The man who, in eight days, will still be here while I get on a plane back to home. "There," he says when he's done, but again, with Nate he shocks the shit out of me when he lifts my leg and kisses the inside of my ankle softly. The lump now sinks to my stomach as it's joined with the little fluttering butterflies. "Now you're ready." He puts my foot down gently. "Now, can I say you look beautiful?"

"No," I say softly, scooting forward, my hand coming up to cup his cheek, "but since I've seen you, I can say without a shadow of a doubt, you will be the most handsome man there tonight." I move my head to touch my lips to his.

"I hope not," he teases once I let go of his lips and wipe off the lip gloss, "I would hate for Macy to cancel the wedding to try and get me to run away with her."

My head goes back as I bust out laughing. "Can you imagine Joshua's face?"

"No." He gets up to his feet and holds out his hand for me. I slide my hand in his as I stand up. He doesn't let go of my hand as he takes a step back. "Okay, now I see all of you." He gives me an up and down. "I was wrong."

"Excuse me?" I say as he holds my hand up and spins me around so he can see the back of the dress.

"You don't look beautiful," he declares once I'm standing facing him, "you look breathtaking."

I try not to look him in the eye while I blush, looking down at my shoes instead. The shoes that are the same burgundy color as the dress I'm wearing. He pulls me to him, the hand that was in mine is now wrapped around my waist. "I don't think you are supposed to look better than the bride."

"Well, it sucks for her, then," I retort as I place my hand on his chest, and it rumbles under my hand from his laughter.

"We should get going," he urges, "so we aren't late."

"I just have to put the final touches on," I tell him as his hand moves from my waist and then down to my ass, where he squeezes it before he steps away.

"I'll go let Whiskey out one more time." He bends and I think he's going to kiss my lips but instead he kisses my neck, exactly where my heartbeat is. "I'll be waiting for you downstairs." He turns and walks out the door, giving me a chance to catch my breath. I put my hand on my stomach and take a deep inhale. The softness of the velvet dress under my hand makes me look into the long mirror that is in the corner of the room. I wasn't sure about the dress when I got it, but after seeing Nate's eyes on me, I know it was the perfect choice. It's long-sleeved, which I took into account in case she wanted to take pictures outside. It goes high to my neck and is tight all the way down until my knees, where it flares out in a mermaid style, but ends at my midcalf. I turn around to see the back that dips to the middle of my back. I snatch up my gold purse that is big enough to just fit my phone in it and my credit card. Even though there is no reason for me to even bring my credit card since I'll be there with all my family.

I walk to the bathroom and pick up my pink perfume bottle, spraying a few times behind my ears and then two at my wrists before applying my lip gloss. My hair is parted down the middle and curled softly away from my face. The makeup is very minimal since I know I'll be in full glam tomorrow. I turn off the light as I head to the stairs. I hold on to the railing as I walk down to the front door where Nate is waiting for me.

His hands are in his pockets as he watches every single move. "I'm going to have fun tonight," he states when I get to the last step, "might not even make it up the steps." He smirks. "Might have to fuck you against the door."

The sound of my laughter echoes in the entranceway. "Good to know I have that to look forward to."

He opens the door for me, holding out his hand for me to walk in front of him. I wait for him on the stoop to lock the door before I slide my hand in his and walk down the steps, watching my every step to gauge if it's slippery. He walks to my side of the truck and opens it for me. I get on my tippy-toes and kiss the side of his jaw before I hold on to his hand and get in.

I watch him as he walks around the front of the truck, the lights from outside glowing around him. I can't help but smile when he gets in. "What's that look for?"

"Just thinking about what is going to happen when we get back home." I say the words and then I want to correct myself. This isn't home. It's his home. I should have said *your* home.

He chuckles as he pulls out of the driveway and heads toward the reception area. The parking lot is full, of course, and we have to park almost at the entrance of the lot. He holds my hand as we walk up to the door and I have the need to pull it away from him, but I don't want to. Even though if someone sees, they might be wondering why we are holding hands. Luckily for both of us, no one is outside.

He pulls the door open for me and I step in, seeing the crowd of people around the door. Joshua and Macy are right next to it, greeting their guests. "I've never seen a rehearsal dinner that has a hundred people," I mumble to Nate, who now has his hand on my lower back.

"How are the two of you the last to arrive?" Joshua's glare goes to me and then to Nate. "You're the best man."

"I don't know if it matters," I say, looking at them, "but the only ones who really have to be here are the two of you." I point to them. "Unless someone is getting cold feet." I look at Macy. "You need a place to escape, you can always come down under."

Joshua pushes my shoulder. "Mom," he throws over my shoulder, "she's being mean to me and it's my wedding day."

"It's not your wedding day," I correct him, "it's your pre-wedding day." I look over at my mother, who comes to stand next to me and wrap an arm around my waist, smiling at me. "He's becoming unbearable."

Someone comes over with a headset on. "Okay, we can slowly get the show on the road." She has short blonde hair that sits on her shoulders. "We can get everyone in place."

"The last of them have arrived." Joshua looks at us.

"Better late than never." I look at the woman, who looks like I just kicked her.

"We don't say anything negative," she scolds, looking around. "We don't put it in the universe." She shakes her head and presses the side of her headpiece. "We have go time."

"She sounds like she's great under pressure," I say, and my mother pinches my side. "Ouch."

"Get into place," she hisses at me, then looks at Nate. "You are so handsome, as always."

"Okay, places, everyone," the woman says, clapping her hands. "If you are part of the wedding party and are part of the bridal party, go over there." She motions to the door. "If you are part of the groom's, you go over there." She points to the back.

"Here we go." I look up at Nate, who smirks at me and slaps Joshua on the shoulder. "Let's get you almost married."

"Shit, the rings," Joshua says, slapping his hand on his forehead. "I forgot them in the safe at my parents' house."

"I have them," my mother assures. "Zack," she calls for my father, who comes over holding a glass of scotch in his hand. "Are you drinking?"

"Say no," I advise him. "Tell her you're holding it for a friend." My mother turns to me. "I'm just helping out."

"Help out by getting yourself where you are supposed

to be," she hisses at me and I raise my eyebrows, walking over to the spot where all the bridesmaids are. They consist of all of Macy's friends, and I think I was given the duty because she had to and not because she wanted to. I smile at the group of ladies who I've spent time with, but that was only because we were at all the events together.

"This is so exciting," one of them chirps and I smile, holding my purse in my hand and then look over to see Evie sitting with my uncle Max, who has his arm around her.

"I'll be back," I tell them, rushing over to the two of them and handing her my purse.

"You know what would be fun?" I ask, handing her my purse and then kissing my uncle. "If you would take my place."

"Are you crazy?" She tries not to laugh. "I think I'm good here with my favorite uncle."

"I heard that," Matthew interjects from behind her and she looks over her shoulder and smiles at him.

"I didn't finish. I was saying my favorite uncle who is wearing blue. You're my favorite uncle who is wearing black."

"Good catch," I tell her and then I hear someone call my name. "Save me," I beg before heading back over. The woman with the headset, whose name is Doreen, gives us a rundown on what we are going to do.

"Any questions?" she asks us and I think about fucking with her and asking her a question, but Macy looks like she's either going to throw up or cry at any minute.

The rehearsal takes over an hour as they make tweaks on who walks down the aisle when. After it's over, the back of the room is opened and we see tables are set for our meal.

"Hey." I look over at Nate, who has come from beside Joshua toward me. "That was fun, right?"

"So much fun I forgot where I was for a minute." I look around. "I wish I had my phone to play a couple rounds of Candy Crush." He shakes his head as we walk toward one of the tables. He points to a table on the side that has Jack and Evie sitting with my cousin Ariella and her fiancé, Jaxon.

"Oh my goodness," she shouts. When she sees me getting close, she gets up, comes over to me, and we share a long hug. "I'm so happy to see you," Ariella whispers and then I close my eyes. "I feel like I haven't seen you in five years."

"It's been a bit under," I counter. "I saw you two years ago when I came for the summer and you were visiting." I let her go. "And now you have a baby."

"Now I have a baby." She smiles at Jaxon, who gets up and comes over to me. "This is Jaxon."

"I think we've met," I say as I give him a side hug and kiss his cheek. "He came to one of the summer vacations, for sure."

"I did," he confirms, then looks over to my side and holds out his hand to Nate. "What's up?" he asks. "I haven't seen you in forever." They shake hands and give each other a side hug. "You look good, man."

"Feel good," Nate says, his hand going again to my

lower back.

"If everyone can grab a seat so we can start the meal," Doreen announces as we walk over to the table. Nate pulls out the chair for me. I smile up at him as I sit down, and he pulls out the chair beside me.

"What is up with you two?" Jack looks at us as he sits with his arm around Evie's chair.

"What do you mean?" I ask him as Ariella sits beside me, and Jaxon sits in the empty chair between her and Jack.

"I mean, neither of you tried to kill each other and we've been here a solid hour, plus he just smiled at you." My palms get sweaty as I think of an excuse to make as to why this is happening. I don't even have time to come up with one because Nate is the one talking.

"We decided we're calling a truce." I laugh nervously at his excuse.

"Yes." I nod my head and swallow. "During the snowstorm, being stuck with him for a day and a half. We decided for Joshua and Macy"—I look at my brother—"that we would be civil to each other for the wedding." I look at Nate who grins, certain parts of me get flutters while other parts of me tingle, one part of me defiantly gets wet. "A truce."

Twenty-Eight

O HOLY NIGHT

NATE

I THOUGHT WE were going to be slick and get away with no one noticing we weren't at each other's throats. I was at least hopeful they would be too busy with the wedding to notice a shift in how we were acting toward each other. I was so wrong. I seemed to be wrong a lot these days. Like when I thought it was a good idea to kiss her in the bathroom. Then the good idea to sleep with her one more time. Then over and over again.

Now I don't think I can walk into my kitchen and make coffee without looking over at her. Next week will be a whole different reality, and it's not one I want to think about. She looks up at me and all I can do is grin at her. I know she's nervously speaking right now and it's so funny that Jack hasn't picked up on it. When she's nervous, she blinks more often than normal. "A truce."

"I smell a rat," Evie accuses, looking at us trying to

see if we'll give anything up. When the door opens, I hear a couple of gasps coming from the aunts' tables in back.

"Is that?" Elizabeth asks, putting her hand on my arm. "Is that Lexi?" She mentions her cousin who, from what I gathered the last couple of months from conversations here and there, left her husband who was controlling her.

"It is," Ariella confirms. "She was nervous about coming."

"What?" Jack snaps out. "Why?"

"This is the first wedding she's been to since she left her husband," Ariella explains and I see her father, Viktor, walking over to her mother.

"Well, trouble just got here," Elizabeth says, pushing away from the table, "Zara is here."

"She's the one with the cowboy husband?" Evie asks Jack, who nods his head.

"He's the definition of save a horse and ride a cowboy," Evie declares, earning a glare from Jack. "I mean he's nothing compared to you, but…." She leans over to kiss him. "He's high up on that list."

"Good to know if I ever kick the bucket," he hisses, "you'll be okay to move on."

She puts her hand on his cheek. "Never."

"Gross." Elizabeth fake vomits to the side as the waiter comes over and pours champagne in our glasses.

Everyone is now in their seats as they stopped on their way to the table, giving hugs and kisses on the way. I put my arm around Elizabeth's chair, as if I've always done it, and she looks over at me. Someone hits their crystal glass and everyone goes quiet while Zack gets up to talk. "Speeches," Elizabeth mumbles, coming to whisper in my ear, "shouldn't we be saving this for tomorrow?"

"Shh." My thumb rubs up and down her side arm as Zack gives a speech, welcoming Macy's relatives into the family.

"Isn't that bad luck?" Elizabeth leans in again. "Like she didn't say *I do*, what if she has second thoughts?" I look down, trying not to burst out laughing. "What happens if she doesn't show up? Will he give another speech?"

I look over at her, seeing the light in her eyes and wanting nothing more than to lean in and kiss her. I'm debating it all when I hear everyone else say, "Cheers."

She breaks the eye contact to grab her glass and then waits for me to do the same before clinking it with mine. "To hoping she shows up," Elizabeth toasts and Ariella chokes from beside us.

I shake my head, taking a long sip of the chilled champagne. The first dish comes out as we talk about everything. Zack and Denise get up from their chairs and head to the dance floor, followed by a few other couples. I put my napkin on the table at the same time Jack puts his. He pushes away from the table and holds out his hand to Evie, who takes it without a question. The two of them head to the dance floor.

I do the same and hold out my hand, Elizabeth just looks up at me. "Yes?" She smirks.

"Can I have this dance?" I ask her and she puts her own napkin beside her plate.

"I guess so, it will keep up the appearance that we're making a truce."

I hold her hand in mine as I lead her to the dance floor, my arm wrapping around her waist, and I bring the hand that holds hers, folding it up as I hold it on my chest. "Isn't this better than the two of you at each's other throat?" Zack says from beside us.

"The answer is yes, Elizabeth," my mother hisses. "Now is when you both answer yes."

"I didn't start it," Elizabeth tries to defend herself.

"Well, you didn't *not* start it," I correct her, and she tries to rip her hand out of mine, but I squeeze my hand to keep hers closer to mine.

"This is about to be the shortest truce in the history of all truces," she hisses and stops when I wink at her. "Don't you even with that."

"Oh, look," Jack says and points up. I look up to see a mistletoe above our heads. "It's customary to kiss."

"They aren't going to kiss," Zack states.

"I don't know," Evie adds, a sly grin on her face, "it's customary to kiss."

I look at her and bend my head, and I can see her eyes widen until I move my head to the side and kiss her cheek. "There, are you all happy?" she says. "Crisis averted. Nothing bad is going to happen. Well, unless Macy decides she doesn't want to be part of this crazy and takes off."

"Bite your tongue," Zack hisses as he moves away from us.

"I thought you were really going to kiss me." She

moves her hand out of mine, wrapping both hands around my neck loosely. "That would have been one way to say the truce is real."

I put my hands on her hips and pull her closer to me. "That would have opened a whole can of worms and a bigger discussion on what we've been doing at home."

She shakes her head and looks down. The song finishes, and Zack comes over and grabs her while I dance with Denise, but it doesn't last long. Jack comes by and we trade partners. By the end of the second song, I've danced with the majority of her aunts.

It's almost eight thirty by the time we get up to leave. "Tomorrow," Joshua reminds me, "you have to be at my parents' house by nine a.m."

"I know," I reassure him. "I got the itinerary you sent last week, along with the daily reminders from my calendar." I slap his chest. "I'll be there as soon as I drop off your sister." I motion with my head toward Elizabeth, who is giving Max a hug. "Text me tomorrow if you need anything." I put my hand on his shoulder. "It's going to be the most amazing day."

"It is." He smiles at me. "It fucking is." He looks down. "I can't wait to repay the favor and watch you get married."

I don't say anything to him as I look over at his sister and realize I've never fucking felt this way before. Not even close. Not even for one fucking day. "I look forward to it," I reply before Elizabeth joins me.

"I'm ready," she announces and I nods at her as I put my hand on her lower back and usher her out of the venue. She takes one step outside and shivers. "It's colder than before."

"The sun was out," I remind her, shrugging off my jacket and putting it around her shoulders.

She uses two fingers to hold the jacket closed in front of her as I put a hand around her waist and walk to my truck. "Thank you," she says when I open the door for her, and for the first time tonight, she leans up and kisses me. A soft kiss on the corner of my lips as she gets into the cab of the truck.

I wait for her to reach for her seat belt before I close the door and head over to the driver's side. Sliding in, I start the car and turn on the heat right way, the cold air fills the cab as I look around, seeing it's just the two of us. Turning to her, I see she's watching me.

"What's—" That is the last thing she says to me because I grab her face in my hands and turn my head to the side. My mouth craves hers. As soon as my lips touch hers, my tongue slides into her mouth. My body, which was tense and on edge the whole time we were in there from the fear I would touch her the wrong way in front of people, or by mistake just kiss her, and then I'd have to explain what the fuck I was doing, escapes me. All of the tension is in this kiss. One of her hands goes to my cheek while the other holds the wrist of my right hand.

"We should really get home," she mentions breathlessly, "so you can do me against the door." My forehead falls to hers as I burst out laughing.

"Yes," I agree, trying not to harp on the fact the way that sentence hit me right in the middle of my chest.

I pull out of the parking lot, looking right and left, when I feel her reach over the center console and put her hand on my thigh. One of my hands automatically goes to hers as I link our fingers together.

The minute I turn off the truck in the driveway, I turn to her. "Wait for me," I tell her as she proceeds to unbuckle her seat belt. I get out, walking over to her side of the truck, the cold night going straight through my white button-down shirt. I open her door and smile at her, holding out my hand. She puts her hand in mine as she takes one step down, her other hand holding the jacket closed in front of her so it doesn't fall off her shoulders.

She steps out of the truck and I slam the door shut and then press her against it. "You look more beautiful now than you did before we left." I push the hair back from the sides of her face so I can cup her face in my hands. "I didn't think it was possible for you to be more beautiful as the days go by." I rub my nose with hers softly, back and forth. "I was wrong." My lips kiss hers gently. "So fucking wrong." Her mouth opens to ask me a question but it just gives me the opportunity to slide my tongue into her mouth.

I use one of my arms to wrap around her waist and pick her up off her feet, walking toward the front door. She lets go of my lips to laugh out. "I can walk, you know."

"You could," I tell her, "but this is faster." I walk up the steps and place her down right in front of the door. Her mouth sucks in my neck as I lift my hand to punch in the code. Her hand rubs my hard cock, squeezing it in her palm.

"If you don't stop, I'm going to fuck you outside the door."

"It's cold." Her voice is soft. "But I'm sure you'll keep me warm."

I bend to take her mouth with mine, her hands now wrapped around my neck. My jacket falls from her shoulders to our feet. My hand moves from her waist to grip her ass, while the other hand opens the door and pushes it open. She steps back into the house, her hands gripping my shirt, pulling me with her.

I step into the house and slam the door shut with my foot, turning her so her back is to the door at the same time her hands frantically pull my shirt out of my pants. Her hands then go to my belt, at the same time I feel something by my feet, then against my legs.

She lets go of my mouth to laugh. "I don't think Whiskey got the memo you are supposed to do me against the door." She looks down at Whiskey, who is going in and out of our legs. The thumping sound of his excited tail hitting the door and then the wall as he moves through my legs and then comes back in. "Whiskey, you are interrupting your father trying to do me." She leans down to rub Whiskey's neck.

"Do you think if we ignore him, he'll go away?" I close my eyes when she asks me that question because I know the answer.

"No," I finally groan out. "Let's get you outside," I tell Whiskey, then look back at Elizabeth. "I want you to stay there." I point to her. "I'm going to let him out and then I'll be right back to bang you against the door."

"I'll be here waiting." She kisses under my jaw.

"Let's go." I motion with my head toward the kitchen door and Whiskey follows me. I open the door, and he looks at me. "Are you kidding me?" I question him as I step outside and he follows me. "Hurry up," I hiss at him as he runs through the snow and I watch him. Turning to look over my shoulder.

"I said not to move!" I shout to her, and she throws her head back and laughs through the door's opening.

"Do you want your jacket?" she asks me and I just shake my head.

"I want you to stay where I told you to stay." I point to her and she laughs again, closing the door as I watch her walk away from the door, my heart clenching in my chest. "It's her," I declare out to the dark quiet night, "it's always been fucking her." There, in the cold, dark night, with a few stars blinking in the sky, I realize I've been holding back over the last seven years for one reason and one reason only. Her.

Twenty-Nine

ELIZABETH

December 24th
Wedding Day

"DO YOU HAVE everything you need?" I ask Nate as he walks out of his closet with the black garment bag in his hand.

"I have the tux." He holds up his hand. "The shoes are…" He looks around the room. "Wherever I threw them last night." He chuckles as he puts the garment bag on the bed next to me, picking up the white shirt he wore last night that he threw over his shoulder before he banged me against his door. "Here's one," he says, picking up his pants and tossing them on the unmade bed.

I curl one of my feet under my leg, as I take a sip of the coffee he just brought up to me as I got dressed in my jogging outfit. My hair is washed and piled on top of my head, ready to be styled for the day. "Where the fuck is the other one?" he asks me like I know.

"This is what happens when you pivot the plan and instead of banging me against the door downstairs, you ordered me upstairs."

"I tried to do you against the door twice"—he walks toward the chair in the corner—"and each time Whiskey thought we were play fighting."

I laugh at the memory because he really thought we were, and at one point he barked at us. "I mean we were play fighting." He looks over at me and I wink at him. "I definitely wanted to play with your toy."

"My dick is not a toy." He shakes his head.

"Um." I put the mug in front of my mouth to hide the smirk I have on my face. "It's kind of like a jack-in-the-box if you think of it. You wind it up and eventually it pops right up."

"Jesus, Elizabeth." He chuckles. "Found it," he says, tossing my dress, landing on his pants.

"Just pointing out the fact," I explain and his phone rings and he groans.

"It's your brother."

"Shocking," I deadpan as he slides his finger across the screen.

"Good morning, Joshua," he greets. "Merry Christmas Eve."

"Yeah," he replies. "Where are you?"

"We just landed on the moon," I tease. "We should be coming back into orbit in a bit."

"Not today," he hisses out, "you cannot fuck with me today."

"So tomorrow I can fuck with you?" I ask and Nate comes over to sit on the bed beside me. My knee is on his thigh as he leans over and softly kisses my exposed neck. "Good to know." I smile at Nate.

"You are supposed to be at my parents' house in thirty minutes," he reminds Nate. "Elizabeth has to be dropped off before you come here."

"Joshua," Nate says in a calm voice, "relax, buddy, it's going to be okay."

"Yeah," I agree with Nate. "Besides, the only person you have to worry about showing up today is Macy."

"Stop saying that," he hisses and then the phone goes dead.

"Did he hang up on me?" I ask, grabbing the phone out of his hand and calling him back.

"What?" he growls instead of saying hello.

"You hung up on me." I gawk at him. "The audacity."

"You would think that would be a sign not to call me back."

"I'm calling you back to say happy Christmas Eve. I've never been more excited for a day in my life like I am for today."

"Aww," he says.

"It's finally fucking over now. I never have to hear about your wedding for the rest of my life." I smile. "See you at the altar," I say and hang up on him.

"As much as I love watching you fuck with him, how about for today you lay off him?" I raise my eyebrows.

"At least until they walk down the aisle."

"Ugh." I roll my eyes. "Fine."

"That's my girl," he praises and I don't even know if he knows what those words do to me. "We should get going."

"Yeah," I agree, and before we get up, he leans in and kisses me. Something that feels like he's been doing it his whole life. Something I feel like I have been receiving my whole life. Something that, come next week, I won't have.

Five minutes later, we're both walking out of the house. He carries his garment bag with his bag of shoes hanging from the hanger and my bag in the other hand. "Close the door, baby." He's called me that a couple of times, usually while we were in the middle of sex. He's never ever called me that outside of bed.

I don't say anything back, instead I just close the door and meet him at the truck. He shuts the back passenger door on his side. He is wearing black joggers and a white sweater, his hair showing me where he ran his hand through it right before we walked out the door. His eyes are bright green with the sun. "Ready?" I ask him and he nods his head. Instead of walking around the truck to the other side, I get on my tippy-toes and kiss his lips softly. My stomach flutters when he opens the door for me, slapping my ass before walking around the truck to his side.

Twenty minutes later, he's pulling up in front of the venue where everything is taking place. "What is going on over there?" I point to the side where a white tent is now up and I see people rushing in with heaters. "This motherfucker is going to get married outside?" I shake my head. "Idiot."

"I'll let him know you approve," he jokes as I reach for the door handle and open the door. I'm about to get out when he grabs my hand. "I'll see you later," he says and his hand comes up to hold my cheek. Something he has done more than once over the last couple of days. Something I've come to look forward to, before he softly kisses my lips.

"I'll be one of the ones wearing green," I tell him as a joke, getting out and grabbing my bag from the back. He looks at me with a smile. "Have fun."

I close the door and turn toward the venue, opening the door and seeing Doreen there with her headset on again as she talks to someone, but stops when she sees me. "Upstairs." She points to the side stairs. "Room numbers four and five are the changing rooms. Your dress is steamed and waiting for you. Rooms one, two, and three are the glam rooms. I think you start with your hair."

I nod to her and head to the stairs, seeing the loft has a long table against the railing with food on it. Everything from pastries to bagels to a man standing there in front of two hot plates that can do either pancakes or omelets. I smile at him before heading to room five first to see if my dress is in there. I find it in room four, hanging right next to my mother's. I put my bag that holds my purse and shoes down in front of it before heading toward where the voices are coming from.

I push open the first room and see my mother there with my aunts, all of them in chairs. The room is transformed into a glam room, to say the least, with six hair stylists getting them ready. "Hello," I say, walking into the room and seeing the eyes all come to me. My mother's eyes light up. "Happy Christmas Eve," I greet, walking to her and kissing her cheek and then grabbing the mimosa out of her hand and finishing it for her.

"Happy Christmas Eve, my love," she replies softly.

I walk over to my aunt Zara, her smile fades and she glares at me. "If you are coming here to finish my drink," she teases me, "think again." I bend to kiss her cheek. "How's my favorite niece?"

I sit in one of the empty seats as a woman comes in with a tray of drinks. She does a quick scan of the room, coming straight to me, and I take one of the flutes from her tray, then look back at my aunt Zara. "I have to ask you a serious question." Her eyes go big and it feels like everyone in the room stops what they are doing and you can hear a pin drop. "Will you answer me honestly?"

"Of course," she says and I can see my mother grip the arms of her chair.

"How many times have you said that to your other nieces?" I wink at her and she throws her head back and laughs.

"Elizabeth," my mother hisses at me, "I thought you were going to ask her something serious."

I roll my eyes as one of the hairdressers comes over and starts to do my hair. "I have a serious question to ask you." Zara turns it around on me as I look in the standing mirror that is in front of each chair.

"Oh, I can't wait for this one," I quip, taking a sip of my own drink.

"When do you think you'll move back home?" she asks, and before I answer, she starts, "I know, I know, you have a whole life there and whatnot."

"And whatnot." I laugh at that part of the sentence.

"Think about it," she advises. "If you get married"—I look at her through the mirror—"you can't get married there."

"Why not?"

"Because you can't." That's all she says, as if that's good enough. "Then what if you have children. What are you going to do, raise them there?"

"Well, I never thought about that," I answer her honestly, "but I don't know if you know this or not, but they allow children in Australia. It's even a happy event when you have them."

"That's not what I meant, smart-ass," she chides. "How can you just raise a child when we all live so far away?"

A lump starts to form in my throat, because I have never not once thought about that. I mean, in all honesty, I wasn't thinking of the future. A future that felt like it was just a wall of nothing. Now if I close my eyes, I see Nate. "The good news is…" I look at her and to my mother, who looks down at her hands. I see her blinking furiously, knowing she's probably going to shed a tear. "I'm not close to that at all."

"But what if you meet someone there?" She asks me

another loaded question. For the first time I admit to myself that I wasn't ever going to meet someone there because the only fucking person I ever wanted was Nate. My heart races and I have a hard time breathing. "Can we not talk about this today?" I try to change the subject. "Let's talk about how amazing today is going to be instead." Zara looks at me, not saying anything. "And can we talk about how Lexi is glowing?" Zara's eyes water as she looks over to my aunt Zoe who just smiles and the tears flow. "Tell me everything."

THREE HOURS LATER, I turn around so my mother can zip up my dress. Turning to look in the mirror, I smile at us. "You look beautiful." She puts her arms around me and hugs me sideways before walking away. I stare at myself, my hair parted in the middle and tucked behind my ears, where pearl drop earrings hang. The one-sleeved, forest-green satin dress is perfectly fit to me. The sleeve is cut down the middle but cuffed at my wrist, showing a hint of my arm. The knot at the side of the dress looks like it's been twisted from the top to the bottom. It falls right to the floor, where my sky-high nude heels peek out of the long slit that comes up my right leg to the middle of my thigh.

"We're ready," Doreen announces, "it's go time."

"I'm ready." I take a last sip of my champagne before grabbing the bouquet of deep red roses that look almost purple. I walk out of the room and see Macy standing there next to her parents. I put my hand to my chest as I smile, and I have to blink my eyes a few times. "You look beautiful," I say softly, and she just smiles at me. Her lace dress fits her like a glove, the sleeves tight until her elbows and then flow long to the side. "My brother is a lucky man."

She looks down at her shoes. "That he is," she admits to me, right before Doreen ushers us down the steps.

My parents wait at the bottom of the steps, my father's face lighting up when he sees me. "My beautiful girl," he says, kissing my cheek, "I love you."

He's told me these words my whole life, but I don't know why today it feels different. I grab his hand before he's told that it's time to walk down the aisle. I get in line where we practiced yesterday, and when it's my turn to walk down the aisle, all I can do is look ahead. I smile at Joshua, who looks like he's going to burst out crying at any second. We share a look and I mouth, "I love you," to him. My eyes then go right to Nate, who is standing beside him wearing the same black tux as Joshua. His eyes are bright, his face more handsome than ever before as he smiles at me. I don't know if it's possible, but my smile just gets bigger. My eyes are on his as I walk down the aisle and stand to the side.

I wait until the song changes and the doors open. Instead of watching Macy, I watch my brother and see the tears running down his face filled with a smile. Twenty minutes later, he kisses her like he hasn't kissed her in a year. Making us roar out with cheers. "It's over." He looks at me. "No more wedding talk."

Thirty

NATE

I WATCH HER across the altar as she trades jabs with Joshua. The two of them making everyone laugh with her teasing him one last time about his wedding. Joshua grabs Macy's hand in his and kisses her fingers before aiming their conjoined hands to the sky. "Married." Everyone laughs as they cheer them on. The two of them sharing one more look before making their way down the aisle. Joshua shakes his father's hand as he walks past him. Zack with that proud look he has on his face most of the time we're all together.

I clap my hands, turning my head to the side to watch Elizabeth, who smiles at them as they work their way down. I'm pushed forward by Jack, who is beside me. "Hurry up so we can get this over with, and I can go and be with my wife." He pushes my shoulder to step forward.

Instead of walking forward, like we practiced yesterday, I tell him, "You take my place." Trying not to let him know I want to walk with Elizabeth and not Belinda.

Belinda steps forward and looks at me, her eyes going big. "Hurry." I push him and he steps forward, smiling at her and then I step forward and hold out my arm for Elizabeth, who looks up at me with a smirk. "Hi," I say, my heart feeling like it's finally beating at a normal pace, unlike when I watched her walk down the aisle. I thought my heart was going to come out of my chest, and the only thing I could think was, *she is beautiful and I want her to be mine.* Mine not just for the time she is here but for longer than that. But then the dread came creeping back up, the back of my neck got so hot I thought someone was pouring boiling water on me. It moved up to the back of my head and all I could do was look at her to calm myself down.

"Hi," she replies softly as we walk down the aisle. Denise holds on to Zack's arm as she smiles at us. "You look very dapper." She turns her head to look at me, and I see the flash of the camera as they take a picture of us.

"You look like a million bucks," I tell her. "More than a million, a trillion."

"Whoa," she jokes with me, looking down at her feet and then straight ahead again, smiling for everyone. Once we get to the end of the aisle, her hand falls from the crook of my arm as she walks over to Joshua.

"Now can I fuck with you?" she asks him and he barks out with laughter. His head goes back before he grabs her in his arms and the two of them share a big hug. "I'm taking that as a yes," she teases and then Jack comes to them and the three of them share a hug.

"We need a picture of this," Macy declares, "a truce has been formed."

"She's just having truces with everyone these days," Jack teases her and then looks over at me, as if he knows what is going on.

"Not everyone." She glares at him and that makes him laugh.

"If we can get everyone to clear out of this area," Doreen instructs, "so the guests can come and congratulate the couple." I step to the side and then look over when Elizabeth comes back to my side.

"She's really bossy," she mumbles and gives Doreen a chin lift.

"Stop making trouble, then," I tease her, and she smirks at me before her face fills with a smile.

"Never," she tells me as we are pulled away to take pictures. There are pictures of just the groomsmen with Joshua and then the bridesmaids with Macy. My eyes never leave Elizabeth's as she smiles for the camera. Then they have one with all of us. I stand next to Jack with Elizabeth in front of me, my hand on her hip. She turns the hand that is hanging from beside her over so I can slide my other hand in hers, our fingers intertwined as we smile at the camera.

After what feels like an eternity, we finally are let go of our duties and we head toward the reception area. "We should get a drink."

"I agree with this," I tell her as we walk over to one of the empty tables that have been assigned for the bridal party. She puts her bouquet down as we walk to the bar.

I order her a white wine and a whiskey for myself. "Well, well, well." We look over when a woman with short salt-and-pepper hair is walking toward us, round black glasses perched at the tip of her nose. "If it isn't little Elizabeth," she says walking to her.

Elizabeth smiles at her. "Dr. Torres," she says her name as she kisses her cheek. "I'm so happy to see you," she adds and then looks at me. "Nate," she calls my name, "this is Dr. Torres, she is one of the reasons I went into medicine."

I smile at the woman. "Oh please." Dr. Torres shakes her head. "Nonsense."

"She has the best emergency clinic I've ever been to." He smiles at the woman. "A place I used to end up frequently with two older brothers."

I laugh. "You were very accident prone," I tease her.

"How is the clinic?" she asks Dr Torres, who smiles sadly.

"I'm shutting it down," she informs her. "It's time for me to retire and I never found anyone I trusted enough to take it over."

"What?" Elizabeth says, her hand coming up to hold on to my arm. "That clinic is…" She shakes her head. "It's the only clinic that I know of in the area."

"I'm sure someone will come around and open a new one once I'm gone," she mentions. "Excuse me, dear, I'm going to go and congratulate Joshua."

"I can't believe it," Elizabeth whispers. "See this scar?" She lifts her bare arm and I see a little V scar. "Joshua threw a plastic chair at me." I roll my lips, trying not to laugh. "See this?" She puts her head back and points to another small scar. "Four stiches, running up the steps from Joshua because I scratched his DVD of *The Fast and the Furious.*" My hand comes up to touch her chin gently. "I can't believe it."

"If we can get everyone's attention," the emcee announces. "We'll be serving the first course in five minutes, so everyone take their seats."

I walk side by side with her to the table and Jack comes over with Evie, sitting down with us. "Did you know Dr. Torres is closing down her clinic?" Elizabeth asks Jack, who looks like he's in shock as well. "I know." She pffts. "She can't find someone she trusts to take it over."

"That's so sad," he replies. "I was wrestling with Joshua once when I was sixteen"—Jack turns to Evie— "and I fucked up my elbow. I told Mom and she ignored me. Said something about not roughhousing."

Elizabeth and I both laugh because she would always say that. "Two days later I went to tell her that I was in pain still. She took one look at it and called me an idiot, but then told me to get in the car. My elbow was fractured. I ended up in a cast and missed my bantam hockey year playoffs."

"What did that teach you?" Evie asks him.

"To never go to my mother when I was in pain. I would go straight to my father." We all laugh at him.

Joshua and Macy are introduced to everyone as husband and wife. The two of them doing their first dance to "Come Away with Me."

Everyone claps when he dips her. "Isn't that sweet?" Elizabeth says sarcastically when they finish and the food comes out.

The plates are cleared when another song comes on and I see people head to the dance floor. I push away from the table. "Will you dance with me?" I hold out my hand.

"Again?" She smiles up at me as she takes my hand and I almost, almost whisper out always. But instead, I just nod my head.

"If you keep this up"—Jack follows my lead, getting up and holding out his hand for Evie—"people are going to think you like each other." We look at each other before laughing at Jack and walking away.

I slide my hand around her waist while she puts one of her arms over my shoulder, her fingers sliding into the back of my hair.

"So on a scale of one to ten," Jack quips from beside us, "how happy are you that in two days you can finally have your room back?" He looks at Elizabeth with a smirk on his face. It's a look I've seen before, many times. A look that says I'm going to fuck with you until you tell me the truth.

"What?" Elizabeth says to him as I look at her, the both of us moving side to side.

"Well, everyone is pretty much leaving tomorrow night, max by the twenty sixth, so your room will be free."

"Oh," she replies softly and I feel the tightness form all over my body.

"You can always still stay with me," I offer. "Baby Cat has gotten used to you anyway."

"Is that why?" Jack asks and then Evie laughs.

"Would you leave them alone?" she scolds. "He thinks the two of you have been hooking up."

My stomach lurches. "What?" I say.

"So," Elizabeth interjects at the same time, "if we were, which I'm not saying we are, what does it matter?"

"If you aren't," Jack teases her, "then what does it matter if we know or not?"

I look down at Elizabeth and see her shake her head. "I guess you'll never know, then."

"The two of you need to knock it off," Evie advises, "it's Christmas Eve and it's Joshua's wedding."

"Please," Jack scoffs, "he's so happy she showed up, he couldn't care less."

"Well, I care," Evie states. "Do you want me to be sad?"

"Yeah, Jack, do you want her to be sad?" Elizabeth jumps on his ass. "She has been looking a little bit sadder every day that goes by. You need to stop worrying about who I'm hooking up with and pay attention to your woman and her needs." I roll my lips. "They are clearly not met." She sighs. "Get away from us before I yell 'stranger danger.'"

"Okay, that's enough," I intervene, moving her away from him. "You are—"

"The best, I know," she fills in for me. "You don't have to say it, I already know. You're welcome, by the way."

"For what?" I ask her, and fuck, the need to kiss her is as strong as it is to keep breathing to stay alive.

"For not telling him that we're hooking up," she answers. "He would kick your ass."

I throw my head back and laugh. "He would not kick my ass." I pull her closer to me. "He would definitely turn around and tell your parents."

"Can you imagine?"

"Yeah," I reply, wanting to be able to kiss her when the fuck I want to, "I can."

"Okay," the emcee says, "it's the big moment."

I let her go a little, turning her in my arms as her back is to me. My arms go around her chest and she leans into me. "It's time for all the single ladies to come up to the dance floor."

"Eeww," she moans out, "absolutely not." She pushes me back. "Move, move, move."

She's about to escape when Denise comes running up to her. "Here is your chance."

"For what?" Elizabeth asks. "I already have a bouquet of flowers."

"Shut up and get on that dance floor and catch the fucking bouquet," she swears and Elizabeth and I just look at each other, trying not to laugh.

"Just move out of the way," I mumble to her and Denise glares at me.

"You're next," she tells me. "He's throwing the garter

and you better fucking catch it."

"I don't want it." I scrunch my nose up and shake my head. "It was on Macy's leg. That's gross. I don't want it. I think it's even a bad omen if the best man catches the garter that was on the bride's leg."

She doesn't say a word to me, she just pulls Elizabeth to the dance floor while Zoe drags Lexi, who smiles at her mother, but it's a smile that says she's not going to catch that thing.

"The best part is she's dating Jaxon's best friend," Jack shares from beside me, motioning with his chin to the guy who is standing at the side, smiling at her. "From what I was told, he helped her get away from her asshole husband," he says. "Whatever he did, she's thriving now."

"Okay, here we go," the emcee starts, "one, two, three." Macys throws the bouquet over her head and it lands right on Elizabeth, who folds her arms to her chest in reflex.

"Noooo," she groans out, "that—" She doesn't say anything because Denise is jumping up and down as if she just won the Stanley Cup.

"She's next." She holds on to Zack's arm, who just smiles down at her. "Oh my God, she's next."

"I'm not next," Elizabeth retorts, moving off the dance floor.

"Okay, where are my bachelors?" the emcee asks.

"That would be you." Jack pushes me to the middle of the floor and I'm surrounded now with some of the men and Gavin.

"You should catch this," I tell him and he smirks.

"I plan on it, since it's customary for the person who catches the bouquet and the person who catches the garter to dance with each other." The minute he says the words, I want to throat punch him. He claps his hands together and I just look at him. "Been trying to catch her attention all night."

I don't listen to anything else because the emcee is counting down. Gavin beside me moves side to side, as if he's getting ready to run a play in football. He bounces up and down on his feet, and when the garter flies through the air, I move my hand up and he may be wider than me but I'm taller, so it falls right in my hand.

Joshua turns around and howls with laughter when I hold up the garter hanging on my finger. I walk over to him and tuck it back in the pocket on his tux. "You can keep that. Thank you very much." I slap his chest, turning and seeing Elizabeth on the side laughing and shaking her head.

"You just had to, didn't you?" she teases me and I smile at her.

"How else would I get you to dance with me again?" I tease her, pulling her to me and bending my head to her ear. "You can thank me later."

Merry Christmas
AND A HAPPY NEW YEAR

Thirty-One

The First Noel

Elizabeth

December 25th
Merry Christmas

I HEAR SNIFFING next to my face before I feel Whiskey's nose in my eyeball. I moan and turn my face to the other side. I don't know why I expect him to walk away but I do. He doesn't. Instead, I now hear him sniffing my hair and licking my neck. "No." I lift my hand and give a little laugh when his nose feels like it's in my ear. "Whiskey," I say his name and he immediately jumps on the bed, stepping on my legs to get over to the other side.

"Whiskey," Nate grumbles in a sleepy voice, "down." Instead of getting down off the bed, all he does is move excitedly to his side of the bed. "What is wrong with you?" I open my eyes to see Nate on his back with

Whiskey on top of him as he pets his head.

"He probably knows it's Christmas and I got him some special treats under the tree." I lift my hand up to rub his neck. "Is that why you are all excited?" I turn on my side and Nate's hand that is under the cover moves to my leg where he rubs it softly. "You want to open your presents?" I ask him and he gets off of Nate and jumps off the bed.

"Great," Nate complains, "now he's really awake."

I laugh as he tosses the covers off him and gets up. His naked body is on full display as he reaches down for the boxers he took off last night after our shower and before sliding into bed after he put out Whiskey one more time. "Come on." He rubs his hands through his hair and looks at me.

"Merry Christmas, Nate." I smile at him and he puts one knee in the bed, followed by his hands on the bed before kissing my lips.

"Merry Christmas, beautiful," he replies softly, giving me one more kiss before moving off and walking out of the door. I hear Whiskey trample down the stairs and toss the covers off myself and stretch. Swinging my legs off the side of the bed, I get up and head to the bathroom. Last night, as soon as we got home, I took off the makeup and took a shower. My hair now looks like a rat's nest and I have some black smudges under my eyes, even though I took off the makeup and then took a shower. I clean up my face with a wet washcloth, grabbing my pajama bottoms and one of Nate's shirts before heading downstairs.

The smell of coffee lingers in the air and the bright sun from outside fills the kitchen. "It's so bright out."

"It's almost eleven," he reports and I gasp.

"No wonder he was all over us," I say, walking to the back door and looking out at Whiskey jumping into the little snow that is left on the ground before running away and then back again.

"Yeah," Nate says, "definitely wouldn't be able to do that if he was a puppy."

"I've never had a puppy," I admit to him.

"Would you want a puppy?" he asks me and I shrug. "It's lots of work at the beginning, and not something that should be done if you aren't home."

"Yeah." I go to the door when Whiskey charges over to the door and I open it, the cool air hitting me right away. "Maybe that's why I never got one. I work long hours and it would be silly to have a puppy and not give it enough attention." Whiskey runs in and heads straight for his food bowl. I walk toward Nate, who is standing right in front of the coffee machine. My arms wrap around his waist as I kiss his bare back, I close my eyes for a moment. "Are you tired?"

"Not as tired as I should be." He puts one hand on my hand on his stomach. "Do you want to do presents before or after breakfast?"

"I have to admit something to you. I hate Christmas."

"I don't think that's a secret, baby," he says softly, his chuckle warming my soul. My stomach flutters from the sound of it.

"I wasn't finished, Nate." I let go of him and he turns

around, his chest to mine. His hand comes up and he holds my hips, making sure I don't go anywhere. I put my hands on his chest, my fingers moving back and forth. "What I was going to say is, I hate Christmas, but I love presents."

He laughs and I can't help but smile at his laughter. He puts one of his hands on the counter beside him but keeps a hold on me. "So I'm always ready to open presents."

"But you hate surprises." I shake my head.

"No one likes surprises, but everyone likes presents."

"So I could buy you a present but I can't surprise you?" He smirks.

"Yes," I agree with him. "If I don't know about it and it magically appears, I'm okay with it. But if you go on and on about 'oh, I have a surprise for you,' then it's a solid no."

"Noted," he says. "So we should do gifts now, then?"

"Yes!" I clap my hands, giddy like a kid in a candy store. "Who is going to go first?" I ask him as he turns to hand me my coffee and then both of us walk toward the Christmas tree.

"As you can see"—I point to the presents under the tree—"I've color coded mine."

"Of course you did." He sits on the couch. "Because not having them the same color makes it more of a surprise for you."

I gasp, "I didn't even think of that." I put my coffee to the side. "Okay, I'm going to give you one first." I get up grabbing the medium-size box. "I want you to keep in mind that I didn't have a lot of time to prepare for gifts."

I walk to him and he opens his legs for me to stand in between them. His hands go to rub up the back of my legs. He looks up at me, his lips in a little smile as I bend my head to kiss him. I hold his cheek with one of my hands while the other grips the box. "Okay." I push the box at him and he grabs it, opening the Santa Claus wrapping and seeing the white box. I sit next to him, almost bouncing in my seat. He opens the top, and when he pulls out the white mug, he turns it over and laughs. "This is going to be my new mug." He looks down at the white mug I had made that says Whiskey, Bean, and Baby Cat's dad, with a picture of them all around the cup. Then in the back it says Best Dog and Cat Dad Ever.

"I might have gotten one for myself also," I mumble to him, "minus the 'cat dad' stuff."

He looks over at me and it's a look he's given me often over the years, but a look I might have locked out of my memory to protect my heart from being more hurt than I was. A look that even now if I wanted to lock it away, I knew I couldn't. "For you to take back home?"

The minute he says that, my eyes get dry and with each blink it feels like I have sand stuck under my lids, and the lump forms in my throat, knowing in seven days this isn't going to be my morning anymore. I don't answer him, instead I just nod my head. He puts the mug to the side and then gets up to grab one of the presents bringing it to me. "I also didn't have time and I scrambled. It didn't help that I tried to ask Joshua and he told me to give you a stocking full of coal."

I laugh as he hands me the thin present, the wrapping paper is filled with Grinch faces, making me laugh. "This is very me." I hold up the soft gift and then I open it and it's a calendar. "What is this?" I open it and every single month is a different picture from this past week.

The tears in my eyes make it blurry to see all the images. Once I get to October I laugh when I see Whiskey with a stuffed pumpkin in his mouth. "That is from last year," he admits, "but the one in December was taken two days ago." I flip to it and the three of them are together.

The cats have red collars on that have white balls at the end of them and Whiskey has a Santa hat on his head. Lying on the ground, he's the only one looking at the camera. Bean looks like she's desperately trying to get the collar off of her, while Baby Cat is glaring at the camera. I can't help the laughter that comes out. "This one has to be my favorite." I hold it up, fighting back the tears. "Thank you." I smile at him. "I'm going to put this up in my locker at work. Might have another one made so I can also have it on my fridge." The tightness starts to form in my stomach.

"My turn," I say quicky, looking away from him, going to the gifts. "This one is a gag gift." I hand him the long box and sit next to him. He unwraps it and the top of the box says Oral Fun: the game of eating out while staying in. "It's a board game."

He turns it around and smirks. "We'll be playing this hourly"—he puts it to the side—"which makes my gift even better." He grabs the small square gift. This one is wrapped with little Christmas bows all over it.

I rip it open and turn it over, the black box with Quickies written in white. "What in the world?" I open the box as he sits there with a smile on his face, every single card is black. One side has a scratch pad, the other side has Quickies in glossy black writing.

"So you pick a card and scratch it off, and you have to do what they tell you to do."

"Ohh, I need something to scratch with." I get up and rush to the kitchen, grabbing a butter knife.

"You really doing that now?" he asks and I look up at him.

"Um, yeah," I reply as the white words appear. "In the next twenty minutes, try at least five different sex positions," I read out loud and then read the rest to myself. "We can't do this one."

"Yes we can," he assures from the couch and I hold up the card.

"The goal is to not climax before the twenty minutes is done," I shriek. "Fuck that."

"So it's a challenge," he goads me. "You are always good with a challenge."

"It's a challenge that is dumb," I retort, walking to him. "There is no way I can last twenty minutes."

"I'll help you," he offers and I laugh at him.

"That is super kind of you. Thank you so much for that. You are such a great friend." The minute I say the words, something changes on his face. I want to take it back as soon as the words are out of my mouth, but what else am I going to call him? My hookup? My holiday fling? Nothing would be good enough, except for the word I should be using. Right person, wrong fucking time, I keep hearing the words play over and over in my head.

"My turn," I say walking back and taking the big box in the back. "It's thin, but—" I say bringing it to him. "I love it, and I really hope you do also."

I hand him the box and he unwraps the paper slowly, the white square box showing him nothing of what is inside. He takes the cover off and then the white tissue paper and the black frame greets him. His mouth opens in shock and he looks over at me. "How the fuck?"

I sit next to him and look at the picture I had professionally made. It's a picture of his clinic and in front, on one side, are his parents that I took from the picture he had on a side table, and then on the other side is a picture of his grandparents. In the middle, sitting down, is Nate with Whiskey and the cats by his side. "How did you do this?" he asks me, speechless.

"I found the picture of you in front of the clinic in my parents' house," I explain to him as he runs his fingers over the image of his parents. "Then I asked if we could add the two other images in there." He looks over at me and smiles, but it's a smile filled with sorrow. "You said that you wouldn't have it without them, and I think that—" I shake my head, correcting myself. "I know they are so proud of you."

"Elizabeth," he says my name, his voice cracking, "this is the best gift I've ever gotten in my life."

I wrap my arm around his shoulders and smile. "So

what you mean to say is, I win." He laughs and his lips come to touch mine in a gentle kiss.

"You win, baby," he agrees softly, "you really fucking win." He puts the picture down and goes to get the small box. "This sucks now that I got that, but—" He hands me the box. "Well, here it is."

"I'm sure it's perfect," I assure unwrapping it and seeing the jewelry box. "What in the world?" I open it, the gold bracelet sits in the middle in a circle.

"It's a customized charm bracelet," he tells me. "The E is obviously for Elizabeth." It hangs in the middle and then beside it is a heart with a diamond it in, another one is a star, and then the last one is a Christmas tree. "I know that you hate Christmas but I put a tree there so you would remember this Christmas and know how much it has meant to me and how I'll remember it forever."

"This is so…" I shake my head. "This is so thoughtful." I take it out and hold it out to him. "Will you put it on me?" He nods his head as he wraps it around my wrist and fastens it.

"There," he says, kissing the inside of my wrist, "now it's perfect." I look down, my eyes going to the heart that is dangling, all the words are stuck in my throat. "Merry Christmas, Elizabeth."

Thirty-Two

ELIZABETH

December 26th

I SHIMMY ON my jeans before snatching the sweater I took out of my bag before my shower. Taking my hair out of the back of it before sitting on the bed, I grab my socks and sit on the edge of the bed that I haven't slept in since we started sleeping together. I look over when I hear him coming out of his bedroom dressed in jeans and a T-shirt. His hair is still wet from the shower he went to take after we had coffee together, sitting on the couch, watching television, and not talking. "Hey," I say when his eyes catch mine.

"Hey back at you." He stands there leaning against the doorjamb. "What's up?"

"My mother just called to remind me about taking me shopping today," I reply, putting the second sock on. "Even though when we went over there for dinner last night, I told her I was not going after–Christmas Day shopping with her." He smiles and looks down. "She says either I get dressed and meet her in the car, or she'll have you carry me to the car." I get up. "I'm going to save us both and just go out and be ready for her."

"Okay," he says softly, "I think I'll go to the office. Catch up on a couple of things before I get back to it after New Year's."

I walk to him and wait for him to kiss me, but he doesn't. He smiles and turns to walk down the stairs. Ever since we exchanged gifts yesterday, he's been quieter than ever. Even at dinner with my parents, his smile never went to his eyes. I waited until we got home to ask him about it but he had other plans. Plans that had my mouth and his occupied. I fell asleep in his arms, and by the time I woke up, he was already out of bed. It was also the first morning I didn't wake up next to him, and I hated every single second of it.

I get up and take a deep breath as I make my way down the stairs and to the kitchen. Whiskey gets off the couch and comes over to me, rubbing himself against my legs. I bend to pet his neck, looking up to see Nate at the coffee machine. My heart pounds nervously as I ask him what I've been wanting to ask him since yesterday, but I've been too scared shitless to ask him, for fear he'll tell me something I don't want to hear. "Are you okay?" I ask him and he turns to face me, his face not giving away anything.

"Yeah," he answers, "I guess I'm just tired."

"We slept almost twelve hours." I laugh nervously,

hoping I can get him to smile at me. Something I didn't know I needed right now in this minute.

"Maybe I need more," he says, his voice tight, and my eyebrows pinch together.

"Seriously?" I say, knowing he's fucking hiding something or he's pissed about something and doesn't want to tell me. I don't know what it is, but I know it's something.

"Seriously," he repeats the word and now I know he's pissed.

"You were quiet most of the night," I mention, my heart hammering in my chest, "and then you said maybe five words to me today. 'Good morning' being two of them and 'hey, what's up' being the other words." My hands start to shake nervously as I place them on the cold island in front of me.

"I don't know what you want from me," he states, "I'm fine."

"You act like I don't know you, Nate." I try to not freak out and keep my voice calm, but as it drags on, the nerves get the best of me and my voice goes higher.

"Do you know me?" he asks me and I have to wonder if he's trying to start a fight with me.

"What the fuck does that mean? Of course I know you. How can you say that?" He shrugs. "Things would go faster if you just said what is bothering you and we can—" I don't finish the sentence because he snorts out angrily.

"We can what?" he snaps. "What can we do?" I don't know if he's asking me or telling me. "We can't do shit."

I see his eyes and they are greener than blue, making them almost look like they are golden. He crosses his arms over his chest, leaning back against the counter. "We can't do shit about shit because this time next week you'll be getting on a fucking plane and leaving."

I open my mouth and then close it again. "Well, yeah, considering I don't live here."

"Yeah, don't worry, I'm reminded every fucking day," he snaps out. "But even knowing it, even telling myself it was just temporary, I fucking did it."

"What did you do?" I wish the question I just asked him didn't have me holding my breath. I wish the question I just asked him didn't have me feeling sick to my stomach. I wish the question I just asked him didn't have my whole body tight with nerves.

"I said I wouldn't say it." He runs his hand through his hair and then holds the back of his head with his hand. "But then I can't not say it."

"Whatever it is, you might as well just say it and get it over with," I push, knowing he's going to say it's not a good idea for me to stay here any longer. That whatever this thing is should just be done with. Knowing when he does say those words, my heart is going to shatter and I'm going to have to pretend I'm fine.

"You want me to say it?" he asks and shakes his head. "Fine, I'll say it." I hold my breath, not sure what he's going to say but not ready for the next thing that comes out of his mouth. "I'm in love with you."

I feel the blood drain from my body. "I'm fucking in love with you and you are going to leave me. I've come to realize I have only ever fucking loved you the way I do. I've realized I've been holding myself back, waiting for you. I didn't know it until everything just clicked into place. How I would stand back and not give myself to anyone. How I would keep whatever it was I had going on at arm's length, knowing subconsciously I was waiting for you."

"Nate," I say his name, shock filling my body as the doorbell rings and I look down the hall.

"You have to go," he states. "Go."

"Nate," I say his name again at the same time the doorbell rings again.

"There is nothing to say, Elizabeth," he says softly. "I live here. You live halfway around the fucking world. I can't do the long-distance thing, not after having you this week. It'll be fine." I look into his eyes. "Unlike seven years ago, we both know what is happening."

The lump in my throat is so big, I don't even think I would be able to say a word. The doorbell rings again and I feel like I'm stuck to the floor. The doorbell stops and now it's followed by knocks on the door. "I'm going to go and get that." He walks around the island and to the front door.

I close my eyes and look down, the first tear falls onto my cheek and I wipe it away as I hear my mother's voice. "I thought she locked you in a room to stop from going out with me," she says laughing.

He chuckles, acting like we didn't just have the most intense conversation of our lives. "I was in the shower." He makes the excuse. "I think she's in the kitchen."

I take a deep inhale, putting my hand to my chest to ease the tightness in it. I exhale a breath before walking into the hallway. "Hi," my mother greets, looking over at me, the smile on her face fading a bit when she looks into my eyes, but she recovers. "I tried to call you," she says, looking at Nate, who is looking at me and who I'm avoiding looking at right now. I'm not sure I can take it without the pain showing on my face.

"I have my phone on the charger in the kitchen," I explain, pointing behind me. "I'll go get it and we can go." I walk away from the two of them. I grab my phone that I plugged in while I had a coffee this morning. I tuck it in the back pocket of my jeans and head back to the door.

"Are you going to go and get your things?" my mother asks me, and I look at her confused. "Well, you have to get out of Nate's hair."

"I'll get them later," I say, hoping she isn't going to push the issue and I'll have to pack up my things.

"Okay, we can swing by after shopping and grab your things." I nod, not willing to get into it with her. I look at Nate. "I'll see you later." I don't know if I'm asking him or telling him, and he just nods his head at me, much like what I did to my mother.

My mother looks between us and doesn't say anything before she turns and walks out of the house. I step out, wanting to turn back and kiss him, which would make things probably worse for us all.

I get into the car at the same time as my mother, both of us slamming the door at the same time. "So"—she starts the car—"should we do coffee first?"

I look at her and nod my head, knowing that she knows something is up. "I think that's best." She pulls away from the house and with each passing minute my heart gets heavier and heavier in my chest. When we get to the small coffee shop, I get out, trying to get my breathing under control, and knowing I'm one second away from a full-on breakdown.

I walk in and head straight for a table. "I'll order for you," my mother says to me. I don't even answer her because of the lump in my throat and anything I say right now I'm pretty sure will come out in a sob. I sit in the back of the coffee shop, looking down at my hands. The bracelet he gave me yesterday slides out of my sweater and I see the heart. My finger goes to touch it at the same time my mother pulls out a chair and sits in front of me.

"They will bring the coffee." She shrugs off her jacket. "I ordered you a cupcake, but I don't think that is going to make you feel better."

I smile and snort a little. "I don't think a cupcake can fix this."

"What is *this*?" she asks me and I look up at her.

"It's…" I start to say and then stop when I feel my bottom lip quiver. "It's—" I exhale. "I'm in love with Nate." I look up and exhale again. "Oh God."

"My beautiful girl," she says and I'm expecting her to freak out, but she smiles at me and holds out her hand on the table, putting it on mine, "we already knew that."

"What?" I ask, shocked. "Who is we?"

"Well, I can tell you who didn't, your father and

Joshua. I'm pretty sure Jack saw it." She smiles. "You've been in love with him since you were a teenager."

"I have not," I shriek. "This just happened."

"No." She shakes her head. "This didn't just happen, maybe you just got your head out of your ass, but it didn't just happen."

"We hated each other," I remind her. "He was involved with someone else," I point out and she rolls her eyes.

"You hated each other because you moved away, and he didn't tell you not to go." My mouth hangs open. "But that's the past, you both had to do what you needed to do in order to be here right now."

"Mom." I stop when the girl comes to deliver our coffee. I wait for her to walk away before I look back at her.

"Elizabeth," she says my name, looking down at her coffee cup. "Seven years ago you hightailed it out of town and went halfway around the world most likely to get away from him."

"I didn't just do it because of him. It was a great opportunity."

"Agreed." She nods her head. "You needed to do what you needed to do and so did he. Now you both ended up here."

"Yeah and now I don't live here," I remind her and she rolls her eyes. "Mom, I can't just get up and move."

"Why not?" she scoffs at me. "You did once before, I'm pretty sure you can do it again."

"I have a life," I counter, and the minute I say the words, the only thing flashing through my mind is Nate.

It's not just Nate, it's also Whiskey, Bean, and Baby Cat. The five of us settled on the couch watching a show, even though it's not a memory I should have.

"What life?" she asks me. "You go to work, you come home. It's wash, rinse, repeat," she snaps at me. "You what, have two friends and barely go out."

"Wow."

"Don't you wow me, young lady." She points her finger at me. "Do you know how hard it is for me to see you not living a full life?"

"Um."

"Um, nothing," she retorts. "How did this happen?"

"How did what happen?" I ask not sure of her questions.

"How did you come to all of a sudden realize you are in love with Nate?" she asks me softly.

"Well, it's technically all your fault," I say with a smile, but the tears form at the bottom of my eyes. "You threw me at him and I was staying in his house." She rolls her eyes. "And then one thing led to another, and we did grown-up things." I put a hand to my mouth to stop myself from bursting out laughing.

"How much do you love him?" she questions, and I tilt my head to the side. "Do you love him so much that you are going to be okay stepping foot on that plane and leaving him, going back home to live without any regret." She smiles and I see her own tears in her eyes. "Or do you love him so much that just the thought alone makes your heart ache? The thought of him being with someone else and creating a family with her makes you violently ill?"

"It makes me violently ill," I admit in a whisper. "Just the thought of stepping on that plane makes me feel this immense pain in my chest that it's hard to breathe." I wipe the tear off of my cheek.

"Well," she declares, picking up her cup of coffee, "it looks like you have a decision to make."

Merry Christmas

Thirty-Three

THE TROUBLE WITH LOVE IS

NATE

I LOOK OUT the window at the trees in the distance. Sitting back in my chair with my feet on my desk, I rock back and forth. I don't even know how. The knock at the door makes me look away from the window I've been staring out of for the last hour. "Nate."

"Hey." I lean back and look at Chloe, who comes in with Whiskey behind her. "I'm about to head out, so I thought I would make sure that Mr. Whiskey was with you."

"Thank you," I say as Whiskey walks over to his bed in the corner and plops down on it.

"How was the wedding?" Chloe asks me.

"Beautiful," I tell her. "Everything went off without a hitch."

"I'm sure Joshua was happy about that." She laughs. "He was a bit of a mess the last time I saw him."

"Good news is that he should be calmed down. They leave to go on their honeymoon on New Year's Day."

"That sounds like fun." I nod at her as she lingers in my office. "Are you doing anything for New Year's Eve?" she asks me and I shake my head.

"To be honest, I didn't plan anything because of the wedding." I fold my hands on my lap.

"If you want," she suggests softly, "we could maybe catch dinner and a movie."

Shit, this is about to get as awkward as it can be. "That sounds like fun," I say with a smile, "but I'm going to have to pass. Us working together and everything, I would hate to get things crossed." She looks down, trying to hide the rejection on her face.

"Of course, I get it." She shrugs. "Thought I'd extend the offer."

"Thank you for that," I say. "Have a great night." I cut the conversation before it gets more awkward.

"See you after the New Year, Nate." She nods at me and turns to walk out of the office.

I look back out the window and all I can do is think about Elizabeth. The phone rings on my desk and I see it's Jack, and I send it to voicemail. It doesn't take much longer for him to text me.

Jack: Are you fucking screening your calls?

I laugh, knowing that he would know. He's not only been one of my closest friends over the years, he's been like a big brother I never had.

Me: Not screening per se.

I press send and the phone rings instead of him texting

me back. I know if I don't answer it, he'll either come and find me or he'll call Joshua, who will then call me or then get Zack. Needless to say, I can't run away from it.

"Yo." I put the phone to my ear.

"Yo yourself," he says. "Where are you?"

"At the office. Why?"

"I just passed by the house to see you and you aren't there."

"I am not," I confirm. "I came in to make sure everything was okay," I explain, even though the minute I got in, I sat in this chair and didn't do anything. My head was whirling after Elizabeth left.

"Funny." I hear the car door close on his end. "I was doing the same."

"You were checking to see how my clinic was going?" I ask him, trying to get him to divert from the real conversation he wants to have.

"Funny," he repeats, not biting, "I was coming to see how you were doing." His voice trails off as he starts his car. "You seemed out of it last night at dinner."

I was out of it. It was a crazy, emotional day when she gave me a gift that means more to me than anything I've ever gotten in my life. It was then and there I knew I was so madly in love with her that I would be broken once she left. I tried to hide it, tried to bury it, but it's bigger than even I know what to do with it. "Yeah, I'm fine, guess I'm just tired."

"Yeah, but you looked like someone stole your dog."

"It's complicated," I finally admit.

"Oh my God," he barks and I can hear the laughter

in his voice. "Are you in love with Macy, and now that she married Joshua, you came to terms she'll never be yours?"

I can't help the laughter that roars through me. "Yeah, that would be it." I chuckle. "You got me."

He laughs with me. "So you going to tell me what's wrong, or are we going to play twenty questions?"

"That's just wasting everyone's time," I huff out, and he doesn't say a word to me. He just sits there on the phone and waits for me to give it up. "It's…" I think about it. "Fuck!" I run my hand over my face.

"I don't know why, but something tells me this has to do with Elizabeth and that truce you guys were talking about."

I look out the window. "Yeah, something like that."

"Ugh," he groans, "I was afraid of that."

"It's fine," I say softly. "It's all good. In a week she'll be gone and it'll be fine."

"You are just going to let her leave?" Jack barks out.

"What the fuck are you saying?" I sit up. "What am I supposed to do?"

"I don't know. My uncle Matthew once handcuffed my aunt Karrie to the bed when she was going to go on vacation without him."

The gasp that comes out of me makes even Whiskey jump. "I'm not handcuffing her to bed, Jack. To some that would be considered kidnapping."

"It was an option."

"It was the wrong one. Can you imagine what your father would do to me if I handcuffed your sister to my bed?" I get up.

"Well, considering the two of you have hooked up, he's going to be kicking your ass for a whole bunch of reasons."

"He loves me like a son, he told me," I remind him.

"Yeah, but that was before you fell in love with his daughter," he tells me. "You can't just let her go."

"There is nothing I can do to stop her. I told her I was in love with her—"

"But did you ask her to stay?" he cuts me off with his question.

"No"—I shake my head—"and I'm not going to. I won't do that to her. I won't have her choose me or her job. I would never do that."

"You could always leave." I look around my office.

"I could but I'd miss your ugly face too much." I smirk and only when he bursts out laughing do I exhale deeply. "I'm going to get going and go home."

"I wish I had the answer for you, buddy," he says softly.

"I wish you did too. Call you tomorrow."

"Call me whenever. I'm here when you need me." I close my eyes and disconnect the call, looking over at Whiskey.

"You ready to go home?" I ask him and his ears go back on his head, his eyes open, and he watches me get up. Only when I'm around my desk do his two front paws get up. He waits until I'm by the door before he saunters off of his bed. "Let's get going."

My stomach feels like there is a lead weight in it as

we pull into the driveway. All the lights in the house off. When I enter the code and open the door, I see she's not here. I try to fight off the pain in my chest but it's beyond my control.

We walk in and I take off my boots while Whiskey walks to the kitchen and then comes back, looking around. "She's not here, buddy," I tell him. I walk to the kitchen and go straight to the Christmas tree to turn on the lights before opening the door and letting him out while I get his dinner in his bowl.

I'm filling his water bowl when the doorbell rings. I look over, turning the water off and drying off my hands before making my way to the door. I don't even check who it is before opening the door and stop when I see Elizabeth standing there. "What are you doing?" I look at her and then look over her shoulder. "Where is your mother?"

"She left," she tells me, her voice soft. "Can I come in?"

I shake my head, confused, and move away from the door to let her in. "Of course you can come in," I tell her, trying to get my breathing down to normal before I start panting.

"I have to let Whiskey in," I tell her, walking away from her instead of kissing her like I want to. I walk away before I get down on my knees and beg her to stay with me. I walk away before she walks up the stairs probably to pack her things. Something I don't think I can take right now. I let Whiskey in and he bypasses me right away, going straight for her.

"Hello, my prince," she coos. I slide the door closed and lock it before walking back to the kitchen, while Whiskey basks in her hugs and tries to lick her face.

I place the water bowl down next to his food and he comes over. I stand with the island between us. It's exactly the same position we were in this morning when I blurted out I am in love with her. I know I shouldn't have said anything, but I just couldn't not say it. It was like I told myself not to say it, but my mouth completely ignored it. "Good day?" I ask her.

"That depends." She looks at me and I wish we would be having this conversation with me touching her. My hand on her neck so my thumb could feel her heartbeat.

"On?"

"Well, on you, really." She gazes into my eyes and all I can do is look at her. My eyebrows pinch together in confusion. "You laid out a pretty big declaration this morning." She puts her hand on the island. I see one of them is shaking a bit and I want to hold it to make sure she's okay. "And then my mother sort of came in and derailed it a bit." I swallow as I just listen to her. "Which might have been the perfect thing." All I can do is take a deep breath in. "Right time, right place." I look down and my heart feels like it's literally going to explode in my chest. "You see, when we left here, instead of going shopping, we went to have coffee." I look back at her. "We had a little bit of a heart-to-heart."

"Is that so?"

"That is so." She smirks. "It was a good talk. You see, she asked me a question that made me violently ill." I stand up straight, wondering if she is sick. "Not physically, metaphorically. You see, she asked me how much I love you." My mouth opens but not a sound comes out, not even a breath. "Then asked me how I would feel if I stepped on that plane and walked away from you. She asked me if I loved you so much, would I be okay with you having a family with someone else."

"Elizabeth," I say her name, my voice cracking.

"I told her that it made me sick. Just the thought of leaving you and you loving someone else, it makes me fucking ill." She swallows down and she lifts her hand to wipe the tear from the corner of her eye. "So I had to make a decision." I walk around the counter to stand in front of her, but not touching her.

"What?" I swear all I can hear at this moment is my heartbeat echoing in my ears.

"I made a decision and my mother sort of helped me with it." She smiles and her tears start to pour down her cheeks. "Well, I made half the decision, the other half stands with you."

"I don't know what you are saying right now."

"I went to see Dr. Torres," she explains and a gasp leaves me, "we sat down and had a nice talk." My head spins. "I wanted to know if she would think about handing over her practice to me." She smiles even bigger. "She said I was the only one she would think of giving it to. Which was good since I had called the hospital and told them I would not be renewing my contract that ends in two months."

"What?" It comes out in a whisper.

"I have to go back for two months, but that will give me enough time to pack up whatever I need to pack up and sell what I don't want and then come back." She taps the counter. "Which now leads me to where the other half of my decision lies with you." I tilt my head to the side. "I'm going to be moving back home," she says the words I've been waiting to hear for the past seven years, even if I didn't know it, "and if it's okay with you, I would like to move in with you."

"I dare you to try to stay somewhere else," I tell her and she looks down and giggles. "Are you sure about this?"

"Am I sure I want to stay with you and I love you? One thousand percent," she confirms and I charge her. My arm wraps around her waist, another one gets lost in her hair. "I love you, Nate," she declares as I put my forehead on hers. "I've loved you since I can remember." Her hand lies on my chest. "I think I'll love you until I breathe my last breath."

"You think?" I question. She smirks and looks down at her hands on me, her index finger tapping my chest.

"I know I'll love you until I breathe my last breath," she corrects herself. "Is that better?"

"Yeah." I nod my head. "That's better. Jack knows about us," I tell her, "he told me to handcuff you to the bed to get you to stay."

"Of course he did." She snorts. "He's a bit dramatic."

"I might have given it more thought than I should have," I admit to her, "but I shut it down. I love you, Elizabeth."

"Is that so?" She looks up at me, her hands going from my chest to around my neck. "Are you finally going to kiss me?"

I grin. "Yeah." I nod my head and turn it to the side. "I'm going to do more than kiss you." My lips touch hers and her tongue slides into my mouth. "It's always been you." I pick her up and her legs wrap around my waist. "It's always going to be you."

"It better fucking always be me," she snips at me before she kisses me and I walk up the steps with her, taking her to my bed.

Merry Christmas
AND A HAPPY NEW YEAR

Epilogue

AULD LANG SYNE

ELIZABETH

Five days later.
December 31st
New Year's Eve

"Explain to me why we have to go to my parents'?" I ask him as I walk into the bathroom with him in the shower.

"Because they invited us," he answers, stepping under the showerhead to rinse the soap out of his hair.

"You could have made an excuse." I cock my head to the side.

"What excuse did you want me to make?" He shuts the water off and runs his hand through his hair. "Did you want me to tell them we were busy?"

"Um, yeah." I watch him step out of the shower and grab one of the white towels that are hanging on a hook.

He wraps it around his waist and covers up one of my favorite things on him.

"They would ask me what we were busy doing." I roll my eyes as he grabs another towel and rubs it over his head on the side and in the back, semi-drying his hair.

"You could have just said we were going to spend it alone."

"We leave in two days," he reminds me. "We won't see the animals for two months, since they are moving in with your parents. Something I don't think they wanted to do but they did only because it meant you were moving back home." The morning after we declared our love for each other, I came down to the kitchen and he asked for my flight information. Ten minutes later he had booked a ticket and will now be coming with me to help close up my house. He then spent the last three days making sure everything was going to be okay at the clinic.

"It's our first New Year's together," I remind him, "and they say what you are doing at midnight is an indication of how you'll be spending your year." He walks to me, putting his hands on my hips.

"And you wanted to be doing what at midnight?" He looks down with a smirk.

"There is a list of things we could have been doing. I could have been doing you. You could have been doing me. I could have been blowing you, you could have been eating me. The list is endless." His head goes back to laugh and I lean forward to kiss his neck, feeling his heartbeat under my lips. "Now we can't be doing that." He looks back at me, picking me up and placing me on the countertop in his bathroom.

His hands go to the sash around my waist of the light pink silk robe, and it falls beside me. The front of the robe falls open, but my nipples stop it from opening all the way. His hand comes up and he places his palm flat in the middle of my chest and moves up to my neck. His lips come to mine as his tongue slides into my mouth. Every single kiss feels like the first one with him. His hand moves the robe to the side and removes it off my shoulders as his tongue plays with mine, going around and around in circles.

He moves both his hands to my nipples, playing with them at the same time. The minute he pinches them both, I let go of his lips to breathe out, "Yes." I reach out for his towel, tugging it off his waist as it falls to his feet. I use one hand to grip his thick hard cock, moving my hand up and down.

He bends his head to take one of my nipples into his mouth, my free hand going to the back of his head as his tongue curls around me. "Need you," I say and he smiles as he moves over to my other nipple. I pull him closer to me, putting both my feet up on the counter, opening for him.

"If you need me," he states, looking up at me as he flicks my nipple, "then put me in you."

I rub his cock up and down my wet slit, coating the tip. Placing his head at my entrance, I move my hands back onto the counter to brace for his thrust. "Going to watch your pussy take my cock?" he asks me and I nod. I watch him slowly slide his cock into me until his balls hit my ass.

"Fuck," I hiss out, contracting my pussy around him. "More," I urge as he pulls out to the tip and then this time he slams into me. "Yes!" My back hits the mirror as he does it again, this time harder than the last. "Again," I tell him, and he moves my ass to the edge of the counter, his cock buried in me as he takes one leg and puts it over his shoulder and then the other one. He pulls out slowly and then he unleashes in me. Fucking me harder with each thrust. I feel him going deeper and deeper each time. "I'm going to—"

"I know." He pinches my nipple and the feeling that I'm going to jump off the cliff is now me free-falling. My toes curl, my eyes close, and my pussy gushes all over his cock. "Fuck," he grunts giving me two more thrusts until he holds my hips, his cock buried to the hilt as he comes in me. My legs fall off his shoulders to his sides as he sits me back up and his cock slides out of me. "Well, that was—" He kisses my lips.

"That was something, all right," I declare as I sit up. He grabs the towel from the floor and wets the corner of it before he hands it to me to clean myself off. "Thank you," I say as I clean up and he does the same.

"I hope you know with this, you are going to make us late."

I jump off the counter and tie my robe. "And you'll have fun explaining why we're late." I tap his bare chest and kiss it before I walk out of the bathroom.

Forty-five minutes later, I'm walking out of the closet where my clothes are now put away. "I need you to zip me up," I tell him as he finishes with his cuff links. His hair is pushed back like I love. The blue pants are so dark they look black, with a white button-down top open at the neck, making me want to bend in and kiss him.

I turn around as he zips my green chiffon dress I bought two days ago when my mother said it was semi-formal. I decided to go for a hunter-green, long-sleeve dress. Once he gets to the top where my neck is, he leans in to kiss me before zipping it. "There," he says and I turn around. "You look beautiful." The top of the dress hangs a little loose and then it tightens up at my waist, until the three-layer ruffled skirt hits my mid-thigh. "I'm going to have fun fucking you in this later."

I laugh as I slide on my sky-high black heels before putting in my diamond stud earrings. My hair is parted in the middle and in a bun at the base of my neck. "I look forward to being fucked in it later." I kiss under his jaw before we walk out of the house and head to my parents'. Right before we pull up to the house, my phone rings and I see it's my mother. "Maybe she's calling to cancel." I cross my fingers before answering it. "Hello."

"Hey, honey," she says and I can tell she's out of breath, "change of plans."

"Yesss," I hiss out. "I'll see you tomorrow," I tell her, then look at Nate. "Turn the truck around, it's cancelled."

"It's not cancelled," she refutes, "but we had to change venues."

"Change venues?" I repeat. "It was supposed to be at home?"

"I know, but your uncles and aunts decided they

wanted to come back to celebrate with us."

"Okay," I reply, not understanding.

"So we called Doreen."

"The party planner?"

"No, well, sort of. We are at the same place they had the reception."

"Mom," I snap, "if he's doing more wedding shit."

"No." She laughs. "Anyway, I have to go. Come here." She hangs up on me and I look down at the phone.

"I say we don't go and see if she notices." I look at Nate, who just shakes his head.

"We have to go."

"But do we?"

"It's going to be the first time we're out as a couple." I turn to face him.

"We literally had dinner with my parents the day after we officially became a couple."

"It's not the same now, your uncles are in town." He pulls into the parking lot.

"Which is why you shouldn't want to go. What if they want to beat you up?"

"No one is going to beat me up," he assures, parking. "They may rough me up a bit. Give me the stern talking-to, like 'if you fuck with her, we'll have you go missing and no one will notice' talk."

I laugh at him, thinking he's exaggerating, but knowing it's something my uncle Matthew would probably say to him. He gets out and meets me at the side of the truck, putting his hand in mine.

I can hear the music from outside the door, and when

I open it, I'm stunned. Completely stunned. Everyone is back here, well, almost everyone. "What is happening?" I mumble. My uncle Matthew looks at me and smiles and then his eyes go to our hands and he glares.

"So it's true," my uncle Matthew says, coming to kiss my cheek and then pushes Nate's shoulder. He still doesn't release my hand.

"It's as true as you standing right here in front of us," Nate confirms.

"This is a little bit over-the-top," I state, looking around at how they decorated the venue in black and gold. They kept the same Christmas trees but now the balls that are hanging on them reflect the black-and-gold theme. Fairy lights hang from the ceiling with big round gold balls.

"You should see in there." He points to the reception area. "It's over over-the-top."

"Well, let's go," I say. We walk into the room, and he was not fucking kidding. Five long tables are set up with black tablecloths and gold chairs. The middle of each table has a gold runner down it with little candles scattered up and down it. A big vase is in the middle with what looks like a bouquet of black and gold balls glued together sitting with fairy lights. Big black and gold balloons hang from the ceiling in different sizes and shapes. Some even sparkle, a couple of them look like they have lights in them. "This is ridiculous," I declare as I look to the side, where a table has a sign that says "Doll Up Your Outfit," with black-and-gold hats that say Happy New Year on them. There are little crowns as well as blow horns.

I scan the room, seeing my parents in the middle of a dance floor and I make my way to them. Nate's fingers hold on to mind. "Don't you think," I say and then look at my uncle Max, who smiles at me big, "that this is a bit too much, even for us?" I ask my mother, who just shrugs. "Hi," I say to my uncle Max. "Was this your idea?"

"Yes," he confirms. "It's a big year for us, we should end it with a bang."

"How is this a big year for us?"

"Well, your brother got married," he starts. "You are moving back home"—he smiles bigger when he looks at Nate—"and this guy finally got his head out of his ass."

"I don't even know what to do with any of this," I mumble. "I'm going to go and get a drink." I look over to where the bar was at the wedding and find it still at the same place, but this time there is a small table beside it that has a banner that says "Time to Drink the Champagne and Dance on the Tables." On the table are glasses of champagne waiting to be consumed.

"Can you believe this?" I look over my shoulder to see Jack and Evie coming toward us. "It's so glamorous."

"Yeah, let's go with that," I deadpan and see a waiter walking around with glasses of champagne, stopping by me to take one. "Cheers," I toast, holding up my glass, "to doing things on the down-low."

The night goes by so quickly, I don't even see it. It's actually a lot more fun than I thought it would be. It's less formal than the wedding, where I didn't have a chance to talk to many people that day and now I feel like I've spoken to everyone. People playing musical chairs, moving to talk to other people. But the whole night is spent with Nate beside me, his hand in mine or draped over my leg. We even get up to dance a couple of times. It is ending up being one of my best nights that I've had in a long, long time.

"The ball is going to drop in about a minute," the deejay announces, "if we can get everyone to the dance floor."

I get up and walk with him and everyone else to the dance floor. He stands behind me with his hands on my hips. "I love you," he whispers in my ear and I bend my arm back to hold his cheek.

"I love you more," I tell him as he turns me in his arms and kisses me before the whole room goes silent. The music shuts off, I hear whispers around me, and I look around, seeing everyone look at me. Then when I look back, Nate is not in front of me anymore. No, he's on one knee.

"Elizabeth," he says my name. "There was a time in my life that I couldn't remember you not being a part of it." He smiles. "But then I remember a time in my life you weren't part of it." My hand goes to my mouth. "I never want to go back to that place again. I lost you once and I'll be fucking damned if I lose you again." He holds out his hand and my father steps forward and hands him a black box. "From this day on, I want every single memory I have to be with you. From this day on, I want every single day to be filled with a memory that we are going to make. From this day on, I want to know you are mine, forever." He opens the ring box. "We may have only been a couple for five days"—that makes everyone laugh—"but my heart has been in love with you forever." I wipe the tear away, "Will you do me the honor of being my wife?"

I don't know if I say yes or if my head nods up and down, but roars erupt from beside me as he slides the ring on my finger. I don't even take a second to look at it, because he's up off his knee and his arms are wrapped around me as he kisses my lips softly. "How's this for starting the year off?" he whispers softly.

I throw my head back. "This was definitely a holiday unscripted." He picks me up off my feet and I wrap my arms around his neck. "I love you," I announce to him right before I kiss him and the clock strikes midnight.

Happy New Year Everyone…

Maybe just maybe…….

Someone else might have a Christmas Wish……

Time will tell………

Visit my website for all the up-to-date announcements.
www.natashamadisonauthor.com

Merry Christmas

AND A HAPPY NEW YEAR